*"I've decided we ___
Zack blurted, bef___
himself.*

August's body stilled like the air before a storm. "I beg your pardon."

He drew a deep breath. "Last night, while you were sleeping, I decided that the best thing for the boys would be if you and I got married."

"Married?" Her expression didn't flicker. "For the boys? Just like that?"

In the deep recesses of his mind, he admitted to a yawning fear that she would slip away from him. She was too independent, too sure. In the dark night he'd realized that if he didn't move quickly to bind her to him, she could easily slip away. But he couldn't make himself tell her the truth.

❤ ❤ ❤ ❤ ❤ ❤ ❤

Dear Reader,

What better way to enjoy the last lingering days of summer than to revel in romance? And Special Edition's lineup for August will surely turn your thoughts to love!

This month's THAT'S MY BABY! title will tug your heartstrings. Brought to you by Ginna Gray, *Alissa's Miracle* is about a woman who marries the man of her dreams—even though he doesn't want children. But when she unexpectedly becomes pregnant, their love is put to the ultimate test.

Sometimes love comes when we least expect it—and that's what's in store for the heroines of the next three books. *Mother Nature's Hidden Agenda* by award-winning author Kate Freiman is about a self-assured woman who thinks she has everything...until a sexy horse breeder and his precocious daughter enter the picture! Another heroine rediscovers love the second time around in Gail Link's *Lone Star Lover*. And don't miss *Seven Reasons Why*, Neesa Hart's modern-day fairy tale about a brood of rascals who help their foster mom find happily-ever-after in the arms of a mysterious stranger!

Reader favorite Susan Mallery launches TRIPLE TROUBLE, her miniseries about identical triplets destined for love. In *The Girl of His Dreams*, the heroine will go to unbelievable lengths to avoid her feelings for her very best friend. The second and third titles of the series will be coming your way in September and October.

Finally, we're thrilled to bring you book two in our FROM BUD TO BLOSSOM theme series. Gina Wilkins returns with *It Could Happen To You*, a captivating tale about an overly cautious heroine who learns to take the greatest risk of all—love.

I hope you enjoy each and every story to come!

Sincerely,

Tara Gavin,
Senior Editor

Please address questions and book requests to:
Silhouette Reader Service
U.S.: 3010 Walden Ave., P.O. Box 1325, Buffalo, NY 14269
Canadian: P.O. Box 609, Fort Erie, Ont. L2A 5X3

NEESA HART
SEVEN REASONS WHY

Silhouette®

SPECIAL EDITION®

Published by Silhouette Books
America's Publisher of Contemporary Romance

Special thanks to Helen Tornadeo, who fights the good
fight every day on behalf of Virginia's children; to the folks
at S.A.V.E., who are doing all they can to make the world a
safer place for the little guys; to Leanne Banks, one of the
most gifted writers I know—who kept saying, "It's style,
Neesa, it's style," until I believed it; and to everyone who
ever experienced the joy of seeing the world through
the eyes of a child.

 SILHOUETTE BOOKS

ISBN 0-373-24122-4

SEVEN REASONS WHY

This edition published by arrangement with Harlequin Books S.A.

® and TM are trademarks of Harlequin Books S.A., used under license.
Trademarks indicated with ® are registered in the United States Patent
and Trademark Office, the Canadian Trade Marks Office and in other
countries.

Printed in U.S.A.

Books by Neesa Hart

Silhouette Special Edition

Almost to the Altar #1080
Seven Reasons Why #1122

NEESA HART

who writes contemporary romance under her own name, and historical romance as Mandalyn Kaye, lives outside Washington, D.C., where, she says, "Truth really is stranger than fiction."

An avid romance fan for years, she got hooked while majoring in international affairs and geography in college. "Romances," she said, "were always more fun, more informative and more relaxing than anything I was supposed to be reading for class." After a brief political career, including a Senate-confirmed appointment to the President's Council on Women's Educational Programs, Neesa abandoned the hectic world of politics to pursue her dream as a full-time author. "Nothing," she says, "could be better than telling stories for a living."

Her interests, other than writing and reading, include volunteering at her church, collecting Barbie dolls and playing the banjo. One day she hopes to learn to pick "Oh! Susannah."

Neesa loves to hear from her readers. You can write to her at: 101 East Holly Avenue, Street 3, Sterling, VA 20164.

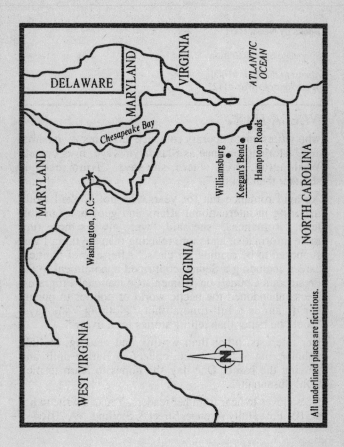

All underlined places are fictitious.

Chapter One

He'd found the address for chaos.

As he watched the unfolding drama across the fence in his sexy new neighbor's backyard, Zack Adriano was certain he'd found the center of chaos in the universe. And it resided in Keegan's Bend, Virginia.

At the moment, it took the form of seven boys—he mentally set their ages between six and ten—chasing a terrified goat. August Trent, the foster mother to at least half the brood, issued orders. Despite the way denim overalls hugged her generous figure and a crop of auburn curls framed her flushed face, August reminded Zack of George Custer at the Battle of the Little Bighorn. Hers might be a picture of pure femininity rather than military prowess, but beneath the guise lay a will of iron determined not to surrender.

As the small town's full-time veterinarian and part-time mayor, August had a reputation for efficiently handling crises. Zack had casually observed her for the past two weeks across the fence that separated their yards. She'd managed every challenge, including the afternoon she came home to find one of her boys trying to walk the clothesline as a makeshift tightrope, with a calm dignity he couldn't help admiring. He knew few women, or men, for that matter, who could juggle even half the tasks August Trent kept up in the air without falling to pieces.

Still, given the little army she had to work with this afternoon, Zack's money was on the goat.

"May Belle," one of the boys yelled, "stand still!" The upended kitchen strainer on the boy's head considerably diminished the authority of the order. Two enormous dogs penned on the far side of the yard had added their howling to the din. With a quick glance in the direction of the pen, Zack estimated that August had another two minutes before the dogs worked themselves loose. May Belle's odds were looking better all the time.

Surrounded by the crowd of boys, the goat lowered her head to charge. One of the little pack of hellions, this one clad in a fuchsia cape and bicycle helmet, dropped a rope around her neck. May Belle, more terrified than sensible, didn't heed the slight pressure at her throat. She charged the house, instead, jerking the boy off his feet.

"Whoa!" He landed on his belly with a loud *whump*. A cloud of reddish dust quickly engulfed him. May Belle raced across the lawn, pulling the kid in her wake. The other boys parted before her like cornstalks in a stiff breeze.

"Chip!" August yelled. "Let go of the rope!"

But Chip either didn't hear or didn't listen. Poor May Belle dragged him halfway to the house before Chip dug his feet into the ground and attempted to jerk the goat to a halt. He might have been successful, had the two dogs not chosen that moment to bolt from their pen and tackle Chip in a flying leap of wagging tales and panting tongues.

The rope slipped from his fingers. May Belle didn't waste time. In seconds, she was galloping toward the small gate. The other boys ran after her, while Chip wrestled with the dogs.

As August rushed toward Chip, the boys managed to corner the goat in the far end of the fenced yard. May Belle was having none of it. Two of the boys grabbed the rope just as she turned and rushed the opposite direction. They managed to stay on their feet, but May Belle strained so hard against the rope, they had to lean back like water-skiers on a towline.

August, evidently satisfied that Chip's wounds consisted of little more than a few scrapes and a grass stain the width of an ironing board across his belly, turned her attention back to May Belle's ill-fated capture. The dogs continued to bark. The boys continued to yell. May Belle eyed August with a look of such distrust that Zack sensed impending doom.

Doom came in the form of a late-model sedan the size of a small cruise ship, turning into the driveway of August's enormous Victorian home.

Zack recognized the car. It belonged to Odelia Keegan, the town's matriarch and, if gossip was to be believed, August Trent's nemesis.

Chip saw the sedan first. He tugged hard on the leg of August's overalls, then pointed to the driveway. Seven heads swiveled to watch Odelia Keegan emerge from the car—seven heads and a goat. Despite the woman's diminutive height, her pale pink suit and white hair, Odelia had an aura about her that Zack figured could stop a tornado in its tracks. Power, money and, unless he missed his guess, connivery had allowed her to run Keegan's Bend for two decades.

August Trent had become the talk of the town the day she defeated Hiram Keegan, Odelia's nephew, in the mayoral race. In the two weeks Zack had been in town, he'd heard at least five different stories of clashes between the two women. Judging from the fury emanating from Odelia's petite body, today he was going to get to witness one.

"August!" she called, her voice rivaling the rusty squeak of a weather vane. "August Trent!"

August's lips pressed into a thin line as she watched Odelia approach the backyard. Chip cowered behind her legs, and Zack watched as the tallest of the seven boys studied Odelia with a look of calculated dislike.

He recognized that look.

He'd used a similar expression in the not-too-distant past, when one of his clients pushed him too hard. In recent months, Zack had found his temper growing shorter as his hours grew longer. The thrill he'd once found in his career as a trial attorney no longer held the appeal it once had. Perhaps, he decided, taking a long sip of his iced tea, that was what he liked most about August Trent. Underneath the exterior package, a package he found entirely too pleasant for his peace of mind, lay a woman who knew who she was and what she wanted.

Reluctantly Zack shifted his gaze back to the tall boy with the hard glare. Clad in black jeans and a T-shirt with Born To Be Wild emblazoned across the front, he was the only one who still had a firm grip on May Belle. The smaller boy had allowed the rope to go slack when Odelia called August's name. In a move casual enough to win Zack's respect, the kid gave the rope a sharp enough tug to ensure that May Belle would still want to bolt, then let the tether slide from his fingers. Sensing her freedom, May Belle jerked free of the other boy's loose grip and charged directly toward Odelia Keegan. The two dogs followed.

Zack watched as August's eyes rolled heavenward, Odelia let out a shriek of outrage as she scrambled for her car door and the boys scattered in seven different directions. With obvious reluctance, August squared her shoulders, called the dogs and started after May Belle.

Zack was so intent on watching the enticing sway of August's hips as she stalked across the lawn, he didn't notice that the boys now stood on his side of the fence until he felt the tug at the leg of his jeans.

He glanced in surprise at the seven faces watching him with a mixture of suspicion and hope. "How'd you get over here?" he asked. He had assumed that the fence fully separated the two yards, and despite the distraction of watching August, he was fairly certain he would have noticed if a group of seven junior commandos had scaled it.

The kid with the strainer on his head pointed to a place ten yards down the fence. "You gotta board out down there. Can't see it 'cause of the ivy."

Zack glanced at the fence, then back at the boys. "So you decided to hide out in my yard until Mrs. Keegan leaves?" he guessed.

One boy, with wire-framed glasses and the whitest hair Zack had ever seen, stepped forward from the small group. In the time he'd had to observe the goings on at the Trent house, Zack had already identified this one as the natural leader of the pack. If memory served, he'd heard the other boys call him Jeff.

"You really a lawyer?" Jeff asked.

Zack's eyebrows lifted a fraction. "Maybe."

"August says you're a lawyer."

"You any good?" asked the kid with the strainer on his head.

"I suppose."

"I heard you were some hotshot lawyer from New York," Jeff persisted. He shoved his glasses up the bridge of his nose with his dirty index finger. "Are you?"

"I work for a law firm in New York, yes."

"But are you *from* New York?"

"I'm from Iowa."

He looked disappointed. "Dang. I thought you were from New York."

The tallest boy of the group, the one who'd turned the goat loose on Odelia Keegan, fixed Zack with a hard stare. "I told you this wouldn't work, Jeff."

"It would work if he was from New York."

"He said he's a lawyer in New York," piped in another kid. His high, squeaky voice reminded Zack of a cartoon character. "What's the difference?"

"Because," Jeff said. "We need a good lawyer. Not one from Iowa."

As the blistering heat of the Virginia sun bore down on Zack's head, a trickle of sweat formed at his nape and ran down his spine. One of the boys, a handsome black kid Zack remembered hearing August call Bo, dropped onto a lounge chair. Zack had noticed earlier that Bo, the smallest of the seven, had seemed the most uncomfortable during the goat-herding escapade. Neatly dressed in khaki shorts and a collared shirt that, by some miracle, he'd managed to keep tucked in, he looked like the kind of kid who'd been told one too many times that children should be seen and not heard. Zack doubted the boy had a lick of temper in him, and it made him wonder how the poor fellow survived in a house run by hotheaded August Trent.

He seemed unaware of Zack's scrutiny. "What are we going to do now, Jeff?" he wailed. "You said we were going to get a lawyer."

"We are," Jeff asserted. "Maybe we'll hire him anyway. I guess an Iowa lawyer from New York is almost as good as a New York lawyer."

"What makes you think you need a lawyer?" Zack asked, despite his better judgment. He didn't have any business getting mixed up with August Trent's kids. Jansen Riley had lent him his large family home in Keegan's Bend on the condition that Zack would find out why Odelia Keegan wanted August Trent run out of town. Getting involved with the woman, or her kids, when he was supposed to be observing her comings and goings was definitely not in his plan. Jansen had told him that his interest in Keegan's Bend was purely nostalgic. He'd grown up there, and knew all too well that the Keegans didn't like to be thwarted. Zack, however, hadn't made a living reading people's faces without learning a thing or two. He had a lot of respect for Jansen Riley—in many ways, the man had been like a father to him. And Zack would have bet real money that Jansen hadn't revealed the whole story behind his motivations. Zack had come to Keegan's Bend wary, and more than a little careful.

With the same methodical precision that had distinguished him as a lawyer, Zack had determined to keep his distance from August until he had more of a feel for the situation. Since his arrival in the small town, all he'd gleaned with his casual questions and feigned curiosity were a few rumors, some choice gossip and a delightful view of August's house. He hadn't planned on her seven little ruffians inviting him to interrogate them. Kids, in his experience, were far more honest than adults. With a little luck, and a few skillful questions, he might start to get some answers.

From the corner of his eye, he could see August and Odelia still embroiled in a heated conversation. If he'd learned one thing about her boys, he knew they were unpredictable, precocious, and bent on trouble. No matter how much August intrigued him, he ought to know better than to get involved with the little mob.

In answer to Zack's question, Jeff pulled up his baggy

jeans, then took a step forward. "We got a good case. We just need a lawyer to help us win it."

Zack dragged his gaze from August. "Is that so?" he asked him.

"Yeah." Jeff gave Zack's porch a pointed look. "Don't you want to ask us some questions or something? That's what they do on TV."

"Why would I want to ask you questions?"

"About our case," he said, his voice taking on an impatient edge. "Don't you want to know about our case?"

Zack threw a final glance at August Trent. Her discussion with Odelia had evidently escalated into a full-fledged argument. With hands waving and face flushed, August was giving her hell. If he entertained the boys for another ten minutes or so, he could at least ferret out just what had Odelia in such an uproar. Now seemed as good a time as any to start earning his pay. His decision made, Zack looked Jeff in the eye. "Maybe."

"We got money, you know," said the tall kid, the one who'd turned May Belle loose on Odelia. "It's not like we're expecting you to do it for free."

Zack had to suppress a smile as he wondered if the boys knew what New York lawyers cost these days. "How much money?"

The kid with the kitchen strainer on his head stepped forward. "A whole hundred dollars."

"A hundred *twelve* dollars," Jeff said.

"And thirty-seven cents," added Bo.

The boy August had called Chip, easily the youngest of the seven, slipped his hand into Zack's. His chubby fingers felt sticky and warm, as though they'd been someplace they shouldn't have. "And a rock," he added solemnly.

He didn't know when he'd had a more enticing offer to take a case. He had a brief image of telling Jansen Riley that the five-figure retainer he'd given Zack to come to

Keegan's Bend had just been bested by a hundred twelve dollars and a rock. He nearly laughed out loud.

Pleasantly enticed by the freshness of the innocence, he tilted his head toward the porch and told the boys, "Why don't we sit on the porch, and you can tell me about your case?"

"Does that mean you're going to take it?" asked the kid with the strainer.

"No," Zack said, "it means I'm willing to consider it."

"You gotta take it."

"Depends on how much you need a lawyer," Zack countered.

Jeff pulled up his jeans again. "Nobody ever needed a lawyer as much as we do," he assured Zack. "Come on." He pointed to the porch. "Let's tell him."

The boys herded onto the porch in a jumble of jeans and sneakers. Only the tall one, the one with the hard glare, sauntered toward the shade with the studied detachment of a kid who cares too much and doesn't want it to show. Zack fell into step behind him.

When all seven boys had found a place to sit—or, in Jeff's case, lean—against the porch rail, Zack propped one foot on the bottom step. "All right. Let's start with your names. You're Jeff."

Jeff nodded, then pointed at the kid with the kitchen strainer. "That's Sam."

"Hiya," Sam said, giving Zack a half wave.

"Nice hat," Zack said.

Sam didn't blink. "Thanks."

Zack looked at Chip. He still wore his fuchsia bike helmet and cape. "You're Chip?"

Chip grinned at him. It was a toothless, engaging grin, that made Zack want to smile back. "Chip Parker," he said.

"Nice to meet you."

Sam sneezed. "Bless you," Zack said automatically.

"Don't pay him no mind." Jeff's tone had the unmistakable authority of a child repeating adult conversation. "He's allergic."

"To what?"

"Everything."

Sam wiped his nose with the back of his hand. "Am not. Just stuff that makes me sneeze."

"I see."

Jeff continued with the introductions. "That's Josh," he said, pointing to the handsomest of the seven boys, the one with the squeaky voice. With his dark hair and eyes, if his voice ever changed, Josh would no doubt be a lady-killer when he hit adolescence. He had a bored, sloe-eyed look about him that the women of Zack's acquaintance generally found irresistible in men. Josh acknowledged Jeff's introduction with a slight tilt of his head.

"Who are you?" Zack asked the redheaded kid closest to him.

"That's Teddy," Sam told him. "He don't talk."

"Why not?"

"Just don't," said Sam. "I reckon he don't want to."

Zack nodded at Teddy. "That's a good enough reason." Teddy stuck out his hand, and Zack gave it a solemn shake. "Nice to meet you."

Jeff pointed to the shy-looking boy who had briefly occupied Zack's lounge chair. With his hands folded in his lap, and his pristine white tennis shoes resting on the ground, he was the picture of perfect behavior. "That's Bo."

He gave Zack a slight wave. "Hello, Mr. Adriano," he said.

His polite retort didn't surprise Zack. Perfect manners seemed in keeping with his subdued, disturbingly mature countenance. "Hello, Bo."

"And that," Jeff said, with a slight tilt of his head in the direction of the tall, hard-eyed boy, "is Lucas."

Lucas glared at him. Zack almost laughed. Long ago, he'd made it a habit to carefully assess prospective clients before taking their cases. His instincts rarely failed him. Lucas's defiant glare reminded him of Eddy "The Pick" Baltucci telling him he'd break Zack's knuckles if he didn't get his prostitute cousin out of jail within the hour. As a rule, Zack never took clients with weapons for nicknames. Lawyers lived longer that way. At Eddy's threat, Zack had called security, and, to the best of his knowledge, some other lawyer had taken responsibility for Maria Baltucci's delinquency.

He thought about asking Lucas if he had a nickname, but decided not to give the kid any ideas. He'd be calling himself Lucas the Spike by the end of the week, and August definitely wouldn't like it. "Okay," he said. "My name's Zack Adriano."

"Yeah, yeah, we know," Sam said. "And you're a lawyer."

"A *New York* lawyer," Bo added.

"A New York lawyer," Zack agreed. "So how many of you guys actually live with August?"

Jeff pushed his glasses up on his nose. "Lucas and Bo and Teddy and Chip are August's kids."

"What about the rest of you?"

"Me and Sam are brothers. We live with our dad."

"But you spend a lot of time with August?"

"Sure. Dad works out at the Hedrick place as the farm manager. This is tobacco season, and he ain't around much. So we stay with August."

"I see." Zack felt a surprising burst of annoyance that their father had allowed August to take on two more kids when she already had a houseful. Some people, he had learned the hard way, were quick to prey on the weak.

Jeff was pointing at Josh. "And Mrs. Prentiss is Josh's grandma."

"Mrs. Prentiss?" Zack frowned. Was this another neighbor who'd dumped her kid on August's already loaded shoulders?

"She takes care of us," Chip supplied. "She comes over when August is gone."

"Ah." He nodded. "So four of you live next door, and three of you are just around a lot."

"That's right," Jeff answered.

"So who needs the lawyer?"

"All of us," said Bo. "We put all our money together."

"What makes you guys think my services are worth your life savings?"

Sam shifted impatiently on the step. "'Cause Ms. Keegan's going to bump off Lucas and Chip and Teddy and Bo if you don't stop her."

"Bump them off?"

Jeff muttered something beneath his breath. "He means ship them off, not bump them off. Ms. Keegan's been bugging August about getting rid of 'em."

Zack nodded, thoughtful. "So I hear."

When Chip shook his head, his fuchsia bike helmet wobbled back and forth. "I don't like Ms. Keegan."

Neither, as far as Zack knew, did anyone else. "Where do you think she's going to ship you?"

Jeff looked thoughtful, then said. "Probably prison."

"Yeah," said Sam. "She's always saying we're all de-delin…"

"Delinquents," Bo whispered.

"Delinquents belong in prison," Sam said.

"And you think a lawyer can help?" Zack asked.

Jeff nodded. "Sure. That's your job. You're supposed to keep people out of prison."

"Truth, justice and the American way," Chip said.

"No, doofus." Lucas gave the bike helmet a gentle whap. "That's Superman."

Chip didn't seem to be offended by the comment. "I don't want to go to prison."

Teddy vehemently shook his head. Bo, Zack noticed, looked terrified.

"So are you gonna help us or not?" Jeff persisted.

"Depends," Zack said. Beyond the fence, he watched as Odelia bustled into her car, slammed the door and roared out of the driveway. He didn't miss the way August's shoulders drooped slightly as she watched the powder blue sedan disappear.

"On what?" Jeff persisted. "We said we'd pay you."

Zack watched as August scanned her yard for signs of the boys. Depends, he thought, on just how mad I get at Odelia Keegan.

"See, Jeff, I told you this wouldn't work," Lucas said. "No one's going to help us."

Zack briefly scanned their faces. "I didn't say I wouldn't help you."

"So we told you we got over a hundred dollars. What else do you want?" Sam asked.

Zack felt his lips twitch. Considering that for two weeks he'd been having some pretty steamy visions about just what he wanted, and about how those wants involved August Trent, he didn't think sensitive ears were ready for the truth. "I want to see the rock," he said, just as he saw August round the corner of her house.

"Boys?" August's voice held a note of irritation. "Where are you?" She was in the process of putting a reluctant May Belle and the two dogs back in their pens.

At the sound of her voice, Bo threw Jeff a panicked look. "Look," Jeff told Zack, "we gotta go. Are you going to help us or not?"

The boys had already begun scrambling for the fence,

evidently recognizing trouble in August's tone. Only Jeff and Chip lingered. Even Lucas had bolted from the porch. "I'll have to think about it," Zack told Jeff. "Can I give you an answer later?"

"Boys?" August yelled again.

Jeff hurried down the steps. "Yeah, sure! Later's fine," he yelled over his shoulder.

Only Chip seemed unconcerned by the sudden, urgent need to retreat. He pressed a blue stone into Zack's hand. "That's the rock," he told him.

Zack studied it a second. It was a plastic gemstone that had seen better days. He put a hand on Chip's shoulder to usher him toward the ivy-concealed break in the fence where the boys were about to crush one another as they tried to cram through the opening simultaneously. Zack reached the fence just as Jeff, the last of the six, stumbled through to the other side. August stood, hands on pleasantly curved hips, facing the house. Had the boys not been escaping as surely as minnows through a torn net, Zack might have taken the time to contemplate the view. This was as close as he'd been to her since he moved into the house. Instead, he held Chip still with one hand while he parted the dense ivy at the top of the fence with the other.

"Boys, come out here right now," August demanded.

"They're over here," Zack announced from across the fence.

Visibly startled, August spun to face him. From the corner of his eye, he noted the disgusted look Jeff gave him. Chip had slipped his hand back into Zack's. "They were visiting me," Zack informed August.

She glanced quickly at the six boys now on her side of the fence. She looked tired and frustrated. Zack figured two run-ins with two old goats in the same hour could do that to a woman. "Where's Chip?" she asked.

Chip tried to jump high enough to see over the fence. "Over here," he told her.

August gave the boys a piercing look before she approached the fence. "I'm very sorry, Mr. Adriano. They know—"

He held up his hand. The minute he released Chip's collarbone, the boy slid free and eased his way through the fence to join the others. "It was no trouble," Zack assured her.

She glanced at the boys again. "What were you doing over there?" she asked.

Lucas gave Jeff a slight whack on the back of the head. "I told you it wouldn't work."

"Jeffrey?" August asked.

"We just wanted to talk to him."

"As soon as my back was turned, you took the opportunity to bother Mr. Adriano, despite the fact that I told you I didn't want you over there?" August asked.

The boys looked sheepish. Except Bo and Chip. Chip grinned at Zack. Bo looked perilously close to tears. August pushed a burnished curl off her forehead. "Darn it, Jeff, I trusted you."

"Sorry," he mumbled.

Zack felt a twinge of guilt. It wouldn't be fair to let her think the boys had intruded on his privacy. He didn't want them in trouble on his account. "It's really not—"

August held up a hand to interrupt him, but didn't take her eyes off the boys. "Do you know why Mrs. Keegan was here?" she asked them. No one answered. "Lucas?" she asked.

Lucas shifted uncomfortably. "She thinks I rode my bike through that new cement she had poured around old man Keegan's statue."

"And you didn't?"

Lucas's expression turned rebellious. "Don't you believe me?"

"If you say you didn't, I believe you didn't," August said. "Does anyone know anything about this?"

In unison, seven heads wagged no. With a heavy sigh, August wiped her hands on the front of her overalls. "That's what I told Mrs. Keegan. All right, I want all of you to apologize to Mr. Adriano, then go inside and wash up for dinner."

Zack was about to protest that he didn't see the need for an apology when August shot him a warning look. He knew better than to counter her authority with the boys. Besides, once the boys were gone, he'd have at least several minutes to speak with her alone, an opportunity that hadn't presented itself in over two weeks. If he hoped to satisfy Jansen, he'd better start getting pretty damn friendly with August Trent. Fortunately, he thought, glancing at her with thorough masculine appreciation, the prospect held a certain element of appeal.

One by one, the boys filed by his position at the fence, muttering apologies. Lucas glared at him so hard, Zack felt his gaze bore through his skull. Last in line, Teddy and Chip approached the fence together. Teddy gave Zack a halfhearted wave before dashing toward the house, but Chip studied him from beneath his fuchsia helmet. "Are you gonna keep my rock?" he asked.

"I don't know," Zack admitted.

Chip nodded. "Hope so," he said, then trotted off toward the house.

A gentle peach flush, the remains of her argument with Odelia, stained August's face. "I really am sorry," she told him. "I told them I didn't want them bothering you while—"

"They weren't bothering me," he assured her. "There's only so much peace and quiet a man can take."

Her eyes widened slightly, and Zack decided the color reminded him of a vintage bourbon, sort of spicy and mellow, all at the same time. "It's just that they're used to playing over there."

"I noticed the 'phone' line." He pointed to the wire that ran between the master bedroom of Jansen's house and August's. "Quite ingenious."

"They can't take credit for that one. It was there when we moved in."

"The coffee can on my side looks new."

"I didn't say they didn't use it, I just said they didn't invent it. Until a few months ago, Mr. Riley had a caretaker living over there. She let the boys play hide-and-seek in the house."

He decided he liked the way August talked to him. She looked at him squarely when she spoke, like a woman with nothing to hide, a woman who didn't play games. He found himself comparing the women of his acquaintance with her straightforward honesty, and thinking that they all fell short. To her credit, she held his gaze throughout his scrutiny. His lips curved into an appreciative smile. "Still, it can't be much fun to be eight and have a stranger take over your playhouse."

"It can't be much fun to be recuperating from a serious injury and have the Mongol hordes invading your yard, either," she said.

"My injury?" he asked. Automatically his hand rubbed his thigh through the fabric of his jeans. "I see news travels fast."

Her flush seemed to heighten. He found himself intrigued by the notion that the peach tint might color her skin from head to foot. "I wasn't trying to pry," she assured him. "It's just that Keegan's Bend is a very small place, and it didn't take long for people to know why you're here."

"Unfortunately, that doesn't surprise me," he told her. "As hard as I tried to keep the incident out of the press, I think it still got picked up by a couple of affiliates."

"It did. I saw it on the national news."

Somehow, it irked him to know that August Trent, and evidently the rest of Keegan's Bend, thought he was sitting on death's door. Just because he was recovering from a wounded leg, that didn't mean he was about to keel over dead. Deliberately he leaned closer to her. When his face was near enough to hers to allow him a whiff of her perfume, he said, "They sensationalized it. It really wasn't all that impressive. I was standing in the district court of appeals in Manhattan when a gunman opened fire in the corridor. The kid was too drugged up to aim at anything. The worst damage he did was the bullet he put in my femur."

She frowned at him. "That's not the way I heard it."

"Gossip isn't always a reliable source."

"The report said you put yourself between the gunman and a child."

"That child was my client's daughter." He shrugged. "People like to make it sound heroic, but it was instinct. What would you do if you had a kid next to you, and some nut opened fire?"

She shook her head. "It's not what I'd do—it's what most people would do. I don't think a lot of folks would have put their lives on the line for a six-year-old."

"I really liked that particular six-year-old." He didn't add that the child's father had just been acquitted of a crime Zack was now certain he'd committed, that for the first time in his career he'd been deceived into defending a guilty client. He wasn't ready to discuss that.

She seemed to sense his determination to keep the conversation light. With a slight shrug, she said, "You should take something like that very seriously. An injury to a major bone can take months to heal."

Zack squelched an irritated sigh. Evidently, nothing he was going to say would convince the woman he wasn't some kind of damned invalid. He didn't like the thought of August Trent thinking he wasn't perfectly capable—of anything. "I assure you, your boys pose no threat to my continued recovery."

She rolled her eyes. "You obviously haven't tried to get them all ready for church on Sunday morning."

Zack recognized the quip as an olive branch. He set aside his unreasonably bad temper and accepted it. "I can imagine."

"I doubt it," she said. "Anyway, I really hope they didn't disturb you. I was preoccupied with Odelia, and they seized the moment."

"It's what boys do. I used to be one. I remember."

"Yeah, well, boys can also wear you out."

"So can goats."

"All kinds," she said, not missing his veiled reference to Odelia Keegan. Tucking a burnished curl behind her ear, she cast a glance in May Belle's direction. "Some are just more stubborn than others." She thrust her hands into the side pockets of her overalls.

Close enough now to look his fill, he indulged the urge he'd been fighting for weeks. As he'd suspected, the baggy fit of her overalls did little to disguise the generous curves underneath. A little too much of everything to be strictly fashionable, it was true, but then, he'd always liked curves, and all the benefits that went with them. His eyes lingered for the barest of seconds on the full curve of her breasts, just visible beneath the front placket of her overalls and the worn fabric of her T-shirt. Belatedly he noticed that a tense silence had fallen between them, as if they'd progressed past the acceptable small talk, and both of them were weighing the ramifications of continuing the conversation. "I think—" he began at the same time she said "Would you—"

Zack smiled the same smile that had reportedly charmed every judge in New York City. "Ladies first."

"Well, I have to get dinner ready, but I just wanted to thank you for putting up with my boys. Mr. Riley probably didn't warn you that you were taking up residence next to the Little Rascals when he lent you the house for the summer."

"He might have mentioned something about it."

"All the same, I'm certain he didn't tell you that you wouldn't get a day's peace while you were here. I appreciate your patience."

"They really haven't bothered me, Ms. Trent."

Her eyebrows lifted a fraction. "Not even the afternoon they tried to hook Boris and Karloff—" she jerked her head in the direction of the two dogs "—up to the wheelbarrow so they could use it for a wagon?"

"Well," he conceded, "I'll confess I've noticed them a time or two." And you, he mentally added. I've noticed you.

"Is that so?" she asked.

"The wheelbarrow incident was the worst."

"So far."

"So far," he agreed.

"Still, we have enough trouble with Odelia Keegan without having to deal with complaints from the neighbors."

He gave her a speculative look, and wondered if he simply imagined the way her flush heightened. "From what I've seen so far, I have no complaints."

He could tell from her slightly flustered expression that she didn't miss his meaning.

Chapter Two

With a wary eye, August watched Fletcher Harrison unload twelve more goats into the pen behind her house. Admittedly, her mind wasn't on the goats that morning. As it had been all night, her thoughts were on the man beyond the fence. To her immense discomfort, she'd been unable to forget the teasing look in his eyes when he wished her goodbye at the fence; nor had she managed to banish the image of dark hair and a silver gaze that made her shiver. She'd dreamed of pirates last night. Pirates who had the same dark, dangerous, determined look she'd seen in Zack Adriano's gaze.

Despite her best efforts, she'd been unable to put him from her mind, and try as she might, she couldn't convince herself that she merely wanted to know what had passed between him and the boys.

Pulling her thoughts back to Fletcher's goats, she watched as he secured the pen. "I'm sorry about this, Fletcher. I wish we could have caught it sooner."

He shrugged. "Nothing you could have done, August."
Slapping his soiled work gloves against his trousers leg,
he gave her a lopsided grin. "I reckon you hadn't planned
on a penful."

"It's all right. It'll be easier to make sure they all get
injections this way."

"Do you need me to stay and help?" he asked.

August thought it over. Injecting the goats wasn't going
to be an easy task, and she could use the extra set of hands,
but she knew Fletcher wanted to get back to his farm and,
more importantly, that he didn't want Odelia Keegan to
see him on her property. She gave him a slight smile.
"Don't worry about it, Fletch. I can handle it."

"You sure?"

"I'm sure. If I run into any problems, I'll call you."

With a grateful smile, he clambered back into his truck.
"All right, August. Thanks for doing this."

"That's why I get paid the big bucks, Fletcher."

He drove away, leaving her to contemplate the thirteen
bleating goats. At least, she thought, Mrs. Prentiss had
taken the boys to the park for the morning. She didn't have
to watch them, too. A glance at her watch confirmed that
she had five hours before she had to be at the courthouse
for a council meeting. That should just give her enough
time to do one round of injections before cleaning herself
up so that she'd look more like a mayor and less like a
goat.

She was in the process of laying out syringes and medicine vials when she sensed the presence behind her. With
a start, she turned to find Zack towering over her. "Oh."
She blinked several times, feeling more than a little off
balance, and not liking it one bit. "You startled me."

"Sorry. I was curious."

His voice had the same velvet quality she remembered
from the previous afternoon. It caused the same goose

bumps to spread over her flesh, too. August gave him a skeptical look. "About the goats?" she asked, not believing for a minute that he was the least bit interested in the symptoms, or treatment, of goat pneumonia.

"Among other things."

The drawl made her stomach flutter. She wasn't precisely sure what Zack Adriano was after, but a strong sense of self-preservation prodded her toward caution. Still, when he leaned on the edge of the pen, she couldn't help noticing the way worn blue jeans hugged lean hips and his blue shirt accented broad shoulders and a narrow waist. His bronzed skin seemed especially appealing where it disappeared into the open collar of his shirt. "What's wrong with them?" he asked.

"They've got pneumonia." She turned her attention back to the vials. "May Belle got it first, and I had hoped to isolate the spread by bringing her here."

"Didn't work?" he asked.

"Nope. Fletcher lost two more goats this week. He doesn't have the space to separate the sick goats from the healthy goats." She pulled on a pair of latex gloves, then prepared the first syringe. "So he brought 'em here."

"Do you have room for them?"

No, she thought. She didn't have room for thirteen goats, and she certainly didn't have room for Zack Adriano. "No, but I didn't have much choice."

"What are you going to do about it?" he asked, and she wondered if they were still talking about the goats.

Holding the syringe, she turned to face him. "I'm going to give them a buttful of antibiotics, and hope they'll soon be ready to go back where they belong."

He studied her for a minute in the bright sunlight. "What will you do if they aren't?"

Panic. "Make do one day at a time and see where it gets me."

Zack's smile was slow in coming, and perfect when it arrived. His teeth flashed white against the strong, tanned planes of his face. With a smile like that, she knew exactly why he'd developed a reputation for a lethal charm that should be registered as a dangerous weapon. The man had enough sophisticated charisma to lube a chassis. Worse, he was easy to like. A lethal combination, August decided. He studied her with a knowing look in his eyes that sent shivers to her toes. He knew exactly what she was thinking, and was enjoying the hell out of it. "Need any help?" he asked her.

She needed help, all right. She needed to be committed, that was what she needed. When she didn't answer, he glanced at the goats, "Giving them their shots, I mean?"

Something in the teasing note in his voice grated her. She might not have his sophistication, but she had ten times his common sense. She'd seen him watching her across the fence, felt the lazy way he observed her from the safe distance of Jansen Riley's house. For two weeks, he'd kept her off balance. August couldn't resist the opportunity to turn the tables. She figured Zack knew as much about goats as she knew about New York lawyers. It seemed like a fair trade. "Sure," she told him. "If you'll hold their heads, I'll inject them."

Two hours later, she reluctantly admitted to herself that he'd fared better than she'd thought. The mess hadn't seemed to faze him, despite the fact that his hundred-dollar running shoes were now ruined. To her surprise, he even managed to maintain a sense of humor while the goats howled, and coughed, and ran, and scuttled about the pen, making the job as difficult as possible. He held each one while she injected the medication, and didn't even complain when May Belle kicked him in the rear in retaliation for the mistreatment.

With his help, a five-hour job was cut in half, and despite herself, August found she enjoyed his company. A little more than she should have, maybe, but enjoyed it all the same. When the last goat had been treated, Zack secured the latch on the pen, then dropped down to rest his back against the outside of the chain fence. August watched him with an amused smile as she stripped off the latex gloves and secured her equipment in her black bag. "So," she asked him, "still curious about goats?"

He propped his forearms on his bent knees. "I think I've seen enough for a while. Don't ever let anybody convince you that what you do isn't hard work."

"Don't worry," she told him with a smile. "People don't usually try."

"I should hope not. What would you have done if I hadn't been here?"

"Done it myself," she said. "It would have taken longer, but I've done it before."

"Can't you get an assistant? Surely some young animal lover would agree to be your goatherder."

She shrugged, snapped her satchel shut, then sat down beside him. "It's tough to get employees in this town when you're on the wrong side of Odelia Keegan."

His eyebrows lifted slightly. "But you're the mayor. You got elected, didn't you?"

"It's a lot easier for people to cast a secret ballot than make a public stand. Odelia hasn't made any secret of the fact that she wants me and the boys out of Keegan's Bend."

"Do you know why?" he asked.

A warning sounded in her mind at the innocent question. She couldn't quite shake the suspicion that Zack wanted to know far more than he was asking. "Not really," she added, hedging.

"But you have a theory?"

She didn't like being interrogated, not even by a man who'd helped her inject a herd of goats. "They're just suspicions, and nothing that I want to talk about."

He took the none-too-subtle hint with easy grace. "I'm glad I could be here to help. I hope you'll let me help again."

She gave his sneakers an amused look. "You sure about that?"

With a slight laugh, he waved one foot in the air. "There are worse fates than ruined shoes."

"You keep thinking like that, and I'll let you tag along when I check on Jack Foltz's turkeys."

"Turkeys? Do I want to know?"

"Probably not. They have infectious sinusitis."

With a slight groan, Zack dropped his head back against the fence. "Is that as fowl as it sounds?"

August laughed. "Absolutely."

"Look at me, I spend two hours with your goats, and I'm reduced to cracking bad puns about disgusting animal diseases."

"Just think what you could do with swine flu."

"No thank you."

A companionable silence fell between them, and August allowed herself to enjoy the rare pleasure of adult companionship. Since she came to Keegan's Bend, since the day she took on Odelia in defense of her boys, she'd made the decision to more or less isolate herself.

Odelia wanted control of Keegan's Bend—she'd never even tried to disguise the fact. August suspected it had something to do with the automobile company executives who were trying to locate a manufacturing facility near the small community. As the area's biggest landholder, Odelia stood to make a fortune if the plant gained approval in the state legislature. But the old woman's dislike seemed to run deeper than greed. For two years, August had wondered just what Odelia Keegan found so distasteful about her houseful of boys, but she'd long since given up on worrying about it.

It got lonely, though, being the enemy of the town matriarch. August had friends, of course, but all of them had made the decision to befriend August Trent to spite Odelia Keegan. She found it difficult to trust friends like that. Zack Adriano had come to her on his own terms, owing nothing to Odelia and, as far as August knew, wanting nothing from her, either. She felt an unfamiliar surge of gratitude as she contemplated the handsome man next to her. He'd closed his eyes and turned his face to the sun, affording August an ample view of his strong profile. She remembered her earlier thoughts, when she'd compared him to a pirate. In the early-morning light, the analogy seemed even more fitting. And she could definitely get used to looking at a face like that. "Zack," she said, figuring she'd better have out with it before she lost her nerve.

"Hmmmmm?" He sounded sleepy.

"I..." She paused. "Well, I've got to get ready for a council meeting this afternoon, but I just wondered if you were doing okay over there by yourself." He turned to look at her, so she indicated the large house with a brief wave of her hand. "I don't know what kind of condition the last tenants left the place in, but it can't have been very clean. Every time the boys play over there, they look like they're returning from trench warfare."

"It's livable," he said. "George Pruitt has been taking care of it for Jansen."

"Is it lonely over there?" Even as she asked it, she wondered at the question. Nearly the same size as her own, the house seemed a quiet sanctuary in comparison. Still, she got lonely, even with four boys in the house and the usual accompaniment of Jeff, Sam and Josh. She wondered if he welcomed the change of pace after the life he'd led in New York.

"A little. I've slept a lot since I got here. Doctor's orders."

"I can understand that, although, professionally speaking, I'm not sure that's the best possible advice."

"I'm not sure I want professional advice from a woman who treats infectious sinusitis in turkeys," he quipped.

"People are animals, too."

He slanted her a dry look. "Men especially?"

"Men especially. And I think the best thing for you is some careful exercise, a good diet, and as little stress as possible. It takes the body a long time to recover from something as traumatic as a gunshot wound."

"I'm doing all right on the exercise," he said. "I walk every morning."

She knew that much, she'd watched more than once as he limped down the long street. His gait seemed to be improving as he continued to work the muscles. "What about the diet?"

"I don't suppose peanut butter and jelly are what the doctor ordered?"

She winced. "Probably not."

"I don't cook," he admitted. "When you live in New York, you don't have to. You can send out for anything you can imagine. I guess maybe I could branch out into frozen pizza or something."

She wrinkled her nose. "Too much fat. Not only is it a nutritional nightmare, but you'll probably die from a heart attack."

"You think so?"

"Definitely."

He leaned closer, and she caught the scent of his musky cologne. "What do you normally do for your patients?"

August inhaled deeply. The clean, masculine scent of

him was doing unexpectedly pleasant things to her insides. "A little cod-liver oil added to their feed usually fixes them right up. Gets the arteries unclogged. For an injury like yours, I'd generally rub them down two or three times a day."

At the mention of a rubdown, Zack gave her a look that threatened to melt her toenails. "Damn. I just ran out of cod-liver oil this morning."

August cleared her throat. "I'll tell you what. In exchange for helping with the goats, I'll make you a deal."

"Does it involve a rubdown?"

She had to fight the urge to blush. "Sorry. Horses and cows only."

"So what's in it for me?"

"Well, Saturday is the Fourth of July. We have an annual fair here in Keegan's Bend."

"How small-town," he quipped. "When you live in New York, you miss things like that."

"Everyone goes. It'll give you a good chance to meet some people. If you think you can stand the noise, I'll let you join the boys and me for the day."

"Are you serving cod-liver oil?"

She shook her head. "Fried chicken. House specialty. The boys will probably even throw in a food fight, just for the fun of it."

"Is the rubdown included?"

"Depends on how you act during the fireworks." Even as she said the words, she felt a little feminine thrill trip down her spine. Dear Lord, how long had it been since she felt free to sit and flirt with a man? It felt good, right.

His smile was slow and sexy, and made her insides quiver. "I'm very good at fireworks."

"I'll bet."

"How could a guy resist an offer like that?"

"If you'd ever had lunch with my kids, you'd know it's

not exactly a generous invitation. I control 'em as best I can—'' she shrugged ''—but they are a mob of boys, after all.''

"Are you as good at being mayor as you are at being a veterinarian and keeper of the mob?"

"I'm not sure I'm particularly good at any of it."

"That's not what I heard."

"Then somebody told you wrong."

"I heard you do it all, and do it really well."

"I think it's more like I do a lot of it and, most of the time, some of it comes out more or less all right."

Zack laughed, and the slightly tense atmosphere instantly dissipated. "So what if I'm still willing to risk that food fight?"

"Be at my house at ten-thirty Saturday morning. We'll walk into town."

"Thanks," he told her. She would have moved away from him then, but his hand came up to tuck a stray curl behind her ear. "I will."

His face was so close to hers, she felt his breath fan across her cheek in a moist breeze. His hand lingered on her cheek as his gaze held hers for several tense seconds. With the barest hint of a sigh, his thumb dropped to trace the full curve of her lower lip, and the breath drained from her lungs.

His lips parted just as a red convertible turned into the driveway of his house. From her vantage point, August saw the car before he did, and felt an unwanted thread of suspicion weave its way into her contentment. Quickly she slid away from him, surging to her feet. At his confused look, she pointed at his house. "You have company."

Zack hesitated, then glanced at the driveway. When he saw the car, he frowned. August felt heartened by the frown. Zack stood, pausing to brush the dirt from his jeans. "What the hell does she want?" he said.

"Who knows?" August said, certain that whatever Betsy May Keegan, Odelia's niece and Keegan's Bend's resident blond bombshell, wanted with Zack Adriano, it would be a hell of a lot more appealing than lunch with a neurotic veterinarian and her foster kids. "Thanks again for your help, Zack. I've really got to get ready now."

He grabbed her hand when she would have fled to the house. "Do you want me to bring anything for Saturday?"

She paused, then nodded. "You can bring the drinks."

"I'll be there," he assured her. "Drinks in hand."

Betsy May had reached the fence and was enthusiastically waving at Zack. August glanced at her, then back at Zack. "If you say so," she said, then walked away.

Zack snatched up the phone on the fifth ring. "Hello?"

"Well, it's about time you got there. Where you been, boy?"

He dropped his keys on the kitchen table. "Hello, Jansen."

"I've been trying to call you all night."

"You have?" Zack wasn't about to tell Jansen he'd been grilling Betsy May for information about August Trent. Jansen would want answers Zack didn't have. "Sorry," he told Jansen. "I was out."

"You gonna tell me where?"

"Nope."

"Has this got something to do with your next-door neighbor?"

"Maybe."

Jansen grunted. "So, you found anything out yet? What's that old bat Keegan doing?"

"I'm not sure. I had a long talk with her niece today. She seems to think that Odelia's got an investment scheme going."

"The Continental Motors deal?"

"Yeah. Odelia's got a lot of time and money invested in trying to get the plant to locate here."

"What's August Trent got to do with Odelia's financial problems?"

"Don't know that, either."

"Well, hell, kid, what have you been doing down there? I'm paying you to take care of this."

"I've only been here two weeks, Jansen. It takes time."

Another grunt. "How's your leg?"

Zack's hand automatically moved to the ever-present throb in his thigh. "All right." Quickly he changed the subject. He wasn't ready to discuss his weakness. "Listen, Jansen, are you sure you gave me everything you know about August Trent?"

"Sure, why?"

"And you have no idea why Enid Keegan left her the house?"

"None. Enid was always a kindhearted lady—a little wacky mind you, but a generous soul. I think she got all the decency in that family. Her will said something about the Keegans owing August's family a debt, but nobody knows what it is. Knowing Enid, some Trent probably helped her cross the street one afternoon. She left August the house just to defy Odelia."

Zack exhaled a long breath. He knew from the file Jansen had given him that August had been orphaned as a young child, had grown up in the foster system, moving from place to place. The more he learned, the more convinced he became that the pieces of this very convoluted puzzle didn't fit. Given August's transitory history, how could Enid possibly have known her family? Even state records didn't indicate August's paternity. Why would Enid have had access to that information, and if she did, why hadn't she done something for August earlier? "I'm going to drive into Hampton Roads tomorrow and search the records," he told Jansen. "There has to be a simple answer to this."

"Maybe. I just know that if Odelia wants that poor young woman run out of town, it's worth our while to save her."

Across the yard, Zack heard the squeals and laughter of young voices, accompanied by a lower, richer, feminine laugh that he found alarmingly attractive. "Sure, Jansen. Don't worry. I'll get to the bottom of it."

"I know you will. And stay off that leg."

"Got it."

"Call me when you know something."

Zack promised he would, then replaced the phone in its cradle. Through the curtained window, he saw the shadows moving about in August's house. A distinctly feminine form wielded a pillow as four small bodies rushed her from behind.

The scene made a slow ache spread through his chest. August, he knew, wasn't the type of woman who dealt in artifice and innuendo. With her, everything was the genuine article. He'd have to be a first-class bastard to deceive her.

His fingers tightened on the window frame as he listened to the sounds of laughter mingling with the night song of the crickets and cicadas. In the shadows, her voluptuous form all but begged for a man's hands—*his* hands. He couldn't remember the last time he'd reacted to a woman the way he reacted to August. One look from her bourbon-colored eyes and his insides went into meltdown. With no effort at all, he pictured her with her lips slightly swollen and damp, a delicate, peach-tinted flush staining her face beneath the enchanting line of freckles that swept the bridge of her nose. Zack felt something clench like a fist in his gut as he remembered her wary I'm-not-sure-I-trust-you expression.

Don't, he'd wanted to tell her. *Whatever you do, don't trust me. You're the kind of woman who wants roots, who makes roots. I could never give you that.*

Already he was torn between his sense of responsibility to Jansen and his attraction to August. As he watched the bedtime ritual unfold in her home, he remembered similar nights, when bedtime hadn't meant a lonely house. In his briefcase sat the files Jansen had given him to study. Some lingering casework for his firm also awaited his attention, but somehow, the thought of falling asleep amid a stack of legal briefs and paperwork didn't hold the appeal it once had.

Without pausing to think, he punched out a number on the phone, then sank into a chair. He'd never thought he'd miss the sound of children playing, but tonight he felt oddly lonely, on the far side of the fence from the joy in the Trent household. Tonight, he'd tell his nieces a bedtime story over the phone. There'd be time enough to worry about Jansen Riley in the morning.

August leaned back against the pillows in her four-poster bed as she thoughtfully contemplated using the coffee-can telephone line between her house and Zack's. She'd deliberately delayed the boys' bedtime tonight, for her sake and theirs.

August had needed the evening's playtime to regain control of her jumbled emotions. The boy's casual affection softened her anxiety. They seemed content. If they sensed her growing frustration with Odelia, they didn't show it. Even Lucas had indulged in the pillow fight. Once, she'd caught him deliberately missing a blow to Chip's midsection. With a smile, she remembered the I-dare-you-to-mention-it look he'd given her when he saw her watching him.

To any casual observer, the raucous play would have

seemed natural enough. Only August sensed the threads of
tension that lay beneath the laughter. As hard as she'd
worked to make her boys feel secure, she still sensed their
fear. She shared it. They'd needed tonight. All of them.
The security and warmth had been as necessary as oxygen.

But during the all-too-short moments of childish joy,
she'd been unable to forget the strangely haunted look
she'd seen in Zack's eyes that evening. Betsy May had
dropped him off just as August was calling the boys in for
the night. From her spot on the porch, she'd watched his
labored progress toward Jansen's house. As if he sensed
her scrutiny, he'd paused to meet her gaze. For the barest
hint of a second, she'd seen an aching loneliness in his
expression. She might have missed it, had she not seen
that particular look staring back at her from the mirror
most of her adolescent life. Across the yard, his gaze had
found hers, and she'd seen the vulnerable spark, an instant
before his lazy smile chased it away.

He'd said good-night with a detachment that left her
feeling strangely hollow. As she watched him limp away,
something in the too-straight line of his shoulders, the
slight tilt of his head, had begged her to soothe away his
ache—an ache she was willing to bet owed little to the
physical pain of his injury.

If there was one human ailment August knew how to
treat, it was loneliness. She'd cured herself out of it enough
times to be America's leading expert on the subject. Instinct told her that Zack Adriano was going to be trouble.
The way she reacted to him gave her proof enough of that.
A tiny voice warned her that he was a grown man, not a
little boy in need of comfort. Zack could take care of himself. But she couldn't put that look from her mind. He
might, almost certainly would, hurt her later, but she
couldn't make herself turn away from him.

Now, as she studied the coffee can, she weighed the

consequences of "calling" Zack, and found them out-matched by her wish to chase away the darkness in his gaze.

Her hand was halfway to the can when it rattled.

A tingle of anticipation raced through her. She pulled the can to her ear. "Hello?"

"August?"

Zack's voice skittered along her skin, leaving goose bumps in its wake. "Hello."

"Did I wake you?"

"No, I was going to call you."

"You were?"

She smiled at the surprise in his voice. "What's the matter, Counselor? Aren't you used to having strange women rattle your coffee can in the middle of the night?"

His laugh warmed her like a buttered rum on a winter night. "There's nothing strange about you."

"You haven't known me long enough."

"Are you kidding? I live in New York. I know all about strange people."

August burrowed deeper beneath the covers. There was something strangely erotic and forbidden about talking to him in quiet whispers through the mouthpiece of the coffee can. To use the connection in his room, he'd have to be seated on his bed. The thought of his big, bronzed body, partially clad, stretched full-length across white sheets, had her pushing the covers back from her suddenly heated flesh. "You, uh, looked tired tonight. I wondered if you were hurting a lot."

"Would I get that rubdown if I said yes?"

"No, but I could give you Jack Rutherford's number. He's the doctor in town. Maybe you might want to have him take a look at your injury."

"I think I just walked too much. If it gets bad, I'll think about it."

"Don't put it off too long."

"Yes, ma'am."

The quip embarrassed her. She should have known better than to interfere. Zack was way out of her league, and the sooner she realized it, the better. If he wanted her advice, he'd have asked for it. "Well, I was just concerned. Glad to hear you're all right. I won't bother you again."

"August." His abrupt tone kept her from hanging up. She wet the corner of her mouth. "Hmm?"

"Don't you want to know why I called?"

"I know why you called."

"You do?"

"Sure. You called to complain about the noise over here tonight."

"You think so?"

"Why else?" she asked. "Bedtime was a little more rambunctious than normal. I wanted to give the guys some time to let off steam."

"As a matter of fact, I didn't even notice the noise."

"Liar. I saw you watching us."

He paused. "Okay, maybe I noticed, but I didn't call to complain."

Her fingers tightened on the can. She had the distinct feeling that the conversation was about to veer out of control. Zack was going to say the kind of thing that normal adult men told normal adult women when they called them in the middle of the night. "You didn't?" She couldn't keep herself from asking the question, despite the warning bells clanging in her head.

"No. I called to tell you I just spoke with Jansen Riley."

Her limbs felt suddenly weak. She couldn't define whether the sensation was relief or disappointment. "Riley?"

"Hmm. He's concerned about what's going on in Keegan's Bend."

August felt her nerve endings tingle. She knew very little about Jansen Riley—had, in fact, only met him once. His antagonism toward the Keegans, however, was legendary. Though August didn't know what had started the feud, the last thing she needed was another adversary in Keegan's Bend. Thus far, Jansen had remained steadfastly absent. And she hoped it stayed that way. "What does Jansen Riley have to do with this?"

"I'm not sure, but I'm going to find out. I just wanted you to know that up front." She wondered if she imagined the soft whisper of his exhaled breath. "Jansen asked me to come to Keegan's Bend and look into this."

"I see."

"I'm not sure you do. I'm here to help you, August. I'm not the enemy."

"I'm not sure why Jansen cares or why he thought you needed to spy on me. I'm not hurting him."

"Odelia is trying to buy his property, too."

"She wants to cash in on Continental Motors. That's not exactly a big secret. If he wants to sell, that's up to him."

"I think there's more to Odelia's plan than that."

"You do?" She clamped down on the swirling fear in her belly.

"Yeah. And I'm going to get to the bottom of it."

"Because Jansen's paying you to watch me?"

"No. It's not like that. I want to help you. I just wanted to deal off the top of the deck with you. Jansen Riley asked me to come here, but that's not the only reason I stayed. I'd feel like I was lying to you if I didn't tell you that."

She squashed an angry retort. "Look, this is all very interesting, but I'm sure by now you have nothing to tell Jansen except that he owns the building next door to a nuthouse."

"I wish you would stop thinking I'm spying on you. I

respect you. And I frankly don't think Odelia has the right, legally or morally, to do what she's doing to you. *That's* why I'm involved. The only thing I'm doing for Jansen is protecting his investment.''

She hesitated. Jansen had a right to protect his property. It seemed absurd to resent him for it. ''Do you really think you can do anything?''

''Yes.''

''Then you're welcome to try. I think I should warn you, though, that I've already had a lawyer look into this. Odelia is determined to prove I've no right to the house. She'll stop at nothing to have her sister's will reversed.''

''You've had a small-town attorney. You haven't had me,'' he said, with a calm assurance that made her heart skip a beat.''

''No, I haven't.''

He seemed to sense the sudden tension in her. She practically heard his fingers tightening on the can, his body shifting on the big bed. ''But you could,'' he drawled. ''You know that, don't you?''

Her mouth went dry. For the first time in a long time, she was left completely speechless.

''August? You still there?''

''Yes.'' Her voice sounded like a frog's croak.

''Sooner or later, we're going to have to talk about this. But for now, I just think we should go into it with our eyes open.''

''Zack, I—''

Before she could finish the protest, he gave the can a slight jerk. It tugged against her hands. ''Just think about it,'' he told her. ''I'll see you Saturday.''

''What if—''

''Good night, August.''

Her eyes fluttered shut. ''Good night, Zack.'' She replaced the coffee can on its peg. Sinking back against the pillows, she lay awake, shivering despite the heated breeze of the warm summer night.

Chapter Three

She must have been out of her mind, August thought on Saturday morning as she dumped three packages of onion-soup mix and two cartons of sour cream into a bowl. She gave the mixture a hard stir. What in the world could she have been thinking, to ask Zack Adriano to share the day with them? Even on their best behavior, the boys were a handful. From her office window, the afternoon he helped her with the goats, she'd seen him walking through town with Betsy May clinging to him like white on rice. She felt quite certain he wasn't ready to experience the boisterous atmosphere of a day with the Trents, when he'd no doubt had the opportunity for a quiet afternoon with the Keegans.

At the thought, August smiled. She could just imagine what the Fourth of July with Odelia Keegan was like. She didn't even know enough swearwords to describe that kind of hell on earth. Still, with Zack living next door for the rest of the summer, life would be easier if he didn't think of her boys as an uncontrollable horde. When a loud crash sounded upstairs, August rolled her eyes. At times, they certainly gave every impression of being a horde, uncontrollable or not.

Resolutely she snapped the lid on the bowl of dip. They were good kids—a little rowdy, but good. They'd made so much progress in the eight months they'd been with her. They didn't deserve to have the Odelias of the world dump on them. As long as they were hers, she'd see hell before she let Odelia, or anyone else, hurt them. Zack Adriano was just going to have to accept his new neighbors the way they were, like it or not.

"Mr. Adriano's on his way over, August." Bo ran from his self-appointed watch on the front porch into the kitchen. He skidded to a stop in front of August. "He just left his house."

August shot a quick look at the clock. He was fifteen minutes early. "Great," she mumbled. She started packing fried chicken in a large plastic container.

"Can I help?"

Despite her agitation, August smiled at Bo. He wore a pair of pressed khaki shorts, an immaculate white T-shirt and a vest with Bugs Bunny embroidered on the back. The vest was a favorite. He wore it when he wanted to impress people. August thought about the three different outfits she herself had tried, then discarded, while dressing for the day. She'd finally settled on a short-sleeved red knit shirt and flattering navy-and-white polka-dot shorts. Evidently, Bo wasn't the only one trying to impress.

"Yes, you can help." She hooked her foot into a high stool and dragged it to the counter. "Up here."

Bo scrambled onto the chair. She handed him a bag of peeled baby carrots. "Here. Take the carrots out and arrange them around that bowl of dip.'' She pointed to the sour-cream mixture.

Bo started laying the carrots in neat rows on the plate. "Like this?"

"Like that."

August was in the process of packing plates and silverware in the picnic basket when she heard Zack's knock on the door. "Boys!" she yelled. "Someone get the door, please!"

"I'll get it!" Chip yelled as he bounded down the stairs.

August heard the screen give an anguished groan. "Hi. Did you decide yet?"

"Hi, Chip. Not yet." The deep rumble of his voice made sweat break out on her palms, and she nearly lost her grip on the stack of plates. Chip's reference to Zack's "decision" wasn't the first she'd heard from the boys that day, but so far, she'd been unable to get information out of them. Even Bo, usually the pushover, had refused to budge.

"Whatcha got?" she heard Chip ask Zack.

There was a rustling of paper. "It's apple cider," Zack said. "I thought maybe we could drink it with dinner."

"Ned always brings wine," Chip told him. He sounded disgusted. August groaned. Leave it to Chip to drag Ned Jacobs into the picture.

"I didn't think you guys would like wine," Zack answered. His voice was closer.

August glanced over her shoulder to see Chip dragging Zack into the kitchen. Just what was a woman supposed to do when a man bribed her kids with apple cider?

Chip flashed her a precocious grin. "Look, August. Zack brought apple cider. Three bottles. Can we have some now?"

August finished stacking the plates in the basket, using the mundane task to help her collect her wits, before she turned around. "Get the glasses out of the cabinet," she told Chip before she finally made herself meet Zack's gaze.

He wore a purple short-sleeved shirt, open at the throat to expose his white T-shirt. His jeans, faded almost white, clung to strong thighs and lean hips. He'd brushed his thick black hair back from his face, but one persistent lock drooped across his forehead. If it was possible, he looked even more like a pirate than he had before. August swallowed. "Hi."

He met her gaze with a steady calm that told her he knew exactly what she was thinking. "Hi. I'm a little early." He set the bottles of cider down on the counter. "Hello, Bo."

He got a shy smile for his troubles. "Hello, Mr. Adriano."

"When you gonna start calling me Zack?"

"I don't know."

Zack leaned one hip against the counter. His close proximity made the hairs on her neck stand at attention. Deliberately she focused on packing the basket. "You looking forward to today?" Zack asked Bo.

"Sure. The picnic's fun."

"What's your favorite booth?"

"I like the horseshoes. I'm real good. Last year I won a medal."

"No kidding?"

"Nope. And wait till you see Sam. He can spit a watermelon seed almost ten feet."

"Ten feet? You sure?"

"Uh-huh. He might not be able to do it so good this year, 'cause his front teeth came in."

"I'm sure that would make it more difficult." August slanted him a wry look. Only Zack could have said that with a straight face. His gaze remained fixed on Bo. "Are Sam and Jeff going with us?"

"They're coming with their dad. They're going to enter a pig in the judging this year."

"And what about Josh?"

"He's with Mrs. Prentiss. They're supposed to meet us after lunch."

"I see."

August rubbed her hands on a dishtowel, then turned to face Zack. "Sounds like a ripping good time, doesn't it?"

His eyebrows lifted a fraction. "Yes, actually."

"I'm sure it's not what you're used to."

"Change isn't always a bad thing. It helps you learn."

She managed a slight laugh. "I'd think after the goat fiasco, you'd have learned all you wanted to know about life in rural America."

He rolled his shoulders. "The goats weren't so bad. I'm a little sore, but that's all."

"No bruises?"

"Just the one May Belle gave me on my butt. I noticed the goats are gone. The dogs, too."

"Yep. Fletcher's goats have all been treated, and I was just keeping the dogs until Caspar Wilding's prize bloodhound went out of heat." She paused, then couldn't resist asking, "How was your week?" She resumed the task of packing the basket. It disconcerted her too much to look at him. There was something in his expression that had her insides shaking like gelatin.

"It was all right," he assured her. "A little dull after the vaccination adventure."

August added a stack of napkins to the supplies. "Sorry to hear that. I would have thought Betsy May would make a good tour guide."

"Euwwwwwwww..." Chip's voice came from inside the cabinet where he was searching for wineglasses.

"Betsy May Keegan?" He stuck his head out to look at Zack. Zack nodded. Chip scrunched up his nose. "Did she try to kiss you? She tried to kiss me once, you know?"

August stifled a groan. Zack slanted her a look that could have melted an iceberg, then glanced back at Chip. "She didn't try it on me," he assured him. "I wouldn't have let her."

Chip shuddered as he crawled back into the cabinet, mumbling, "She's gross."

"Besides," Zack drawled, "I'm partial to women with red hair and needles," he said.

August changed the subject. "Bo, would you please go upstairs and tell the guys we're waiting for them?"

He slipped from his chair, then gave Zack a shy wave as he hurried from the room. Chip crawled from the cabinet with a handful of plastic wineglasses. He studied Zack as he placed them in the basket. "When are you gonna make up your mind?"

"I told Jeff I'd let you know today," Zack told him. "And I will. Right after lunch."

August frowned. "Does somebody want to let me in on what's going on?"

"'Fraid I can't," Zack said. "It's between me and the boys."

Just barely, she refrained from pressing the point. He'd drawn his line in the sand, and it would do her no good to cross it. She'd have to wait and confront him when the boys weren't listening. "Well, then," she told him, "let me go get my shoes, and we can go."

"Good. I'm getting hungrier by the minute."

He watched in masculine appreciation as August retreated through the swinging door. By the time he arrived that morning, he'd lost any semblance of patience he once possessed. In the past three days, he'd spent countless hours in Hampton Roads, examining court documents and custody records. He'd seen things that made his hair stand on end. From the paper trail, he knew that August had been surviving Odelia's threats to take her house and reverse her custody of the children on wits and bravado alone. If she had the first clue as to how tenuous her hold on the boys' future was, she should have been running scared a long time ago.

As far as he was concerned, he'd given her more than enough time to prepare for today. She was a smart woman. There was no way she wasn't aware of the electricity between them. Each time he thought of her in the past few days, he'd found his body heating. The sensation was simultaneously disconcerting, frustrating, and arousing as hell. He wasn't used to this, and wasn't at all sure he liked it. In the years he spent in New York, he'd carefully cultivated a few well-managed relationships. The women in his life were sophisticated, cultured, disciplined.

All had lacked the impulsive fire he sensed in August.

Yet he'd been unable to set thoughts of her aside as he delved into the mountain of legal red tape. An inner voice warned him that he was getting in way over his head, that the nagging sense of loneliness, of aimlessness, that had plagued him since he reached Keegan's Bend was about to create havoc in his life. But an irresistible urge to know her, to understand all the complexities and facets of the woman across his fence, was irrevocably drawing him further into a vortex of uncontrollable want.

And he was losing his mind over it.

In the past three days, he'd dodged three phone calls from Ginny DeLark, a New York business associate who'd made it quite clear that she hoped to deepen their relationship when he returned to the city. Sheer connivery had helped him avoid Betsy May Keegan. But no amount of willpower could keep his mind off August Trent.

In three days, he'd learned enough about her past and the boys' future to go from impatient to downright frustrated. August owed him answers, and he wanted them today.

The sight of her, barefoot in her kitchen, with her red shirt hugging her breasts, and her blue-and-white shorts clinging to her luxuriant curves, had undone him. In an instant, he'd remembered why he found her so irresistible. She probably hadn't meant the outfit to be alluring, probably hadn't even thought about it. That combination of innocent and seductress had him dragging his gaze from the place where the cuff of her shorts lay against her peach-tinted thighs.

The fact that she appeared to be as nervous as a cat soothed him somewhat, but he still found himself oddly on edge as he imagined spending a day with her and her four chaperons.

As if on cue, Teddy bounded into the kitchen. He gave Zack a friendly wave.

"How you doing, kiddo?"

Teddy shrugged. Chip walked over to join them. "You know what, Zack?"

"What?"

"We got five whole dollars to spend on games and stuff," Chip told him. "I'm gonna win a bear."

Zack glanced at Teddy. "You got five bucks, too?"

"Sure he does," Chip explained. "August gave us each five dollars to spend."

The heavy fall of sneakered feet heralded Lucas's arrival. He entered the kitchen, with Bo trailing a few paces behind, then gave Zack a sullen look. "Where you been?"

"Working on your case," Zack told him.

Lucas seemed to consider the information. "Found anything out yet?"

"A few things."

"You gonna tell us?"

"Not till I discuss it with August."

Lucas looked like he wanted to protest, but Chip was tugging on the leg of Zack's jeans. "Will you show me how to win a bear? I want a red one."

"You can't win at those things," Lucas told him with pained patience. "They're all rigged."

"Are not," Chip insisted. "August said I could win if I threw the ball hard enough."

Lucas snorted. "August believes in the tooth fairy."

As if on cue, Chip's mouth dropped open to show Zack his toothless gums. "The tooth fairy brought me a quarter when I lost my front teeth."

"No kidding?"

"Yeah. Lucas said it was really August, but I don't believe him."

"Then you're a doofus," Lucas said.

"Am not."

Zack moved quickly to head off the brewing argument. "Lucas, give him a chance," he warned. "Somebody brought him a quarter. Might as well be the tooth fairy." Before Lucas could protest, Zack looked at Chip. "And, yes, I'll help you win a bear."

"What are you going to win?" Bo asked him.

August chose that moment to reenter the room. Zack watched her approach with a growing sense of heat and want. "I'm thinking of spending my money at the kissing booth."

August leaned back against the wide oak at the top of the hill. During the short walk to their picnic spot, the boys had maintained a constant stream of chatter, keeping Zack occupied. She'd been all too aware of his eyes on her, however. There was a promise in his gaze that made her knees feel week. She'd almost dropped to the ground in relief when they finally reached the top of the hill. She didn't think she could have taken another minute of the close tension. The easy camaraderie they'd shared while injecting the goats was gone, replaced by an awareness that made the air seem to sharpen and sizzle.

After studying her for several seconds, Zack had stretched out on the blanket. He was close enough that she felt his heat, close enough to make her nerve endings sparkle like fireworks.

His expression told her he noticed her discomfort. His lips twitched into a knowing smile as he calmly began filling glasses with bubbling cider and glanced at Bo. "So, when you boys aren't chasing goats around your backyard, what do you do to stay out of trouble?" he asked.

The tension broken, the boys immediately took Zack's cue, leaving August the rest of the meal to study Zack's interaction with her small brood.

Lunch, she had to admit, was a surprisingly lively and pleasant affair. Zack concentrated most of his attention on the boys. He had a remarkable camaraderie with them. When he made casual references to his brothers and sisters, who seemed to have an endless stream of names and anecdotes, she started to understand why. He'd obviously grown up in a large family, and he was used to interacting with children.

The boys chatted amiably with him through most of the meal. He seemed at ease with the conversation, casually asking questions that were sure to elicit detailed responses. He charmed them just as easily and fully as he'd charmed her. When he admired Bo's Bugs Bunny vest, he earned an adoring smile.

For her part, August marveled at his instant rapport with her kids. All of them had come from difficult family situations. Despite their precocious nature, they rarely formed attachments to other people, with August being the one notable exception.

Yet they seemed inclined to trust Zack. Even Lucas, the wariest of them all, entered the conversation. Except for the veiled references to whatever bargain had been discussed that afternoon in Zack's yard, she couldn't find fault with Zack's easy responses to their questions.

August fiddled with her fork while she listened to Chip rattle on about his rock collection. Zack was giving the discussion all the gravity of a lecture from the National Geographic Society. Occasionally, he would slide a smoldering look at her, or roll a carrot on his tongue in such a way as to make her toes tingle. His comments, while innocent enough, held an unmistakable double meaning. The longer he toyed with her, the more tense she felt. His generous interaction with her boys made him an easy man to like, but she still wasn't sure she trusted him.

The final straw came when she felt his fingers settle on the bare skin of her forearm. A jolt of pure desire raced from the spot where his fingers were rubbing lazy circles on her skin to the pit of her stomach. With a measured calm she hadn't known she possessed, she put her fork down, afraid she'd throw it at him if she didn't. While the thought of her fork protruding from his forehead was mildly amusing, the heated sensations traveling up and down her arm were not. "Boys?" she asked.

Four heads turned to look at her. Chip stopped in the middle of an explanation about how applesauce was only good if it had pieces of peel in it.

"Are you through eating?"

They answered in yeses and nods.

"Then go ahead and scrape your plates. I'm sure Josh, Sam and Jeff are waiting for you."

"You want to come with us, Zack?" Chip asked. "You can show me how to win a bear."

Zack studied August for a few long seconds before he turned his gaze to the boys. "If you give me a couple of minutes alone with August, I'll meet you down the hill."

Before August could protest, the boys began scrambling from the table. Plates were scraped and dropped into the picnic basket in rapid succession. In seconds, the boys were fleeing down the hill. August's strict warnings about good behavior and staying clean fell on quickly retreating ears.

"Is it safe to let them wander off on their own?" Zack asked.

"Emma and Henry will look after them."

"Emma Prentiss?" he asked, referring to Josh's grandmother.

"And Henry Derden. He's Sam and Jeff's father."

"Can they control them?"

"Can anyone?" She gave him a wry look. "Now, you want to tell me what you were thinking when you told the boys you were going to spend your money in the kissing booth."

He chuckled. She felt the sound in the tips of her toes. "I was watching you. What do you think I was thinking?" Reclined back on one elbow, plucking fat red grapes from a laden cluster, he looked every inch the decadent temptation she'd been trying to ignore for the past three days.

"No telling what the boys thought."

He plopped a grape into her mouth. "I'd wager Chip, Bo and Teddy thought it was a terrible waste of five dollars, and Lucas, who probably knows a lot more about kissing than he should at his age, still doesn't trust me."

The tangy juice of the grape tickled the roof of her mouth. She visually searched through the milling crowd at the foot of the hill for sight of the boys, but her attention remained firmly focused on Zack's solid heat. "Why should he trust you?" she asked. "There hasn't been a

single man in his life who's given him reason to trust anybody.''

"What about you?'' In a sudden motion that dragged
her gaze from the crowd and fixed it firmly on his face,
he shifted so that his body trapped hers against the tree.
Though he wasn't actually touching her, his compelling
presence held her captive. "Who do you trust, August?''

"This isn't just about me, Zack. I've got four lives to
consider.''

"I know.''

"Odelia is ready to do just about anything to get rid of
me. Even worse, she'd use any excuse she could to hurt
my boys.''

"Tell me why, August.''

"Because she wants us out of here.''

"That much is obvious.'' He laid one hand on her
shoulder. "Don't you want to tell me what you've done
to get that woman to dislike you so much?''

"I'm not exactly sure,'' she confessed. "I just know that
since the day I got here, especially since the day the boys
got here, she's been determined to run us out of town.''

Zack frowned. "The boys didn't come with you to Keegan's Bend?'' he asked.

"No. They came later.''

"Why did you bring them here?''

She thought about answering him, then changed her
mind. "That's none of your business.''

"Would it be my business if I told you I want to go to
bed with you?''

His eyes had turned a smoky gray. "Are you always
this blunt?

"Not always. Just when it seems more prudent to lay
my cards on the table than try and hedge around the conversation. I've been thinking about what it would be like

between us since the first time I saw you across the fence. Unless I miss my guess, you've thought about it, too.''

''All right,'' she said. ''Since you asked, no. It wouldn't make a difference. My boys like you. They really like you, and I'm not going to let you violate their trust.''

''What's between you and me has nothing to do with the boys,'' he said. He stood so close, the spicy tang of his aftershave tickled her nostrils. His voice had dropped to that low, rumbly tone that always made her insides quiver. He had the barest hint of an accent, something she couldn't place. It was slightly foreign, dark—exotic, even.

And it always made her mouth grow dry. ''What do you want from me?'' she whispered.

''I think you know the answer to that.''

''Things you can't have.''

''You don't know that. You don't even know what they are yet.''

''I'm not going to let you hurt my boys.''

''Are you protecting the boys, or yourself?''

Both, she thought. ''It doesn't matter. All they've got is each other and me.''

With a slight smile, he leaned close enough for her to feel the warm whisper of his breath on her cheek. ''And you don't want to talk about it?''

''That's right.''

''Good,'' he said. ''As it happens, I've got other things on my mind right now.''

''Other things?'' she asked, before she could stop herself.

His eyes twinkled. ''You want to know what they are?'' His voice had that note in it again. She couldn't take her gaze from the firm contours of his mouth.

A sliver of heat that had nothing to do with the weather worked its way down her spine. She couldn't seem to tear her gaze from the challenge in his. Even her hair seemed to have come alive under his close scrutiny. A warning note sounded in her head, telling her that she was way out of her league with this man. His was a life of sophistication and culture. She sharpened her wits on a small-town council and a pack of kids. Still, he held her under a spell, as if she were a captive feather on a summer breeze. His closeness pulled her into an unfamiliar vortex. With a strange sense of inevitability, her lips parted around the question "What?" but she didn't think any sound emerged.

Something forbidden flared in his eyes. In their depths, she saw the pirate she'd fancied him to be, a man who plundered and stole, who ruthlessly took what he wanted. "For two weeks," he drawled, his breath fanning a moist caress on her face, "I've been consumed with wondering things like whether or not your hair is as soft as it looks." His slight accent seemed to thicken. "I wonder if all the curves under your clothes are as sexy as I think they are. About what it's going to be like when I make love with you. Are you the quiet type in bed, or do you purr a lot?"

The words made her breathing turn shallow as they skittered across her already sensitized nerves. "I don't think—"

He interrupted her by flicking a curl off her cheek. "I'll bet you're a purrer. I love that in a woman."

She was quickly losing control of the conversation. "This isn't right," she said. "Someone might see us."

"No one will see, *querida*." he insisted. The Spanish endearment wrapped around her like a hypnotic cloak. He was no longer the man living in the house next door. He was a pirate come to sweep away her world. Her heart seemed to stop beating. He leaned closer, to mask her view of the crowded fair. His presence blotted out everything but the roar of her pulse in her ears. "You make my blood heat, and my skin tingle, and my pulse race, and my—"

"Stop, Zack. I want you to stop."

He paused for the space of several heartbeats. "Why don't you tell me about Ned Jacobs?" he prompted. She should have known he wouldn't miss Chip's allusion to Ned. His lawyer's mind was practiced at remembering conversational details. "Does he affect you like I do? Does he make you quiver when he's got his hands all over you?"

"You've never had your hands all over me," she said. "How would I know?"

"Want to find out?" he whispered.

Like she wanted to keep breathing. "This is insane."

With a gentle push, he fully pinned her against the tree. The rough bark pricked at her flesh through her knit shirt, but the sensation paled in comparison to the extraordinary feel of him leaning over her body. He planted a palm on either side of her shoulders. "It's insane, all right. Totally, mind-shatteringly, arousingly insane. From the first time I saw you standing in May Belle's pen, all I could think about was the way it would feel to touch you."

She struggled for equilibrium. "If I was in May Belle's pen, I was either giving her a vaccine or taking her rectal temperature."

The quip dimmed none of his intensity. "It was the vaccine," he said. "The sight of you sticking that needle in her butt really turned me on."

"You're teasing me."

"Oh, no, I'm not. You've been thinking it, too. Ever since the beginning."

"I have not."

"Come on, August." He rubbed his thumb over her lower lip. "Don't play games. I don't want to play games."

"You *are* seducing me," she said.

"I'm sure as hell trying."

"I don't want you to."

He bent his head to touch his tongue to the sensitive whorl of her ear. "Tell you what," he said, his voice a husky rasp against her ear. "I'll make you a deal."

"A deal?" She was fast losing her concentration.

"Yep." He lifted his head to meet her gaze. The glare of the sun seemed to sharpen the angles of his face. "Let me kiss you one time. If you don't like it, we'll quit. I mean really quit. I'll go back to Jansen's place and stay there. But if you do like it, we'll just see where things take us."

"You're pretty sure of yourself."

He flashed her a wicked grin. "You scared?"

"Of course I'm not scared."

"So you accept?"

"I didn't say I—"

"Oh, shut up, August," he said. He lowered his head and took her lips in a long, soul-searing kiss.

August thought she'd been kissed before, thoroughly kissed. But Zack Adriano was fast changing her mind. His kiss stripped away every reserve, every layer of normalcy, of civility. His firm mouth moved over hers in a hot, liquid caress. He rubbed against her lips while he coaxed her into responding. When his tongue slid along the curve of her lower lip, she gasped in surprise.

Zack didn't waste any time pressing his advantage. He slid his tongue deep into her mouth, stroking her in a way that was so intense, so seductive, so suggestive of a deeper intimacy, that August's lungs stopped working.

He trailed one hand down the length of her arm, until his fingers laced with hers. Bringing her hand to his hard chest, he pressed it against him. "Touch me, *querida*," he whispered, before he covered her mouth again.

Her fingers slipped inside the open neck of his shirt to skate along the muscled plane of his chest. She felt his heat through the worn cotton of his T-shirt. He groaned when she found his flat nipples. Inflamed by the small sound, she pressed closer to him. With a muffled expletive, Zack cupped her bottom in one hand, and brought her fully against his solid length. With his other hand, he found the hem of her shirt. In seconds, his warm fingers were sliding over naked flesh. When he encountered her lace-covered breast, she heard him suck in a ragged breath.   She was drowning in sensation. He'd destroyed any thought of caution, of sanity. His warm hand rubbed against the aching peak of her nipple. It sent a streak of lightning through her blood. She moaned and leaned into him, pressing her breast into his palm. She needed him, needed this. How long, she wondered, since she'd felt this sweet sense of obliteration? How long since she'd allowed herself the purely physical satisfaction of touch? Zack's caress awakened a long-suppressed hunger in her soul. Now, he could pay for it. He'd deliberately tempted until he knew she'd turn to putty when he touched her. If her response shocked him, so be it. August needed him, needed this. He'd offered. Now he'd have to give it to her.

Her thighs were wedged against his, her fingers were tangled in the hair at his nape, her lips and tongue were greedily sucking at his mouth, when she heard the footsteps coming up the hill.

Footsteps. With a guilty start, she pushed at Zack's shoulders. He eased slowly away. Her entire body trembled at the loss. Chip stood watching them with avid curiosity.

"Whatcha doing?" he asked. "Kissing?"

August choked. Zack reached over and calmly helped her adjust her clothes. "Sure were," he said.

Chip wrinkled his nose. "Kissing's gross."

Zack grinned at him. "Tell you what, Chip, I'll check

back with you in about ten years. We'll see if you still
think it's gross.''

"You had your tongue in her mouth," Chip insisted.

August buried her face in her hands. Zack gently rubbed
his fingertips on the skin at her nape. She'd had no idea
she was so sensitive there until she felt the scalding heat
of his touch. She raised her head to look at Chip. "I
thought you were at the fair," she said, hoping her voice
sounded at least partially normal.

Chip scooped up the ball and glove he'd left by the
picnic basket. "I forgot my lucky ball. I need it to win a
bear." He glanced at Zack. "Are you gonna come help?"

"In just a minute," Zack said.

"August says you gotta throw the ball real fast."

"It's not speed that counts." He gave her a smoldering
look. "It's accuracy."

She frowned at him. "Stop it."

Zack chuckled in her ear. She felt the warm rumble all
the way to the soles of her feet. He leaned down and whispered, "If you behave, I'll show you my technique."

She scooted as far away from him as she could, turning
her attention to Chip. "Go on back, Chip. We'll be down
in a minute."

He glanced from Zack to August, then mumbled something beneath his breath before racing down the hill. August had to fight the urge to press her fingertips to her
tingling lips. His scent lingered on her skin, as if he were
still leaning over her, still kissing her. Soap and aftershave
and something indefinable mingled to form an intoxicating
lure. That, August guessed, was the smell of testosterone.
She wiped a hand through her tousled hair. "I'm sorry.
Things got out of hand."

His eyebrows lifted a fraction. "Don't apologize."

"I don't usually jump on men like that."

A slight dent—did she dare call it a dimple?—appeared

in his left cheek. "Last time I checked, you weren't doing all the jumping."

"Still, I let things get out of hand." She met his gaze, refusing to be embarrassed. "I promise it won't happen again."

Zack's chuckle sent her pulse to the moon. "God, I hope you don't mean that." He gently tucked two stray curls behind her ears. "For what it's worth, I've never liked women who play games. I'm attracted to you. Unless my instincts are completely haywire, you aren't exactly oblivious to me, either."

August had just opened her mouth to reply when the sound of shouting carried up the hill. With a frown, she glanced past his shoulder. "What in the world—"

Zack scanned the crowd for the source of the confusion. When he spotted a large pig barreling through the crowd, with seven little bodies in its wake, he gave August an amused look. "What were you saying about trouble?"

"Oh, no." She surged to her feet. "That's Sam's pig."

"And she's headed right for the reviewing stand."

"Where Charlotte Anne Keegan is reciting the Gettysburg Address."

Chapter Four

By the time Zack and August reached the reviewing stand, hell had broken loose. Henry Derden skidded to a stop next to August.

As Luanna, Sam and Jeff's pig, ran laps around the stand, Zack counted seven heads. Chip was dragging his baseball glove behind him. Even Bo had managed to get a smudge on his usually spotless clothes. Sam was sneezing as he battled his way through the dust Luanna left in her wake. Lucas glared at young Charlotte Anne, who steadfastly continued with her recitation of the Gettysburg Address, despite the chaos.

Wiping his sweating forehead with a bandanna, Henry gave August an apologetic look. "I'm sorry, August. Emma and I were letting Jeff and Sam show Luanna to the boys when she got out of her pen. Something must have spooked her."

August's expression turned to one of comic horror as

Lucas tried to corner Luanna between the reviewing stand and the dessert table. Charlotte Anne had stopped reciting and started yelling orders at Lucas. Lucas was telling her to keep quiet, and Luanna was squealing at both of them. Sam had managed to work his way around to the other side of the table. Luanna took one look at the rope in his hands, then darted toward the dessert table, her head bent low. When she rushed the table, cakes, pies and jelly molds soared into the air. A large dish of ambrosia splattered down the front of Charlotte Anne's dress.

Confused and frightened, Luanna began turning circles as the boys closed in on her. With dirt streaking their clothes, and sweat dampening their hair, they looked like a street gang.

Huffing and puffing, Emma Prentiss joined them. "Land sakes, that pig sure can run."

"Emma—" August put a firm hand on her shoulder "—you shouldn't be running around in this heat."

"Somebody's got to catch that pig."

"Don't worry about it," Zack said. He glanced over his shoulder as August steered Emma toward a shaded park bench. Fifteen men, and most of the town's children, were now trying to help corner poor Luanna. "Luanna's going to be fine."

"Why don't you sit here, Emma?" August guided her down on the bench. "It's cooler."

Zack snatched a water pitcher from a picnic cloth and poured out a glass. As he pressed it into the older woman's hand, Luanna let out a frightened squeal that carried on the balmy afternoon air. Amid the howls and shouts of the crowd, the frightened pig took off toward the stables.

"Oh, God," August groaned.

"This is worse than May Belle," Zack told her. "Renegade animals are becoming a habit with you."

"I'll get her, August!" Henry shouted as he started off after the crowd. "Don't worry!"

"August Trent."

The screech of Odelia's voice was easily recognizable over the din. With poor little Charlotte Anne in tow, Odelia marched over to their spot by the bench. "You've really done it this time," she said. "You've managed to ruin a perfectly fine holiday celebration."

August met Odelia's acid stare with a weary look. "Looks like everybody's having fun to me." She indicated the throng chasing Luanna through the streets. With a kind smile at Charlotte Anne, she said, "I'm sorry about your dress, sweetheart."

"It's okay," the child said. "I didn't—"

Odelia gave her arm a jerk that looked strong enough to wrench it from the socket. "Hush up, Charlotte Anne. This is adult talk." When she turned on August again, a dark anger burned in her gaze. "I told you something like this was going to happen."

"Odelia, I think you're overreacting. There's no damage done."

"Overreacting?" Odelia's lips pulled into an ugly frown. "Only you would say something like that, August Trent. You've allowed those little demons of yours to completely disrupt a town event, and you say I'm overreacting?"

August dragged a hand through her already unruly hair. "They're little boys. They act like little boys."

"They're delinquents. And they belong behind bars."

August's temper snapped. Between the heat of the day, and the way her body still trembled from Zack's touch, she simply didn't have the stamina to maintain her calm. This time, Odelia had pushed too far. "This has gone far enough," August snapped. "I have tried everything I know to get you to lay off my kids, but if you can't see reason, then I'll have no choice but legal recourse.''

The older woman's eyebrow arched so high, it disappeared beneath the curled fringe of her beauty-parlor hair. ''Legal recourse?'' she said, her voice southern syrup laced with steel. ''Surely you aren't so naive that you think there's a judge in this county who'd rule against me? You're a smart woman, August Trent. You wouldn't be sitting in this mayor's office if you weren't. Why don't you use that brain of yours and admit you can't win this battle?''

''Because I still have a few tricks in my hat.'' August paused to rein in her temper. ''I've got the environmental impact study for Continental Motors sitting on my desk. The council still hasn't voted on it, you know. You could lose millions if the plant doesn't locate here.''

Odelia didn't bat an eyelash. ''And your point, August?''

''From the beginning, you've wanted me out of Keegan's Bend because I stood in the way of your financial success. It's got nothing to do with your dislike of my boys, or a pig loose at the Fourth of July picnic. The house and land Enid left me, plus Jansen Riley's property, are the last two pieces of land you need to turn yourself a tidy little profit. If you could, you'd probably stalk poor Enid in her grave to make her give you back the house.'' She squared her shoulders. ''Well, I'm not selling, or leaving. Neither, as far as I know, is Jansen Riley. So that puts you in a bit of a spot, doesn't it?''

''You have no idea what you're talking about.''

''No? Then why don't you explain the phone call I got from Jameson Oaks at Continental Motors, thanking me for the increased financial incentives Keegan's Bend offered his company to locate here? Last time I checked, I was still mayor in this town. The council didn't make any additional offers. I assume, therefore, that you did."

Odelia's lips pressed into a thin, unpleasant line. "You think this is about money, don't you?"

August struggled to maintain her composure. "Of course it's about money. You're furious that Enid willed a family property to an outsider. You're furious that I won't sell it back to you. You're furious that her will was so airtight that even the judges you supposedly have in your back pocket won't reverse it. And you've decided the only hope you've got is to make my life miserable enough so I'll leave town. Am I getting it so far?"

"Not precisely."

"Well, let me tell you something, Odelia. You can push me really hard. Generally, I just ignore people like you. You aren't worth the time and effort to dislike. But this time, you've threatened my kids."

"Those delinquents you call children are out of control. If you wouldn't let them run rampant through the town, I wouldn't have to chastise them."

"Chastise?" August's fingers tightened into fists. "Chastise? They're scared to death of you. They're convinced, all of them, that you're going to ship them off to some orphanage where they'll end up back in the foster system."

"And you're willing to do anything to prevent that?"

"Absolutely."

"Including leave town?" Odelia asked. A spark of triumph glowed in her eyes.

"This is my home." August took a step closer. "This is their home. And if you think you can run us out of town because of some business—"

"You're really a very foolish child, do you know that?"

August refused to be intimidated. "Drop the southern charm, Odelia. I'm not fooled."

The older woman's lips curved into a smirk. "You honestly believe that I'd go to this much trouble over something as paltry as the few thousand dollars I have at stake in Continental Motors?" Her shoulders moved in a slight shrug. "If they locate here, it'll create jobs, stimulate the economy. The Keegans stand to gain a great deal, but my battle with you has nothing to do with money, August. You should have figured that out by now."

August's breathing had gone shallow. Perspiration beaded on her skin. The world was suddenly too confining to accommodate her frustration and Odelia's presence. The condescension she heard in Odelia's tone threatened to snap the fragile rein she had on her temper. "Then why," she said with a deadly calm, "don't you tell me why your sister left me the house?"

The flicker of anger in Odelia's eyes told August she'd hit her mark. "Enid was a foolish child. She was prone to do irrational things."

"Like give her house and land to a complete stranger for no apparent reason?" August shook her head. "I don't think so."

"It clearly stated in her will that she owed your family a debt for their kindness to her."

"Come on, Odelia. You don't believe that, do you?"

"Don't play games with me, August. I always win. If you're smart, you'll take the money I've offered you, pack up your little horde and leave here. Someone is going to get hurt if you don't."

"Is that a threat?"

"It's the hard truth. I will have you gone, at any price. You might as well accept that."

"No one messes with my kids."

Odelia fixed her with an icy glare of contempt. "And no one challenges Odelia Keegan and wins."

August opened her mouth to reply, but then Zack's fingers clamped on her elbow. "That's it," he said. "I've heard enough." The determination in his voice seemed to impress even Odelia.

Odelia glared at him. "I don't see that my business with August is any of your—"

"I'm making it my business."

"You," she told him, her voice pure acid, "are a stranger in this town. You know nothing about our traditions, our history."

"I know that you're overreacting to a little boyish fun. So the desserts got ruined. Worse things have happened."

"This is not an issue of a ruined picnic." Her face pinched into a tight line. "It's one more example that August cannot control those boys she has brought into this town. It's only a matter of time before something serious happens."

"Aunt Odelia..." Charlotte Anne began.

"Speak when you are spoken to," Odelia told her.

Zack's expression softened when he glanced at Charlotte Anne. "We'll replace the dress, Charlotte Anne," he told her. "I'm sorry your speech got ruined."

She beamed at him. "I didn't like it, anyway," she said. "Mama made me wear it."

"Enough," Odelia spit. "There are more important things going on here than your dress."

August stiffened. "Save the venom for me, Odelia. I'm the one you're mad at."

"Oh, you have that right. I'll have you gone yet, August Trent, you mark my words."

Zack held up a hand to silence the tirade. "If you're going to be threatening my clients, Ms. Keegan, you'll have to deal directly with me."

"Your clients?"

"I'm an attorney."

If August hadn't been so agitated, she might have

laughed at the look of stunned outrage on Odelia's face.
"Don't tell me, Mr. Adriano," Odelia snapped, "that August has convinced you she has a case?"

"I'm more than convinced."

"Mr. Adriano, are you even licensed in Virginia?"

"I have several clients with financial interests in several states. I maintain licenses in all of them."

August recognized the dangerous flare of anger in Odelia's gaze. "And just what," she asked, "did August have to do to win your loyalty?" The innuendo was unmistakable.

August gasped. "How dare you!"

"What's the matter, dear?" Odelia drawled. "I haven't shocked you, have I?"

Zack's fingers tightened on her arm in a silent warning. His piercing gaze remained firmly fixed on Odelia. "When you run out of tangible threats," he drawled, "do you always resort to insults, Ms. Keegan?"

To her credit, Odelia didn't flinch. "If necessary." She studied Zack through narrowed eyes. Her gaze dropped, briefly, to his hand on August's elbow, then returned to his face. "I can see I underestimated you. Betsy May assured me you weren't going to be difficult."

"Betsy May was wrong."

Odelia seemed to gather her composure around her like a cloak. Behind her, August saw the boys chasing Luanna down the main avenue of town. Odelia stood rock-still, like a monument to distaste. Her attention was focused solely on Zack. "Evidently. I never should have sent a child to do a woman's work, I suppose. I've no doubt that Jansen Riley is behind this."

"Jansen is an old friend," Zack conceded. "When he asked me to come to Keegan's Bend, I complied."

"And as part of the arrangement, you've taken on August Trent and her pack of delinquents?"

"As it happens, August isn't my client."

That seemed to ruffle Odelia's calm. "But you said—"

"I said, I wouldn't have you threatening my clients. I never mentioned August. I don't represent her. I represent her kids."

Odelia's outraged oath acted like a balm to August's soul. She could have kissed Zack for putting that look of stunned disbelief on Odelia's face. The crowd chasing Luanna was making so much noise now, it was difficult to hear the quiet thread of calm in Zack's voice.

"Those boys?" Odelia sputtered. "You can't be serious."

"I'm completely serious. The boys have me on retainer."

"This isn't a game, Mr. Adriano. This is a very serious matter. If you think I'm going to let you get away with this, you—"

"I assure you, I'm completely serious. And because August is the children's legal guardian, I'm going to have to insist that any further interaction you have with her be directed through me."

Odelia seemed to have recovered some of her calm. She gave poor Charlotte Anne, who'd been watching the exchange with wide, wondering eyes, a hard shake with her lace-gloved hand. "Surely you realize you can't win this battle. I *own* this town."

Zack's expression turned stone hard. He reached into the back pocket of his jeans and produced a folded piece of paper. "Maybe you own the town, but I've got the law on my side."

"The law?" Odelia's laugh was as cold and lifeless as a snowbank. "Mr. Adriano, *I* am the law."

August saw the gleam of satisfaction in Zack's eyes as he handed her the folded paper. "Well, then, you've just issued yourself a restraining order."

With an outraged gasp, Odelia snatched the paper from his hand. "You will hear from my lawyer."

"I'll look forward to it."

She spared August a final glare before she dragged a complaining Charlotte Anne away from the fair.

Emma made a disgusted sound beneath her breath. "The old prune," she said. "Goes to show what can happen when you've got nothing to love but money."

"Are you feeling better, Emma?" August asked her.

The older woman nodded. "I'm fine. I'm sorry we lost control of Luanna."

With a heavy sigh, August sank onto the bench. Zack saw the expression on her face as she watched Luanna make another lap around the town. The resignation he saw in her eyes bothered him. Some of the fight seemed to have drained from her.

As Luanna headed for a side street, several men moved to head off her progress near Pete Flannery's stable. Evidently, they were going to try to corral her in the paddock.

"Don't worry about it, Emma," August was telling the older woman. "If it hadn't been this, it would have been something else." Her gaze met Zack's. "But nothing's going to hurt the boys. You can count on it."

August's words echoed in Zack's mind for the rest of the afternoon. After poor Luanna was captured and penned, the remainder of the day passed in relative calm. Mitchell Watson rescued the town from the dessert debacle by opening his ice cream parlor. After cleaning up the boys as best she could, August seemed content to spend the afternoon trailing them from booth to booth while each of them spent what remained of his five dollars.

Odelia had disappeared after the pig incident, and Zack couldn't help noticing that the festivities seemed to take on a lighter tone in the wake of her departure. Emma and

Henry left the seven boys with August and Zack as they headed off to finish judging the various categories for live-stock and produce.

With August's attention absorbed with the boys, Zack was grateful for the chance to study her. On the surface, she appeared to be having a good time. Casually Zack watched her as she helped the children win games. She moved about the town with an easy grace, a joy of life, that fascinated him. Everywhere they went, she stopped to say a kind word, to inquire about a problem, to ease the burden of the people around her. She did everything with an abundance of passion, a passion he desperately wanted to feel, to bask in.

When she laughed, the throaty sound set off sparks in his blood. The firm curve of her chin, the strength in her fingers, the casual elegance that marked her gestures, prac-tically begged him to touch her. Twice, he caught her look-ing at him with a suppressed heat. Both times, he had to battle the urge to drag her home, where he could make slow, easy love to her. August Trent was the kind of woman who came awake in a man's arms. He'd have staked his life on it. Like Snow White, he mused, in a rare moment of poetry. Surrounded by her seven little men, all she needed was a lover's kiss to awaken the passionate woman inside.

He wanted that passion desperately.

Perhaps that yearning sharpened his senses. Only he seemed to know that her light spirit masked a deeper, driv-ing fear. He sensed the tension in her. Noted the way her hands would dart out to compulsively straighten Josh's shirt collar, or smooth Bo's hair. Her gaze continually scanned the crowd as she watched her boys make their way through the fair. By late afternoon, she was like a walking time bomb. Zack decided the time had come to interfere when she jumped a good six inches at the touch of his fingers on her arm. It was early evening, and she'd declined to eat dinner with the boys, claiming that the afternoon's heat had stolen her appetite. In the waning sunlight, Zack saw the lines of tension around her eyes. "Nervous?" he asked.

"Of course not." Her smile was a bit too bright, too assured.

"Liar. You're about to combust."

"Don't be silly." She pointed to the boys. "They're having a great time."

"But you're not."

She shrugged. "I'm a little worried about how I'm going to get the chocolate out of their clothes, but other than that, I—"

"August." With a gentle pressure, he guided her to a secluded spot between two tents. "Honey, you're wound up like a watch spring. Odelia really upset you this afternoon, didn't she?"

She watched him for long seconds. As if it were a glacier slowly crumbling, he watched her facade slip away. "What am I going to do?" she whispered.

Zack didn't waste any time. He pressed her back against the tent, then gave her a quick reassuring kiss. "Wait here," he said. "I'll ask Emma to watch the boys, and we'll go somewhere and talk."

Her stricken expression tore at him. "I can't leave the boys."

"They're going to be fine," he assured her. "You don't have to be the Rock of Gibraltar every waking hour."

Her hands clamped onto his forearms in a compulsive grip. "She can't have them, Zack. She can't."

"I know." He eased away from her. "Just give me a few minutes. I'll be right back."

He took less than thirty seconds to locate Emma, and another minute or so to round up the boys. With a stern warning that they'd better be on their best behavior, he left them drinking lemonade and watching Luanna compete. By the time he returned to August, she was leaning against the side of the tent. The color had drained from her face, and her eyes had a lifeless expression that worried him.

"Okay," he said. "Let's go."

"Where?"

"Follow me."

In silence, he guided her through the crowd to the base of the hill. With a firm hand at her back, he walked with her back to the shady spot beneath the wide oak tree. August sank to the ground with an exhausted sigh. "I'm sorry, Zack. I didn't mean to ruin everyone's day."

"Stop apologizing." He seated himself next to her. "Odelia's little tirade would have disconcerted anybody. You don't have to take that from her."

"I appreciate your interference. What was that paper you gave her, anyway?"

"Just what I said. It's a restraining order."

She frowned. "What?"

Zack tangled one hand into her hair. The curls were slightly damp from perspiration. He rubbed the pads of his fingertips on her scalp. "Your boys just got themselves a lawyer, August."

"A what?"

"A lawyer," he said, "and a damned good one, if I do say so myself."

August blinked several times. "They can't hire a lawyer."

"Why not?"

The question was so ridiculous, she almost laughed. "Why not? Let's start with the fact that they don't have any money, then work ourselves around to things like the age of majority."

"I'm on retainer."

"Retainer?" She lifted an eyebrow.

"Yep. Twelve dollars, thirty-seven cents, and a rock. That's my price for cases like this. They offered me more, but I decided to give them a break on my hourly fee."

"This is the bargain you guys have been alluding to since the other day?"

"Yes."

"They hired you? They offered you a case?"

"Right the first time."

She studied him for several seconds. "If word of this got out in New York, your clients would probably mutiny."

"Probably. Jansen Riley pays me five hundred dollars an hour."

"Well, isn't he a fool?"

"I'm worth every penny."

"As the boys' guardian, I think you're probably legally required to tell me what's going on."

He gave her a lopsided smile that did strange things to her insides. When he twined a curl around his index finger, she felt the light pressure all the way to her toes. "They're a little worried about Odelia," he said. "They asked me to defend their interests."

A flutter of dread tripped down her spine. "They said that specifically? They're worried about Odelia?"

"Ummm." He didn't seem to be paying much attention to the conversation. Something about her ear seemed to fascinate him. He traced the curve of it with the tip of his finger. "They think she's going to run them, and you, out of town."

At his words, she felt a wave of bitter anger wash through her. Those fears, she knew, were terrifying to a child. Boys like Bo and Chip and Lucas and Teddy, especially, lived in terror of being sent "back." The remembered agony of sleepless nights, horrifying dreams and wrenching disappointments made sweat break out on her palms. "She wouldn't," she whispered. "I won't let her."

Zack's fingers moved over her face in a restless caress. She felt the probing strength of his eyes as he tried to gauge her mood. "August? Is there something you want to tell me, here?"

"When?" she asked. "When did they tell you that?"

"The day they came through my fence while you were talking to Odelia."

She knew the color had drained from her face, had felt it wash out of her. "I've got to talk to them—" She would have moved away from him then, but he stayed her with a firm hand on her shoulder.

"Wait a minute. Just wait a minute. Tell me why you're so upset."

She gave him a startled look. "Upset? Do you know what they're going through? They're scared to death." She'd had no idea they harbored those fears. She'd tried so hard to protect them, to make them feel safe. "Have you got any idea what it's like to be eight years old, to have lived in three different states with eight different families, and spend every waking minute worrying that you're going to be out on the street again?"

His gaze narrowed. "Do you?"

"Yes. Yes, I do. And it's terrifying. If they think—" she shuddered "—if they're even slightly worried that I'd let that happen to them, then I've failed them. God, they've got to be scared out of their minds. Why didn't you tell me this right away? I had a right to know."

"I didn't tell you because my business is with the boys."

"This isn't a game, Zack." His hands had begun to knead the tight muscles in her shoulders. "This is serious. When those boys came to me, everything they owned fit in a shopping bag. Hell, their life is so mobile, they don't even own suitcases. They just stuff two pairs of jeans, a couple of shirts, and a baseball into a bag and drag off to the next place that'll take them. You can't even imagine how terrifying that is to a child."

"I know that." His strong fingers refused to yield to the pressure of her smaller hands.

"Sure you do. That's why you just glibly informed me that you're their lawyer."

"There wasn't anything glib about it. I decided to take their case."

"They don't have a case." She couldn't seem to keep the slightly hysterical note from her voice. In some dim corner of her mind, she knew that remembered fears were clouding her judgment, but she couldn't seem to keep the demons at bay. In her mind were visions of finding a bag with her meager belongings sitting on a small bed, of buses and trains that had led to scary new places, of cold nights in dark rooms with nothing and no one to hold the fears at bay. She pictured that happening to her boys and felt her sanity slipping away.

"The way I see it," Zack said, his voice strangely calming, "if four kids are worried they're going to find themselves on the street because of a nasty old lady's personal vendetta, they've got a case. The law takes that kind of thing very seriously." He paused. "So do I."

August met his gaze, found a strange sense of comfort in the clear intent she found there. "You're serious, aren't you?"

He nodded. "I told you, I'm on retainer. Nothing's going to happen to them as long as I have anything to do with it."

"I want to believe you."

"But you don't?"

"Zack, I—"

He pressed his thumb to her lips. "Why don't you let

me start?'' he said. ''I've been going over the legal records regarding your fostership of the boys. There's a lot of sketchy information in there about your past, August. I think it's time you leveled with me.''

Chapter Five

His thumb traced the curve of her lower lip. "Whoever did the paperwork on the boys evidently wasn't too concerned about procedures. You've got a tenuous hold on them, at best."

August's eyes widened. "What?" she whispered, as his fingers moved to trace the path of her jaw.

"You didn't know?"

"No." She felt a soul-deep panic. "No. I assumed Kaitlin had taken everything through the proper channels. Why would she cut corners?"

His thumb had found the curve of her ear. "Probably because those poor kids had already been bumped around a few times. She figured the chances of a challenge were slim to nothing. If she's like most social workers, her first concern was getting them placed somewhere safe. She could worry about the paperwork later."

"Only she never did?" August asked, starting to feel

queasy as she thought of the possible consequences. What if Odelia knew? What if her lawyers learned that legal maneuvering could force her to give up her boys? The thought made her blood run cold.

Zack dropped his hand to take one of hers. "Only she never did. So we don't have a lot to work with. I'm going to need you to level with me."

Reluctantly, August met his gaze. "What do you want to know?"

"I want to know why you agreed to take on four kids the system didn't want, and why you refused Odelia's financial offer to leave town."

"I couldn't run away."

"August—" his thumb moved along the sensitive skin of her palm "—she offered you more than the value of your house. You could have taken that money, and the boys, and relocated somewhere she wouldn't bother you. You want me to believe that the only thing that kept you here was determination?"

"Would you let Odelia run you out of town if you didn't want to go?"

"I wouldn't let her break up my family."

"Don't you dare accuse me of endangering the boys' future! You know I'd do anything for them!"

"Damn it, August, I need answers from you. I'm not the enemy."

"No?" She tried to move away from him, but he stopped her with a firm hand at her shoulder.

"No." His gaze held hers. "No," he said, more quietly, "I'm not. I'm going to help you, but you've got to help me first. We're not playing a game here. We're talking about four young lives. They need you."

She fought an internal battle and lost. Zack was going to make her admit things she longed to keep buried inside. He would want to know everything, the stories, the fears, the motivations, all of it. "You can't let her take them away from me," she whispered.

"Help me," he urged.

"What do you want to know?"

He seemed to sense the importance of the concession. "What are you willing to tell me?"

"Most of it. Maybe not the gorier details, but I'll tell you how it started."

"Fine. We'll start there. Why don't you tell me how you ended up in Keegan's Bend?"

"Inheriting the house from Enid was a like a miracle. I had no idea why. I had just graduated from veterinarian school, and was ready to set up practice. I got a call from Odelia's lawyer telling me I should come to Keegan's Bend right away."

"I assume Odelia's attorneys investigated the provisions in Enid's will."

August managed a slight laugh. "*Investigated* isn't the right word. *Scrutinized*, maybe. *Dissected*, even. Odelia was furious."

"And no one found out why Enid left you the house?"

"Not that I know of. Everything was iron-tight. Odelia even tried to question Enid's state of mind when the will was drafted, but the lawyer in Hampton Roads who drew it up had witnesses. There was no way around it."

"So what about the boys? Where do they fit in?"

"As soon as I knew the house was mine, I called Kaitlin. She had them waiting for me."

"She'd been having trouble placing them?"

"Yeah." August shook her head. "That's a major flaw in the foster system. People want kids they can turn around in a night, but most of the children are so emotionally scarred, it can take months, even years, to reach them. Most foster parents don't have that much patience."

"Or love."

She met his gaze. He was watching her with a tenderness that tugged mercilessly at her heart. "I suppose."

"How much do you know about the boys?"

"Lucas, he's fairly typical of kids in the system. His father abandoned his mother. She couldn't take care of him, so she turned him over to the state."

Zack's eyes narrowed to dark slits. "There's maternal instinct for you."

"Actually, it's better for a woman to recognize she can't care for the child than neglect him, or worse, because she doesn't want to admit she can't hack it. Social workers have to take too many battered kids out of too many homes. Lucas has scars—who wouldn't—but his are the emotional kind. They'll heal in time."

"What about Chip? He's—" Zack paused, as if searching for the right word.

"Simple?" August supplied.

"I guess. Not slow, I don't think. Just different."

She nodded. "He's brighter than he seems. He's the youngest. He just turned six. As I said, Lucas is fairly typical of the kids in the system. They're hurt, and the only way they know to express that hurt is with anger. But some kids react like Chip. He can't stand what's happening to him, so he just switches it off. He's got an internal protective mechanism that enables him to ignore whatever's happening around him."

"Is it dangerous?"

"It could be. If he's not nurtured out of it, he could explode one day. That generally happens to kids in their adolescence, when they lose some of their ability to escape into fantasy."

Zack exhaled a long breath. "How do you keep from wanting to kill their parents?"

August waited while a warm breeze rustled the leaves overhead. She gently squeezed his hand. "I concentrate on the kids and try not to think about how they got that way. Bo's a good example."

"I've never seen an seven-year-old with better manners."

"He entered the foster system after his mother was killed in an automobile accident. When Kaitlin found him, he was living with a foster family in Norfolk. He'd been there a year. She's still trying to locate his younger sister, but the case files are missing. There are hundreds of children in the system who fit his sister's description, and the only way Kaitlin can find her is to check each one individually."

"Great."

"Exactly. Here's this kid, completely traumatized by the death of his mother, and the first thing social services does is separate him from his only living family member."

"If Kaitlin finds her, are you going to take her in?"

August looked at him in surprise. "Of course. I doubt Bo will even begin to heal until he knows his sister is all right. That's part of his problem. Unfortunately, a lot of families take in foster kids for the money. I get an allowance from the state for each child. Some foster parents see it as supplemental income."

"Damn."

"It's enough to make your blood boil," she told him. "The family Bo was with kept telling him that if he behaved, if he didn't give them any trouble, or tell his social worker that he didn't have enough food, or enough clothes, or enough blankets, they'd find his sister and let her live with them." She saw the way Zack's jaw tightened into a rock-hard line. "He's convinced that if he manages to be perfect enough, he'll get his family back."

With a muttered exclamation of disgust, Zack wiped his hand over his face. "This is repulsive. How does this happen?"

"The courts are just now getting to the place where they're starting to believe the kids. It happens to hundreds of foster kids every day. There are some good families out there. Some kids make it through the system relatively unscathed, and social workers like Kaitlin do everything they can for each child. But she's overworked and underpaid. As much as she wants to, she can't give every child the personalized attention they need. There's not enough time, and not enough money. Kids fall through the cracks."

"Did you?" he asked quietly.

August drew a deep breath. The afternoon sun had made the air thick with humidity and heat. Even in the shade of the tree, she felt the dampness seeping through her clothes. "Don't you want to know about Teddy?"

"Yes, but I'm not letting you off the hook, either." He reached for the pitcher of lemonade where it rested in the shade of the tree. Filling a glass, he pressed it to her lips. She took a greedy swallow. A drop of the icy liquid spilled from the corner of her mouth. Before she could wipe it away, Zack bent his head to catch it with his tongue. At her gasp, he smiled at her. "Tell me about Teddy," he prompted. "We'll get to the rest later."

"Then stop touching me. I can't think when you do that."

A flare of heat that had nothing to do with the warm afternoon sparked in his eyes. "That's the best news I've had in weeks."

With a disgruntled frown, she leaned slightly away from him. "You said you looked at the kids' files this week in Hampton Roads. Wasn't this stuff in there?"

"Some of it. I'm getting a clearer picture from you, though."

"It's not pretty, is it?"

"It's making me furious." Zack shook his head. "People have no right to treat children like this."

"Teddy's case is the worst, I think. He comes from an abusive home. The social worker who first handled his case had been called out to his stepfather's house on four separate occasions. Each time, despite the evidence, she left him with his father."

"Oh, hell."

August shrugged. "That's one of the flaws in the system. The courts are very adamant about trying to keep families intact."

"Even when the kids are getting knocked around?"

"Unfortunately, yes. There's a philosophy that removal from the home will be more traumatic for the child. The emphasis is on family counseling to end the abuse."

"How often does that work?" He bit out the question.

August shook her head. "I don't know the statistics, but I doubt it's very effective. Generally, when a child is abused by a male figure in the home, the male is either the boyfriend, or the second husband, of the mother. Natural fathers are rarely inclined to physically abuse their own children. It's territorial."

"It's criminal."

"That too. In Teddy's case, he was living with his stepfather. Kaitlin still hasn't determined what happened to the mother, but two years before she took over Teddy's case, the courts had given the stepfather legal guardianship."

"If he was beating him up, why did he want to be his guardian?"

"My guess would be the added welfare money he could get from the state."

Zack swore again. August ran her thumb over the tense lines of his hand. "When Kaitlin went to check on Teddy's progress, she found him locked in a closet. He had several very obvious signs of previous abuse, and he'd stopped talking."

"Has he ever said anything?"

"Not since Kaitlin has been his caseworker. We're not sure when he stopped." Two unexpected tears welled in her eyes. She shook her head to prevent them from falling. The tears she cried for her boys, she'd always cried in private. Through the years, she'd learned to scorn the pity of others. She would never subject her kids to the same cloying false concern she'd endured so many times. She'd always been able to tell their stories without feeling it personally. Only when she sat alone in her bedroom did she weep for them. But now she met the tender look on Zack's face and realized why her throat felt suddenly clogged. She'd never told their stories to a person who responded to them as he did. "I guess," she whispered, still fighting the tears, "I guess he just ran out of things to say."

"Ah, August..." Zack's hands closed on her shoulders. He guided her to a comfortable position against his chest. "Don't cry."

"It's so unfair."

"I know."

"They're just little boys, Zack. They've never felt safe in their lives."

"But they're safe with you."

"Only if Odelia doesn't win."

"She won't." Gently, he tipped her away from him. With the rough pads of his fingers, he brushed away her tears. "She won't," he promised again. "You're not going to let her, and neither am I."

August drew comfort from his quiet assurance. "Thank you," she told him, "for understanding."

He regarded her for several long seconds. "Are you going to tell me your story, too?" he asked. "Or do I have to wait for that?"

A familiar feeling of panic lodged in her throat. She didn't tell this story to anyone. The secrets were hers alone. "I'd rather not talk about it."

"I want to understand you," he persisted. "Not just because of the boys, either. I want to understand who you are. Please, August, trust me."

In her entire life, she'd never been urged to trust anyone. Her survival had depended on her ability to trust only herself. Zack's persuasive plea was almost hypnotic. She couldn't take her eyes from the strong set of his face, the compassion in his gaze. More than she wanted her next breath, she urgently wanted to believe in this man. Perhaps it was the way he'd listened and responded to her stories about the boys. Maybe he'd seduced her with his quiet confidence. More likely, the feeling that Zack Adriano was a man who got what he wanted had lured her into a rare tranquillity. Beneath the sheltering limbs of the tree, she allowed herself to relax.

His presence soaked into her troubled spirit like the first drops of rain on parched earth. With an almost alarming sense of ease, the words came. "I grew up a foster kid," she began. "I was born in Nashville, and bounced around from place to place while the state tried to find somebody who'd take me."

She felt the warm strength of Zack's hand close on hers. He waited in silence, offering her the slight physical comfort. Her fingers tightened on his. "I was an ugly kid," she said, with a slight self-deprecating laugh. When he opened his mouth to protest, she shook her head. "I mean, really ugly. I was skinny, and my hair was so red, it looked like a shaggy carpet. I had more freckles than skin, and I had some physical problems nobody knew how to fix. I was sick all the time. Colds, flu, viruses, you name it. I don't think I was well more than twenty or thirty days a year.

"The state kept trying to place me, but in those days, they handled things a little differently. Usually, families would come to the state homes and look us over. Everybody wanted babies, and if they were willing to take an older kid, they didn't want one that looked like a red-headed skeleton.

"When I was about six, I finally got picked. I went home with this young couple." She met Zack's warm gaze. "You know what I remember most about them?"

He shook his head in mute denial.

August managed a slight smile. "She smelled good. Up until then, the only smells I knew were the stenches of the streets, and the antiseptic odors of the state homes. This lady smelled really, really good." She fell silent for several long minutes as she remembered what it had been like to put her shopping bag of meager possessions on the large bed in her airy new room.

"What happened?" he prompted.

"I don't know." August shook her head. "I never knew. I lived with them for about three weeks. I tried so hard to make sure I did everything right. Then, one day, I came home and found my stuff, packed in a shopping bag, sitting on the bed. That meant it was time to go back to the home."

Zack swore beneath his breath. Startled, August realized she hadn't been paying attention to his reaction to the story. Her fingers tightened on his hand. "It's all right, Zack."

"The hell it is. How many times did this happen to you?"

"I don't know. I lost count." She wondered if he'd find the lack of emotion in her voice odd. She'd long ago lost the ability to grieve about those moments in her life.

With the pads of his fingers, he softly pushed her damp bangs off her forehead. "I'm so sorry, *querida,*" he whispered, and somehow, the words didn't carry the same pity she usually heard. There was a wealth of understanding in him that she struggled to understand.

"It's over," she said. "I survived."

"No kid should have to go through that."

"That's why I'm a foster parent."

"Yeah. I guess it is."

"When I was in high school, I realized that the only way I was ever going to have a life for myself was if I made one. I got a job working in a pet store after school to save some money for college. There was this doctor who came in twice a week to care for the animals, and she was the one who really encouraged me to become a vet.

"By working weekends, and waitressing, and just about every other odd job I could get, I managed to put myself through college in five years. That's where I met Kaitlin."

"Kaitlin Price—the social worker who handled the boys' paperwork?"

"That's the one. She was my sophomore roommate, and we lived together until she graduated. She majored in sociology, and I had told her that as soon as I got established, I wanted to become a foster parent. Kaitlin understood, knew my history, so when I inherited the house from Enid Keegan, she already had Lucas, Chip, Teddy and Bo lined up. I guess she figured the paperwork wasn't nearly as important as getting them out of the system."

"That would be my guess," he concurred. "So you came to Keegan's Bend, and the boys came to live with you?"

"Three months later."

"And when did your troubles with Odelia start?"

"Before they even got to town. She was furious that Enid had left me the property. It's the first time since anyone can remember that a Keegan property didn't get left to a Keegan."

"Had you ever met Enid?"

"No."

"So a complete stranger left you a family home?"

"Yes."

"And you don't know why?"

"The will said she owed my family a debt." August glanced away again. He was probing too close to the truth.

"Did you believe that?"

She shrugged. "Why wouldn't I?"

"Because a woman who spent her whole life trying to figure out where she belonged wouldn't just accept that as an answer."

"It's the only answer I have, Zack."

He tapped on her chin until she faced him again. "Why do you think Enid left you the house?"

"I don't know."

"Don't tell me it's never occurred to you that you could be related to the Keegans?"

"Of course it's occurred to me," she said. She'd already laid herself bare for him. His probing was beginning to grate her already vulnerable nerves. "That's every orphan's fantasy, Zack. There was a mistake at the hospital. Somebody switched the babies. My real family is rich, and beautiful, and they wanted me. But that's the fantasy, not the reality.

"The reality is, nobody knew who my parents were, and for whatever reason, I was turned over to the state. Hell, I don't even have a real birth date. Whoever my mother was, she didn't even bother to record the day I was born. If Enid Keegan cared so damned much about me, then why did she leave me in the state home to rot?"

"Ah, *querida*," he reached for her then. She went easily, naturally, against his chest, where she drew solace from the solid press of his body. "It's okay."

To her horror, she felt her shoulders lurch with fresh

tears. She simply would not cry. She was stronger than the memories. She'd spent a lifetime proving it. Zack's hand found the nape of her neck, where he traced a slow, easy pattern. "We're going to fix it," he promised. "I swear to you, we're going to fix it."

"Why is she doing this?" she whispered. "Why does she care?"

He didn't have to ask to know she was talking about Odelia. "I don't know. Some people come into this world mean to the bone. I think she's one of them."

"What are the chances that she could take my boys?"

"It's not going to happen."

"But you think I should take her money and leave here?"

"I think you'd have a better chance of keeping your kids without a battle if you did." He tilted her away from him so that he could study her face. With excruciatingly gentle fingers, he brushed away the two tears in the corner of each eye. "But you need to be here, don't you?"

She searched his face. "How do you know that?"

"Because this is the first real chance you've ever had to find out who you are. That's the reason, isn't it?"

She paused, then nodded. "I've never been this close to an answer."

"And I think Odelia knows what it is."

Shivering, August pulled away from him to lean against the tree. "They're just little boys," she said. "She's got no right to terrorize them."

Zack shifted so that he could sit shoulder to shoulder with her. To the west, the setting sun had streaked the sky with orange and lavender wedges. "I asked Emma to bring the boys up here for the fireworks," he told her. "Do you want to go back to the fair, or would you rather rest here awhile?"

Her head dropped heavily onto his shoulder. "I should go back."

Zack encircled her with his arms. "Stop fighting the battle on your own, *querida*. You don't have to anymore."

Her answer came as a whispered sigh as she settled against him. Emotionally drained as she was from the afternoon's events, her eyes drifted shut just moments later.

Zack leaned against the tree, holding August while she dozed in the cradle of his arms.

The soft feel of her against him reawakened every fantasy he'd had for the past week. Inside, a burning anger tore at him as he considered the stories she'd told him. He had the same nauseating disgust for the people who'd done this to her and her boys as he'd had the day he looked Joey Palfitano in the eye and knew he was lying. His hands trembled with it. He ached in an almost physical way to find the people responsible and force them to confront the emotional damage they'd inflicted.

Holding her brought out every protective instinct in him. She was so soft, so vulnerable, in her sleep. The curve of her neck, the downy soft hairs that curled around her face, the trusting way she leaned into him, made him think of a time when she'd faced her fears alone with no one to comfort her. He refused to think about the consequences of the feelings that ripped through him. He'd spent ten years avoiding commitments. If he took on August and her kids, he'd be up to his eyeballs in promises he might not be able to keep, but each time she sighed in her sleep, each time she shifted against him, resolve drowned out common sense. He couldn't turn his back on her, when everyone else in her life had. Damn the consequences, he wouldn't let her get hurt.

By nightfall, he was almost glad the throbbing pain in his thigh had dimmed the sharper, more insistent ache that centered in his groin. During the evening's fireworks display, he gingerly massaged the tender flesh around his wound. August had awakened when the boys joined them. She seemed refreshed, more relaxed, as she shared her boys' enthusiasm for the spectacular light show. He, too, found he could put the unsettling thoughts from his mind as long as he concentrated on August. Watching her, however, had its own price. Twice, Zack actually groaned out loud as he saw the wonder on her face.

Emma collected an exhausted Josh as the last of the fireworks twinkled away. Sam and Jeff stumbled down the hill with their father. Zack helped August pack up the remains of the picnic as the boys gathered their things.

On the short walk back to her house, the boys trudged along in tired silence. Zack was relieved to have an excuse not to make conversation. His leg was burning now. He'd seriously overtaxed the injured muscles, and had to concentrate to walk. Zack waited while the boys filed through the gate and headed for the back door. By the time he dropped the latch into place, he'd broken into a sweat. When they finally reached August's back porch, he collapsed onto the swing with a dull thud.

She glanced sharply at his face, then at the fingers of his right hand massaging his leg. "Oh, Zack, your leg..."

"It's fine."

Chip's worried face peered at him over the arm of the swing. "Are you all right?"

He nodded. "Just a little sore."

"What happened?" Bo crowded in. Teddy stood in front of him, wide-eyed, watching Zack with obvious concern.

"I'm fine," he told them again. "My leg hurts a little."

"You should have said something." August set the picnic basket down on the porch. "Lucas, would you go get the ice pack?"

Without comment, he raced into the house. She reached for Zack's hands and firmly moved them away from the sore spot. "Is it cramped, or just throbbing?"

Throbbing, he thought, was the operative word. When her firm, slender hands settled on his thigh, most of the pain in his body shifted in a new direction. He groaned.

August interpreted the sound incorrectly. "Am I hurting you?"

He managed to shake his head. Lucas returned with the ice pack. She placed it firmly on his leg. "We could have gotten a ride home."

"Are you going to be all right?" Bo asked, his eyes huge and worried.

"Sure," Zack told him. "Nothing to worry about." Just because he might spontaneously combust, that wasn't cause for alarm.

Chip looked at August. "Can you fix it?"

Zack almost laughed out loud. She could fix it, all right. She could take him to bed and stay there for a week, and he'd be just fine. August smiled at her four boys. "He's fine. Honest. I'm going to give him some aspirin, and he'll be good as new by morning."

They seemed to accept her reassurance at face value. Teddy gave Zack's hand a reassuring pat. "Now," August told them, "while I work on Zack, I want everybody upstairs in the bath or shower in the next five minutes."

"Why do we have to take baths?" Chip asked. "We went swimming in the duck pond."

"Because I said so." She waved them in the direction of the house. "Let's go. Tomorrow's Sunday, and you have to be clean."

Amid grumblings and a minimum of fuss, the boys herded through the door. "I'll be up to inspect faces and hands in ten minutes," she told them. When they disappeared up the stairs, she turned back to Zack. "Is that helping?" she asked, indicating the ice pack.

"Some."

"Let me get you some aspirin."

"I don't need any. I'll be all right. I just need to sit for a while."

"Are you sure?" She frowned at him. "You were limping pretty heavily."

"I'm sure." He patted the bench next to him. "Just sit with me for a while."

She gave him a skeptical look, then lowered herself into the swing, next to him. "You should have told me you were hurting. I'd have done something about it."

"So far, everything I've seen you do on an animal has been some revolting procedure. Next thing I know, you'll be coming after me with one of those three-and-half-foot needles you're so fond of."

She laughed. The throaty noise had its usual effect on him. "Don't tell me you're grossed out by my job."

"Completely. I thought being a vet meant wading out through ten-foot drifts of snow to deliver a calf in the middle of the night."

"It does, sometimes. But most of the time, it's like pediatrics. Pretty much every treatment I administer is disgusting. The only thing that makes it worthwhile are the patients."

He smiled at her then. In the moonlight, her hair glistened a dark auburn. Because he couldn't resist, he lifted a hand to twine his fingers in the silky curls. "Thank you for tending to me," he said. "And thank you for telling me your story today. I know it wasn't easy for you."

She put an infinitesimal distance between them. The shrill chirp of a cricket punctuated the still air. "You know," she said, clearing her throat on a nervous laugh, "it certainly got hot today."

His lips twitched at the none-too-subtle change of subject. "Sure did," he drawled.

Her slight cough told him she didn't miss the innuendo. "If you'll be quiet a minute, I can tell you just how hot it is."

"No kidding?" He brushed his fingertip over the arch of her eyebrow.

"Un-huh." She wedged her forearm between them so that she could glance at her watch. Zack watched the intent expression on her face as she concentrated on the dial. The color was rising in her cheeks even as she made every attempt to ignore him. He moved his finger to trace the path of freckles on her nose.

"Seventy-eight," she announced a few seconds later.

"Hmmm?" His hand had found the satin-soft skin of her throat.

"Seventy-eight. It's seventy-eight degrees."

"Is that a fact?" He pressed his thumb to the throbbing pulse at the bend of her collarbone.

"The cricket," she muttered, though the words were stifled on a gasp of surprise when his lips replaced his thumb. "I counted the chirps of the cricket."

He rubbed an openmouthed kiss on her neck while his hand found her nape. "How many chirps?" he prompted, when she seemed to lose the thread of the conversation. He nipped the sensitive skin on the underside of her jaw.

"Oh." The word was a sigh "Forty-one. Forty-one chirps." Her back arched against the armrest of the swing as she tried to move away from him. Zack pressed his body more fully to hers, pinning her against the pine seat. "You—" She gasped again. "You count the number of chirps in a fifteen second period, then add thirty-seven to get the air temperature."

This time, he did laugh. With a warm chuckle, he raised

his head to meet her gaze. "August, why are we talking about crickets?"

He saw the wariness in her gaze. "I just wanted to show you that not everything about vets is revolting."

With a wicked smile, he raised both hands to cup her breasts. "It certainly isn't." Slowly, he dipped his head so that he could rub his mouth against hers. "You feel so good," he told her. "I love watching you move. It makes me wonder what you'll feel like when we make love." He ran his hands down her back to cup her behind. He'd already decided the woman had the sexiest fanny in the world. He should know. He'd looked at an awful lot of fannies.

"Zack." She pressed her hands against his chest.

He lifted his head a fraction of an inch. "What is it, *querida?*"

"Please tell me you don't feel sorry for me."

He heard the thready note of panic in her voice. "Sorry for you?" Deliberately he shifted against her so that she could feel how much he wanted her. "Does that feel like pity?"

"I couldn't stand it," she confessed. "I just couldn't stand it."

"You're the strongest woman I know. I feel a lot of things for you, but pity isn't one of them." He pressed his lips to hers and whispered, "I wanted you all day today."

Chapter Six

August gasped against the gentle pressure of his mouth. "Oh, Zack."

His name on her lips fueled the passion pulsing through him. "All I could think about was the way you tasted, the way you sounded, when I kissed you." He pressed a hungry kiss to her lips. "I wanted…"

Another kiss.

"…to hear…"

And another.

"…you moan again."

This time, he swept his tongue inside and swirled it with hers until the sound he'd waited for was wrenched from her chest. "Like that," he whispered. "Just like that."

Her body went pliant against him, but she still didn't give him the response he wanted. Slowly, he lifted his head. "You can't tell me you don't feel it. I saw it in your eyes today." He swept a hand along her spine. "I can feel it in the way you respond to me."

August's breath came in soft pants. The flush on her face, the confusion in her eyes, made him frown. "This is happening so fast," she told him. "I hardly know you."

"But you want me." He pressed his lower body against her. "And I want you. You've got to know that."

"I'm sure, in your experience, that lots of women—"

He intercepted her thought process before it completed the circuit. "Hold on," he said. He moved his hands to her waist, then flexed his fingers to make her sit still. Every time she squirmed, he died a little inside, but he wasn't going to let her retreat in fear. She'd already shared so much with him today, he didn't dare let her pull away. "I want to clear this up right now. I'm not going to pretend that I'm inexperienced, but I don't want you to think I'm some kind of Lothario, either."

"What am I supposed to think? I've only known you a few days, and you're already trying to maneuver me into bed."

"Do you want to know the truth, or do you just want to jump to conclusions?"

"I know I sound like a prude to you, but I, well, I'm not used to all this innuendo." She paused before admitting, "You're making me nervous."

That pleased him more than it should have. Slowly, he reached for her hand. "August, I want you to listen to me for a minute."

"Is this the part where you tell me that there have been hundreds of women but none of them meant anything?"

He frowned at her. "There have *not* been hundreds of women."

"Dozens, then."

"Not even dozens."

"Am I supposed to believe that?"

"I know I've come on to you pretty strong." At her

brief snort, he conceded, "All right, really strong, but I don't make a habit of doing that."

"No?"

Her voice was so soft, he couldn't tell whether she believed him or not. "No. Contrary to popular opinion, it is not the practice of every red-blooded American male to sleep with every woman he encounters."

"Half the women?" she asked.

He almost believed she was teasing him. "Not even ten percent."

"That's not what they told us in school."

"I'll bet you went to Catholic school, didn't you?"

"Our Lady of Virtue just to name one," she said.

He groaned. "I should have known."

August shifted on the porch swing to look at him more closely. "I'm sorry if I gave you the impression that I think you're some kind of womanizer."

He raised an eyebrow at that. "Don't you?"

"No. It's just because this—" She made an absent gesture between them. "It's happening so fast. It's overwhelming me. I'm worried about the boys. I'm stressed about Odelia, and now this. It's a little more than I can handle all at once. I've never been through anything like this."

"Neither have I," he said.

Her eyes widened. He wished he could decipher her expression. "But surely you—" She trailed off.

"I've got a healthy enough sex drive, if that's what you mean. Hell, you of all people ought to know that. But it's not like I'd hop into bed with some woman just because she was available."

"Never?"

He felt a twinge of irritation. "No. I'm not going to lie and tell you I've had nothing but meaningful relationships, because I haven't. I've never had a meaningful relation-

ship. What I've had are arrangements between two mutu-
ally agreeable adults. Safe, clean, and protected."

"I wasn't inferring that you were irresponsible."

He ignored her. "Despite what you might think, I
haven't even lost count. I know exactly how many women
I've slept with."

"A laudable accomplishment."

"Maybe they'll put that on my tombstone."

August's relenting laugh was soft, a gentle caress on the
night air. She turned to watch the stars. "I'm sorry I can't
be more blasé about this. It's just that I don't know how
to handle it. You're so…so…you. You're Zack Adriano,
world-famous defense attorney, protector of the innocent.
I mean, you're even a celebrity since that shooting incident. As mayor, I probably ought to give you the key to
the town. But I'm the vet and part-time mayor in Keegan's
Bend, Virginia. I know you think I'm terribly unsophisti-
cated. Let's face it, I'm not in your league."

He shook his head. "I don't think you're unsophisti-
cated," he said. "I think you're August Trent, and you're
in a league of your own."

"I couldn't just sleep with a man I didn't care about."

He could tell the admission embarrassed her. He reached
up to run his thumb along the line of her cheek. "I'm glad.
I like you more because I know that." He realized, with
something of a start, that it was true. Shaken, he turned
the idea over in his head. Yes, definitely yes. Always before, he'd never particularly wanted his lovers to care for
him, not in any real sense. Caring meant commitment.
Zack didn't give commitments. But watching August with
her kids, seeing the look in her sea-green eyes when she
told him the story of her past, had started to thaw something in the region of his heart. He was increasingly afraid
that he was rediscovering his soul, and equally powerless
to do anything about it.

"So what are we going to do?" August asked him.

He gave her a light kiss. Deliberately, he made sure it was dramatically different from the first one they'd shared. There was nothing sexual in it. He lingered over the full curve of her mouth before he raised his head. "We're going to spark."

"What?"

"Spark. Isn't that what people do in this part of the world?" The idea absolutely amazed him. He found himself simultaneously charmed and aroused by the concept of courting August Trent.

"I haven't heard that term in years."

"Neither have I, but it doesn't mean I don't want to try it."

"You're serious."

He shrugged. "I said I wanted to make love to you. And I do. But I didn't mean it had to be tonight." He flashed her a brief smile. "Although I wouldn't complain if the wind blew that way."

"It doesn't."

"Didn't think so. So we're going to spark."

"What exactly do you have in mind?" Wariness laced her tone.

"Well, for starters, I'm going to finish fixing the mess you've got on your hands with the boys' fostership papers. He paused to smooth the frown off her forehead with his thumb. "And when I'm not playing lawyer, we're going to spend time together, and play with the boys, and sit on the front porch and swing."

"Just swing?" she asked.

"Depends," he said, flashing her a wicked smile.

"On what?"

"On the sparks."

"Zack—"

He pressed a finger to her mouth. "We'll just see what happens. Agreed?"

August searched his face in the moonlight. His eyes held that intense glow that mesmerized her. Perhaps it was the moonlight, or the sultry heat of the evening. Perhaps the crickets drowned out her common sense. Or maybe the heavy smell of gardenias and the lingering acrid smoke from the fireworks gave the moment its sense of unreality. Maybe she merely found herself seduced by the memory of the tenderness she'd seen on his face when she told him her story. Whatever the reason, she felt the resistance in her give way in a flood of longing. Slowly, she enfolded his hand in both of hers, then lowered it from her face. With the distinct impression that she was getting in way over her head, she whispered, "Agreed."

At ten o'clock the following day, Zack was restlessly pacing the confines of Odelia Keegan's foyer. Deliberately, he'd left August wanting last night. He'd felt it in the slight tremor of her lips, the tension in her body. She'd wanted him as much as he wanted her. He'd been sure of it.

But standing in the way had been the empty threats Odelia had hurled at her that afternoon. Instinctively Zack knew that as long as August felt the need to protect her kids from Odelia, they'd always come first. He would take a back seat, in her mind, to saving her boys. An unusually strong determination, one he didn't dare scrutinize, drove him to resolve the crisis. Once Odelia was out of the picture, August's commitment to the boys wouldn't seem as threatening.

During the long, sleepless night, Zack had pored over the files Jansen had given him. Slowly, a theory had begun to take shape, and with it had come a strategy. As he dressed that morning for his impromptu visit on Odelia, he'd felt a strong sense of satisfaction.

Now, waiting restlessly in Odelia's foyer, he found his determination growing. He had only to picture the boys to feel his jaw grow tense. One thought of a young August sitting in a state home had his blood running hot. He'd have staked his reputation on the fact that Odelia was somehow behind the tragic circumstances of August's life. And if it killed him, he'd make her pay for it.

"Mr. Adriano?" At the sound of his name, he glanced at Odelia's maid. She beckoned to him from a large wooden doorway off the foyer. "Ms. Keegan will see you in her study now."

His temper kicked up several degrees as he strode into the room. Odelia stood at the end of the long, heavily decorated room, studying her reflection in the mirror. Wood shelves, filled with leather-bound volumes, lined the walls. The furnishings had a distinctly masculine feel. Leather chairs and a Persian carpet gave it a formal look that seemed somehow inappropriate on the hot Sunday morning. A dour portrait of a white-haired gentleman hung above the fireplace. *Oppressive opulence* best described the ornate room. Juxtaposed with it in his mind was the image of August clutching a shopping bag as she sat, alone, on a bus ride to nowhere. His jaw clenched so hard that his teeth hurt.

Odelia turned from the mirror with an utterance of distaste. "Mr. Adriano," she said, acknowledging him. "I see you're admiring Father's portrait."

Just barely, he refrained from telling her that *admiring* wasn't the right word. Instead, he pulled his gaze from the large oil. "Naturally," he said. "I see the family resemblance."

She indicated one of the leather chairs across from the desk. "As I assume this isn't a social call, I'd like to get directly to business. I am expecting a caller this afternoon."

Zack snapped open his briefcase without comment. He pulled a large folder from inside, then dropped it on her desk. "You're aware by now of the validity of the restraining order I gave you yesterday?"

She snorted. "That damned Fulton Cleese," she said, referring to the judge who'd issued the order. "I never have liked that man."

"The feeling is mutual," Zack assured her.

Odelia leaned back in her chair. "You aren't foolish enough to believe your histrionics will have any effect on me, I hope."

"No." He flipped open the folder. "But you aren't foolish enough to believe I'm going to stop with a restraining order."

With tightly pursed lips, she studied him across the desk. "What's in this for you? How much is Riley paying you to do this?"

"That's between me and Jansen."

"Does August know that you're being paid to champion her cause?"

"Jansen didn't ask me to come to Keegan's Bend because of August, Odelia. He sent me here because of you." He found the paper he wanted and slipped it from the folder.

"Is that so?"

"Yes. He wants to know why he's had three offers from your attorneys in the last six months for his house and land."

"Surely they explained that I'm interested in turning a profit when Continental Motors builds its plant here."

He flipped the paper to her. "They, however, did not explain this memo that Jameson Oaks sent you eight months ago stating that he wasn't interested in an additional land investment."

Her cold gaze flicked over the paper before returning to

his. "I don't suppose it would do me any good to ask where you got that?"

"No."

She pushed it back to him with a red-nailed hand. "Then it won't do you any good to ask me to explain it."

"Then why don't you explain why you want August Trent run out of town?"

"That's my business, Mr. Adriano."

"I'm making it my business," he warned her. "You've got no legal grounds." He tapped the paper with his forefinger. "Evidently, you've got no financial grounds. That leaves a personal vendetta, and I'm going to get to the bottom of it."

To her credit, Odelia's expression barely twitched, but an unmistakable spark of irritation flared in her gaze. "What's in this for you?" she asked him.

Zack shook his head. "The only thing that's in it for me is making sure August and those four little boys don't get stomped on."

"That's very noble." When she reached beneath the desk, Zack heard the whirring turn of a combination lock. "Are you certain you aren't enjoying side benefits?"

He frowned. "Ask another question like that, and you'll find yourself wrapped up in so much legal red tape, you might never get out."

She plopped a bundle of hundred-dollar bills on the desk. "I assure you that my interests are strictly academic." Two more bundles followed. "I want to know how much it's going to cost to get you to leave this alone."

Zack looked at the money with distaste. "You can't buy me, Odelia. Don't even try it."

"Really?" She added more money to the pile. "I understood that you were in the habit of selling your services to the highest bidder. Isn't that what Joey Palfitano thought?"

He drew a deep, calming breath. Like any well-trained enemy, Odelia had done her homework. Joey's trial had been well publicized, as had Zack's role in it. Odelia had knowingly zeroed in on what she assumed was his soft underbelly. He grudgingly conceded a mental point to her, but forcibly retained his composure. "You're not even in Joey's league. You might as well accept the fact that I'm not going away. There's a skeleton in your closet, Odelia, and I'm going to find out what it is." He dropped the folder back in his briefcase.

"Don't be melodramatic," she snapped. "Just because I want that woman and those four hellions out of my town, does not mean I have something to hide."

"Maybe not," he said, deliberately snapping his brief-case shut. "But if you do, I'd carefully consider how much you want to keep it hidden. If you keep pushing August, you have my word that I'll make you pay for it."

Abruptly Odelia stood. "Then we have nothing else to discuss."

With a slight nod, he rose from his chair. "Evidently not." He didn't bother with the usual niceties as he exited the study. He'd accomplished what he came to do. With a deft stroke, he'd reversed the tables. Odelia was now on the defensive, and he aimed to keep her there.

As he crossed the wide foyer, Betsy May intercepted his progress. "Zack. I heard you were here."

"Morning, Betsy May."

"I don't suppose you'd like to stay a while and have breakfast with me?" When he opened his mouth to reply, Betsy May held up her hand. "Don't answer. I already know what you're going to say. I'd have to be a fool not to know your attentions were already occupied."

He gave her a lazy grin. "As smart as you are, what are you still doing in Keegan's Bend?"

She tipped her head toward the study. "Aunt Odelia

puts on a good show, but she's getting old. She couldn't live here by herself. God knows Hiram wouldn't do anything for her.''

"Hiram?"

"Her nephew. My first cousin."

"Charlotte Anne's father?"

"Yes. He's the one August defeated in the mayor's race." Besty leaned closer to Zack and muttered in a low voice, "He's a shiftless drunk, if you ask me. He lives with his wife just outside of town, in the house Odelia bought for him."

"Who'd you vote for in the election?" Zack asked.

"I'll never tell." She gave him a coy look as she buffed her nails on the front of her gingham jumper. "Anyway, if it was up to Hiram, Odelia would just sit out here and die. All he wants is the money. Somebody's got to take care of her. She's not all that well."

"Doesn't she have children of her own?" he asked.

Betsy May shook her head. "She never married, couldn't have had kids even if she had." At his raised eyebrow, Betsy May nodded. "You need to understand what her life was like to understand why she is the way she is. Grandfather was married twice. Odelia was his only child by his first marriage. Her mother died in childbirth. When he married my grandmother, she was considerably younger than he, and I don't think Odelia ever adjusted to her. Maybe that's why she was so close to Grandfather. Even though there were two boys, my father and Hiram's father, Grandfather left most of the money and the businesses to Odelia. He raised her like his oldest son. I think that's one reason she's so bitter."

Zack's brow furrowed as he concentrated on the story, searching for the missing pieces. "How do you know she couldn't have children?" he asked.

"There was an automobile accident. One Sunday afternoon, Grandfather took Odelia and Enid into town for ice cream. On the way back, there was an accident. Odelia bled internally for quite some time before anyone found them." Betsy May laid a hand on his sleeve. "It's very hurtful to her, Zack. I think she thought she failed Grandfather by not having a family. Surely you can understand that."

He frowned. "How old was she when this happened?"

"Oh, she was just a child then. Maybe eleven or twelve. Enid was only two."

"Are your parents still living?"

"My mother is. She lives in Charlottesville. Hiram's mother is still living, too. She's in a nursing facility in Richmond. Odelia outlived all of her siblings."

Shifting his briefcase to his other hand, Zack muttered, "I see."

"I hope so. She's not as bad as you think, you know. It's mostly just for show."

"Don't push your luck," he told her with a rueful grin.

Betsy May shook her head. "Oh, I know the shell is hard as nails. She's always felt a certain sense of family responsibility, especially since Grandfather died. In a lot of ways, she's just a lonely old woman."

"She brings it on herself."

"A lot of it, she does. But she needs me." She glanced at the door of the study. "So I stay."

"You're a good person, Betsy May."

"Oh, I'm not all that good," she said with a slight, tinkling laugh. "I just pretend real well. Besides, there are certain advantages to living here. I get to know all the scandals in Keegan's Bend long before they happen. Odelia knows everything, and I overhear most of it."

He gave her a thoughtful look. "I don't suppose you know, then, who the visitor is that your aunt is expecting this afternoon?"

"I just know her lawyer is coming with some man they've been looking for. I don't know what it's about, though. Do you think this has something to do with August?"

"Maybe."

"I'll see what I can find out."

"I don't want you to do anything you feel uncomfortable with."

"I said I cared about my aunt, I didn't say I thought she was perfect. I don't know why she resents August so much, but it's not fair. If Aunt Enid left her that house, she did it for a reason."

Chapter Seven

When Zack found August a few hours later, he was still pondering his conversation with Betsy May. He'd have given his eye teeth to know who Odelia was expecting that afternoon. Betsy May had only puzzled him further. Another phone call to Jansen had yielded little, and even Fulton Cleese, Zack's college friend who served as a judge in the Virginia Superior Court, was at a loss to explain Odelia's inexplicable dislike of him. Fulton was notoriously well-informed about Virginia politics, but Odelia eluded him. Frustrated, Zack had decided to question August about Enid's house. There had to be something, anything, that would indicate why Enid had named her in the will. At this point, he'd even listen to ghosts.

At August's house, he'd found the typical chaos. Emma had been alone with the boys. She'd told him that August had left, distressed by a phone call she received shortly after they returned from church. Odelia's attorney had phoned to tell her he'd arranged a court hearing in Hampton Roads to challenge August's right to keep the boys.

Emma had pointed him in the direction of the stable, where he found August treating a large chestnut mare. Zack deduced from eavesdropping on August's conversation with the mare, that the horse, named Scarlet, had a fairly severe case of actinomycosis. All he knew about actinomycosis was that it required August to stick a syringe in Scarlet's mouth to withdraw a nasty-looking yellow fluid. Just as revolting, he thought, as usual. Scarlet didn't seem to like it, either.

Zack laid the sheaf of papers on one of the tack benches, then eased up behind August. All it had taken was one good look at her to bring the memories of the previous day flooding back. His frustration with Odelia was instantly forgotten as he studied August's back. Her green T-shirt disappeared into the narrow waistband of khaki shorts, and the sight of shapely legs tapering to narrow ankles had his pulse accelerating. He couldn't resist the urge to touch her. When he wrapped his arms around her from behind, she jumped six inches. "Didn't mean to startle you," he said against her neck. "I thought you heard me come in."

August squirmed. "I was talking to myself."

"I heard." He turned her gently away from the mare. "Feeling agitated?" He bent his head to kiss her.

"Zack, not here," she gasped.

He ignored her protest. "Want to tell me about it?" He nuzzled the corner of her mouth.

"Someone might come in."

The grooming brushes she held in each hand limited her mobility. Zack took advantage by pressing her lower body more closely to his. "Feel any sparks?" he asked.

"Zack, really."

"I do," he said, then slanted his lips over hers. He

rocked his mouth back and forth until she moaned for him. With a satisfied grin, he nipped her lower lip. "Have I told you how much I like that noise?"

Her head dropped back to give him access to her throat. "No," she whispered.

"No, I haven't told you, or no, stop?"

When her eyes fluttered open, he saw the momentary confusion in their depths. "I don't know," she admitted.

Zack pried the grooming brushes from her hands. "I think we'd better continue this somewhere else. I wouldn't want to shock Scarlet."

"I have to finish brushing her," came the weak protest.

"Later. We need to talk, and I think we'd better do it in private. Do you have a key to your office?"

"Yes."

"Good. That'll do." He took her hand and guided her quickly from the stable, pausing only to scoop up the sheaf of papers. In silence, they made their way across the busy street to the town hall, which housed August's office. Zack hurried her up the single flight of stairs. The building was deserted. Their footsteps echoed eerily on the marble floors.

Zack waited while August dug her keys from her pocket. When they slipped into the stuffy interior of her office, he shut the door with a satisfying click. A flick of his wrist sent the sheaf of papers sailing through the air to land on the padded sofa. With a hand on either side of her face, he pulled her against him once more. "Let's try this again," he said. "I already know about the phone call. I talked to Emma."

"Oh."

"Why didn't you come to me with this?"

"You weren't home."

"So you went and hid in Pete Flannery's stable."

"I wasn't hiding."

He shook his head. "Yes, you were. You going to tell me about it?"

"Of course."

"Can I kiss you first?"

"Zack—"

"Don't bother saying no." He bent his head. "I'm going to do it anyway." Before she could protest, Zack captured her mouth with his. He took his time with the kiss. Leisurely, he explored the soft contours of her mouth, rubbing his lips against hers in a gentle caress. Long seconds passed before he felt her hands creep up his chest to encircle his neck. When she twined her fingers in his hair, he felt the gentle friction in the soles of his feet. With one hand at her back, and the other cradling her head, he walked her slowly backward until her thighs bumped the side of her desk.

Zack lifted her onto the desk with a slight growl, then pressed her legs apart so he could step between them. "Hold me, *querida,*" he urged. "Squeeze tight."

In reflex, her legs clamped around his hips. "Zack."

"Like that." He took her mouth again, this time with an insistent, marauding pressure that had her clutching his upper arms for balance. His tongue swept between her lips. His hands skimmed her ribs, her breasts, through the soft fabric of her T-shirt. "Oh, yes. Just like that."

August sought solace in the obliterating pleasure of his kiss. The insistent fear that had torn at her since she spoke with Odelia's lawyer slowly gave way to the molten sensations that spread through her body. Why did he have to look so damned appealing? In black jeans and a short-sleeved red shirt, he was six feet, four inches of male potency. When his hands pressed flat against her hips so that he could mold her to him in an intimate embrace, his hardness pressed into her softness. His heat matched hers. And her will to resist flew right out the window.

When he finally wrenched his mouth from hers, her breath came in ragged little gasps. His callused fingers skimmed her face, pausing at her closed eyelids, rubbing her dampened lips. "Sparks, *querida*," he whispered. "Like an inferno."

August's eyes drifted open. The intensity in his gaze seared her. A raw, driving want burned its way from his eyes into her soul. "How do you do this to me?" she whispered.

"Do what?" His fingers caressed the arch of her nose.

"Make me forget everything else. I lose myself when I'm with you."

His smile made her stomach flip over. "That's how it's supposed to be."

August stole several seconds to let her breathing return to normal. Her heart rate still threatened to gallop away. The feel of Zack's corded strength beneath her fingers, between her thighs, had her insides quivering. "Are you always this insistent?"

"Only with you," he said. He took a slow step backward. Her legs, bare beneath the fabric of her shorts, trembled at the friction his jeans caused on the sensitive skin inside her thighs. The sudden loss of his heat seemed startling in the air-conditioned office. Unconsciously August swayed toward him. "Don't tempt me," he urged. "If I touch you again, we'll end up on the couch."

Her eyes darted, against her will, to the blue sofa. Guilt stabbed her when she saw the heavy folder he'd carried into the office. "Are those for me to sign?"

Zack glanced at the sheaf of papers. "Yes. I finished going over everything this morning." He assisted her down from the desk. "I went to find you, and Emma said you were at the stable."

August struggled to regain her composure. If she could muster just a tenth of his unflappable calm, maybe she wouldn't feel as if the world were getting ready to spin out of orbit. "She told you about Odelia's lawyer?"

"Yes."

The clock on her desk chimed a soft three o'clock. Reflexively, her gaze traveled to the window. As anticipated, she saw seven small heads bobbing along the crowded sidewalk. At five minutes to three each day, a well-meaning Emma settled onto the sofa to watch cable reruns of "Lawrence Welk." Two minutes later, she promptly fell asleep. The boys rarely failed to capitalize on the opportunity.

August watched them from her office window almost every afternoon. Today was no different. They hurried along on their self-appointed mission, oblivious to her gaze. Josh pulled at Sam's arm when Sam would have paused to pet Homer Peterson's dog. Chip dragged the enormous red bear he'd won at the Fourth of July picnic along the sidewalk while he chatted, nonstop, to a worried-looking Teddy. Lucas and Jeff led the pack. They paused at each street corner for signs of prying glances, then raced along toward Buddy Booth's candy shop. Bo stopped once to right a garbage can they knocked over in their haste.

August knew this particular routine of theirs by heart. They'd hurry into Buddy's shop, pool their money for as much candy as they could afford, then race home in time to slip back into the house before Emma noted their absence. She'd watched them execute the raid at least a dozen times. Today, it held a certain poignancy for her. She was barely holding at bay a growing sense of dread that she was losing the war. In a tense voice, she asked Zack, "Should I be worried?"

Zack's hands settled gently on her shoulders. "Maybe. It depends on how much he knows about the mess Kaitlin created."

"Odelia's got every judge in this county in her pocket." Reluctantly, she turned from the window. "Just ask her."

"I wouldn't bet on that. I got a restraining order issued, didn't I?" He gave her shoulders a quick squeeze, then released her to pick up the folder. He pulled the sheaf of papers from it and handed them to her.

"I suppose." With a feeling of dread, she began flipping through the documents. "Do I need to read these?"

"You can if you want to. Essentially, they're petition papers, verifications of employment, confidentiality agreements, and some housekeeping stuff Kaitlin should have prepared for your signature."

She picked up a pen. "Give it to me in a nutshell."

"Your signature says you promise not to physically, emotionally or mentally abuse your foster kids, to provide them with an education, and make sure they're well cared for. I flagged everywhere you need to sign."

She flipped to the first orange flag. "Does it say anywhere in here that I'll put my personal feelings aside and take Odelia's financial offer to leave town?"

"August." He approached the desk with measured steps. "This is not your fault."

"You don't think so?" She flipped to the next flagged page.

"No. Sooner or later, this situation was going to explode. At least it happened now."

She raised haunted eyes to his. "You mean now, while I have you to bail me out?"

"I mean now while you aren't alone."

August's eyes remained firmly fixed on the papers as she muttered, "You can't possibly understand."

"You know," he said, "I have had just about all I can stand of you telling me I don't get this. Just because you've spent most of your life analyzing your own problems does not give you the right to analyze everyone el-se's.''

"Well, thank you, Sigmund Freud."

He ignored her sarcasm. "For your information, I know exactly what they're going through."

"Don't be trite," she snapped. She hadn't meant to sound so irritated, but his kiss had her seriously off kilter. "I don't mean to be rude, but unless you've been there, you just can't get it."

"You don't think so?"

"No."

"Well, then, try this on for size."

At the anger in his voice, her head snapped up. He was restlessly pacing her office, and she sensed a deep turbulence in him that she hadn't seen before. "Zack?"

"When I was fourteen years old, my mother delivered my twin baby sisters. They made siblings number eleven and twelve."

"You have twelve brothers and sisters?"

"I do."

She studied the square set of his jaw. Only the slight ripples beneath the skin indicated his tension. And that look. That same sad look she'd seen across the fence was back in the depth of his gaze. Picturing him amid a laughing, squirming heap of younger siblings, she wondered how that look had found its way into his expression. All her life, she'd figured you could never be sad if you had family. "Were you the oldest?" she asked, already knowing the answer. His air of authority was unmistakable.

"Yes. There were four boys, then eight girls. I was the oldest. But eleven was the magic number for my father. We were living in Cedar Rapids, Iowa, where Pop had taken a job in one of the mills. After the twins were born, he went out for cigarettes one night, and never came back."

August felt a stabbing sense of loss on his behalf. Zack, then a young man, had been left to cope with the desertion of his father. Like most abandoned children, she'd found some strange solace in never having known the parents who'd left her. Zack hadn't been afforded that small refuge. This was the side of him where that haunted look fed on his remembered pain in a fountain of bitterness. "My God, Zack."

"Here was my mother, the abandoned Spanish-speaking Catholic wife of an Italian-American husband, with thirteen kids, no job skills and no money, living in the Protestant-middle-class capital of the world. For the next four years, she slaved away at three jobs, trying to make ends meet. I was the oldest, with three brothers after me. We all got jobs after school. Everybody who was old enough to work, did. We lived in constant terror of being separated."

"Somebody should have hung your father," she muttered. "Nobody should be allowed to do that to his family."

Zack didn't seem to hear her. The memories appeared to be holding his attention captive. "When I turned eighteen, my mother got ill."

"Oh, Zack."

"Six months later, she died of pneumonia because we couldn't afford the antibiotics."

"And you were left with twelve kids to raise?"

"Something like that. My brothers were sixteen and seventeen at the time. They were old enough to help, and—" he shook his head slightly "—except Rafael, who was old enough and didn't want to, they were good about it. Rafe and I argued a lot, until he finally left home a year later. The rest of us scraped by. I put myself through night school for college, and managed to get a scholarship at Columbia University Law School. So I moved us to New

Jersey, where my sisters could go to school while I commuted into the city."

"Your brothers were in college by then?"

"College or trade school. Rafael was putting himself through the University of South Carolina. He's an ocean archaeologist now. Miguel's in the navy. Sebastiano is a master carpenter." Pride, and something else, something close to awe, rang in his voice when he talked about his brothers. Even the prodigal, Rafael, she realized, had earned Zack's respect.

"The girls?" she prompted.

He glanced at her, as if suddenly remembering her presence. "Oh, the girls. The twins are in college. Lucita is at Syracuse, and Amanda is at Duke. The rest are out of school and working, or married, or both. I've got seventeen nieces and nephews, whom I adore, and six brother-in-laws who are terrified of me."

"Sounds like you did a wonderful job."

He shook his head. "We all did. Everybody worked hard to keep us together. I've washed enough diapers, made enough trips to the emergency room and held enough midnight vigils to last me a lifetime." After a long pause, he braced both fists on the desk. He leaned so close to her, she could feel his breath on her face. "So don't tell me that I don't understand what your kids are going through. I spent the better part of the last twenty years lying in bed at night, scared stiff that my family was going to get ripped to shreds."

"I'm sorry, Zack."

"Don't tell me I can't understand the fear, or the uncertainty, or the pain. I may be a man—hell, I'm even a lawyer—but before you jump to any more of your conclusions, make sure you have your facts straight."

"I didn't mean—"

"You did." He bit out the words. "Sometimes I think

you're so busy feeling sorry for yourself, you don't take the time to notice what's going on right under your own nose."

She'd just opened her mouth to respond when Sam, sweaty and scared, crashed through her office door. "August! August, you gotta come quick!"

The alarm in his panting voice made her blood pressure shoot through the roof. "Sam. What's wrong?"

"That man." Sam sucked in a breath. "He's at the house."

"What man?" Zack asked.

"He says he's Teddy's father."

August didn't wait to see if Zack and Sam would follow. She headed for the house at a full run.

Zack reached the porch as August wrenched open the door. Pain lanced through his thigh like a knife wound, but he ignored it long enough to do a mental count of six small heads in the den. Sam stumbled into the house after him. Lucas, who was doing the best job of looking brave, had the boys corralled on the couch, while Emma Prentiss used her rolling pin to hold off a burly, menacing-looking man.

The stranger spit a dirty stream of tobacco juice onto the carpet just as Zack dropped into one of the ladder-back chairs. "That's my kid," he mumbled around the large wad in his cheek. "And he's coming with me."

The boys closed ranks around Teddy. Lucas glared at Zack. "Do something," he demanded. "You said you'd do something."

Zack rubbed the pain in his thigh with one hand, then reached for August with the other. She appeared to be on the cusp of attacking the stranger. Beneath his fingers, her forearm felt tense as a bowstring. "Who are you?" he asked.

"I'm George Snopes, and that—" he pointed a dirty, cracked finger at Teddy "—is my son. I've been looking all over for the boy since last year."

Teddy gave Zack a look that threatened to rip his heart out. "You can document your paternal claims, I assume?"

"What?" Another stream of tobacco juice hit the carpet.

Zack levered to his feet. By keeping most of his weight on his left leg, he could minimize the pain in his right. His height, he knew, gave him an intimidating edge. At any moment, the situation could soar out of control, and defusing it before someone got hurt was his first priority. "I assume," he repeated, "that you can prove you're the boy's father."

"'Course I can. Besides, he remembers me." He fixed Teddy with a beady-eyed stare. "Don't you, boy?"

Teddy's eyes grew huge in his small face. "Then I'll have to see the papers," Zack said, extending his hand. "Now."

"What papers."

"Your documentation that you're his father. He's not leaving this house until I see your papers."

"I ain't got no papers."

"Then you'd better leave before I call the police."

When Snopes took a step toward the boys, Emma raised the rolling pin. "You come one step closer," she warned him, "and I'll knock you cold."

"Get outa my way, old woman," he snarled.

Emma brought the rolling pin down, hard, on his shoulder. When he howled in outraged pain, August rushed to insinuate herself between George and her family. "She hit me!" George yelled, spewing a stream of obscenities.

"That tears it." Ignoring the pain in his leg, Zack crossed the room in three long strides. He clamped a large hand on George's shoulder. "Get out, or I'll throw you out."

"Who the hell do you think you are?"

"I'm your worst nightmare," Zack said. "And you have about ten seconds to get five hundred yards from this house."

Snopes looked from Zack to Teddy. "Tell 'em, kid," he said. "Tell 'em I'm your daddy."

"He don't talk," Jeff said. "He ain't never talked since he got here."

"'Course he talks." Snopes tried to break free of Zack's grasp.

August stepped closer to him. "Don't touch them."

"Get outa my way."

"August," Zack warned, "he's leaving."

"I ain't going nowhere without my kid." Snopes lurched to the left, and the pain that lanced through Zack's leg loosened his grip on the man's shoulder. Temporarily free of the restraint, Snopes brought a beefy fist down on August's collarbone. The force of the blow sent her to the floor. With an outraged howl, Emma cracked him on the head with the wooden rolling pin, and he collapsed in a groaning heap.

"August!" Chip rushed forward, sobbing, to throw chubby little arms around her neck. Six more bodies enveloped her as she rubbed the rapidly bruising spot on her shoulder. "It's all right." She gathered them under the sheltering protection of her arms. "I'm all right."

Zack grabbed Snopes's grimy collar and hauled him to his feet. "You set one foot on this property again, and I'll personally see to it that you don't walk out of here in one piece."

"Are you threatening me?" he sputtered.

"Yes." Zack shoved him toward the door.

Snopes searched for, and found, Teddy's tear-filled eyes. "You tell 'em," he said. "You tell 'em right now, or I swear to hell I'll get you."

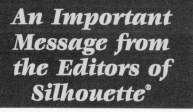

Dear Reader,

Because you've chosen to read one of our fine romance novels, we'd like to say "thank you!" And, as a _special_ way to thank you, we've selected _four more_ of the books you love so well, _plus_ a lovely gift, to send you absolutely **FREE!**

Please enjoy them with our compliments...

Candy Lee

Editor

P.S. And because we **value** our customers, we've attached something extra inside...

FREE GIFT EDITOR'S SEAL THANK YOU

Peel off seal and Place inside...

How to validate your
Editor's FREE GIFT "Thank You"

1. Peel off gift seal from front cover. Place it in space provided at right. This automatically entitles you to receive four free books and a beautiful Cherub Magnet.

2. Send back this card and you'll get brand-new Silhouette Special Edition® novels. These books have a cover price of $3.99 each, but they are yours to keep absolutely free.

3. There's no catch. You're under no obligation to buy anything. We charge nothing—ZERO—for your first shipment. And you don't have to make any minimum number of purchases—not even one!

4. The fact is thousands of readers enjoy receiving books by mail from the Silhouette Reader Service™. They like the convenience of home delivery...they like getting the best new novels BEFORE they're available in stores... and they love our discount prices!

5. We hope that after receiving your free books you'll want to remain a subscriber. But the choice is yours— to continue or cancel, any time at all! So why not take us up on our invitation, with no risk of any kind. You'll be glad you did!

6. Don't forget to detach your FREE BOOKMARK. And remember...just for validating your Editor's Free Gift Offer, we'll send you FIVE MORE gifts, *ABSOLUTELY FREE!*

GET A **FREE** CHERUB MAGNET

This charming refrigerator magnet looks like a little cherub, and it's a perfect size for holding notes and recipes. Best of all, it's yours ABSOLUTELY FREE when you accept our NO-RISK offer!

Teddy's whole body had begun to shake. Zack took one look at the terror in the small blue eyes and lost what fragile threads remained of his temper. Before Snopes had time to blink, Zack slammed his fist into the man's jaw. The force of the blow sent him staggering over the threshold. "Out!" Zack snarled, and slammed the door with a force that rattled the windows.

Behind him, the soft sound of sobbing filled the sudden quiet in the room. August's gently whispered words of comfort floated softly on the tense stillness. Zack had to suck air into his constricted lungs to force his anger aside. Part of him still wanted to bury his fist down Snopes's throat. When he finally forced himself to face them, he found Emma's eyes trained on his. "You did what was right," she assured him. "What needed to be done. I'm sorry I didn't hit him harder with the pin."

"Thanks, Emma." His gaze swung to August. She was watching him with a quiet desperation that knotted his insides. He made his way across the room to where the boys still huddled around her in a heap. He looked at the small heads and felt his stomach clench. Everything August had told him came back to him in a rush. Despite the consequences, despite his best intentions not to care too deeply or feel too much, they'd wormed their way under his skin, just as easily as they'd crossed his fence. He dragged a hand over his face with a sudden feeling of weary relief. He'd been fighting his instincts too long. "Gentlemen," he said. "You just hired yourself a lawyer."

Seven pairs of eyes met his. In them he saw a mixture of fear and hope and disbelief. "What are you gonna do?" Sam asked.

Zack glanced at August again, "Can you give me a few minutes to make sure August is okay?"

Chip's arms remained locked around her neck. "You're okay, aren't you?" he pleaded.

Bo's head peeked out from beneath her arm. "Did he hurt you a lot?"

She dropped a soft kiss on Chip's forehead as she ruffled Bo's hair with her fingers. "I'm fine. Everybody's fine."

Teddy, Zack noticed, didn't look fine. His face was colorless and pale, and his eyes remained fixed on an invisible point in space. "Emma," he said, "why don't you take Teddy in the kitchen and see if you can find him something to drink? Boys—" he glanced at the rest of them "—if you'll give me a few minutes with August, we'll meet back here to discuss your case. Deal?"

Jeff watched him through wire-framed glasses. "You aren't gonna let him take Teddy, are you?"

"No."

"What if he has papers?" Lucas asked.

"Yeah." Sam shuffled to the front of the pile. "What if he gots papers?"

"I'm still not going to let him do it." As Emma led Teddy toward the kitchen, the child turned to watch Zack. The pleading look in his eyes begged for solace. "I promise."

The boys seemed momentarily content with the answer, and filed in somber procession toward the stairs. As Lucas passed Zack, he muttered, "Ten minutes. That's all you get."

"Fine." When they disappeared, he reached out a hand to August. "Come on," he urged. "Let's have a look at that bruise."

"It's fine." She let him assist her to her feet. "Really."

"It's bleeding," he told her, pointing to the spreading red stain on the collar of her coveralls.

She glanced at it in surprise. "Bleeding?"

"I think he cut you with his ring. You need some antiseptic, a bandage, and some ice." With a firm hand at the small of her back, he pressed her toward the kitchen.

"How's your leg?" she asked.

"Not as bad as your shoulder."

"That's not funny. It was really hurting you when we got here."

"It's fine." He pushed open the swinging door with his free hand. "Quit stalling."

"I don't think—" She glanced at the counter, where Teddy sat, holding a tall glass of tea, while Emma bustled around the kitchen laying out baking ingredients. "I don't think Teddy should see the blood."

"I do," he said. "Trust me."

Teddy sensed their presence. The pallor still dominated his face, but his eyes appeared to have focused. He stared at them, heartbroken. "It's okay, buddy," Zack said as he urged August into the kitchen. "It's just a little cut and a bruise."

"No worse than when you fell off your bike on Pine Ridge," August assured him.

"Sit." Zack swung one of the kitchen stools into position near Teddy. "Emma, where's the first aid stuff?"

"In the bathroom medicine cabinet," she said. She was creaming butter and brown sugar with the force of a tornado. Zack noted the tense set of her face as she used the distraction of baking to work off her frustration. He envied her. He still felt the need to hit something—someone—but he fought for the calm facade he sensed Teddy needed. The child was in desperate need of reassurance, and the quicker the adults in his life got back to normal, the quicker he'd find it.

Zack fetched the first aid kit from the medicine cabinet, pausing to brace his hands on the sink as he fought for control. When he returned to the kitchen, his hands were trembling so much from his lingering anger, he wasn't sure he could pull off the simple procedure of cleaning August's wound. "Here we go," he said with forced cheer as he set the kit next to August on the counter. "Let me see it."

She eased the coveralls off her wounded shoulder. Teddy's eyes remained fixed on the blood. Gently, Zack swapped the small cut with a cotton ball. "Not too bad," he said. "Not even a half inch long."

Teddy scrambled to his knees so that he could look closely at the cut. "See." Zack pointed to it. "It's just a little thing." He finished cleaning it. "Hurt much?" he asked August.

"No." She smiled at Teddy. "I'll bet it doesn't hurt even half as much as the time you slammed Bo's finger in the closet door."

That won the barest hint of a smile. Zack applied a tiny gauze pad and a plastic bandage to the cut. "Bleeding stopped," he assured them. "All we need now is ice."

Teddy jumped off his stool and headed for the refrigerator. Zack used the opportunity to ask August, "How does it feel?"

She frowned at him. "Hurts like hell."

"I know." He stroked a finger on her jaw. "The ice'll help." Behind them, Emma continued to mutter as she dropped eggs and baking soda into the cookie dough. Teddy returned with the ice pack. "Thanks." Zack scooped it out of his hand. "Here you go," he told August. "Put that on, you'll be as good as new."

She winced when he pressed the cold bag on the large bruise. Zack gave her an apologetic look, then turned to Teddy. "Now," he said, placing his hands on either side of the child's small waist. He lifted him until he sat on the counter, then leaned down so that his face was at eye level with Teddy's. "I want you to listen to me," he told him. He saw the way Teddy's eyes widened, and wished he could hit George Snopes all over again. "You don't have to go with him," Zack said. He kept his gaze on Teddy's.

A mixture of disbelief, hope and fear reflected in his blue eyes, like pebbles in a mountain stream. ''No matter what happens, you don't have to go with him.''

The child searched his face for long seconds, then tossed his arms around his neck with a heart-wrenching sob.

Chapter Eight

The boys watched him more intently than any jury as he paced August's den and searched for words. Teddy sat on August's lap, shivering. With his head buried against her neck, he was the only member of the small audience not raptly listening to what Zack had to say.

"I'm going to level with you," he told them. "I'm going to tell you exactly where I think we are, and exactly what I think we have to do, and then you can ask me anything you want. Deal?"

They looked to Jeff for guidance. He nodded. "Deal."

"All right. First of all, I want each of you to know you don't have to be afraid of George Snopes."

Chip tugged on Zack's pants leg. "Can he take Teddy?"

"No," Zack said. "According to the files, Teddy's father surrendered custody to the state three years ago."

Lucas snorted. "The files. That don't matter. If some kids' parents come looking for 'em, you don't think the judge is going to send 'em back?"

"Not this time," Zack said. "This kid has a lawyer."

Bo's small hands moved backed and forth on the carpet in nervous agitation. "But he said he would. He told you he'd come get him."

"He won't, Bo." With a sigh, Zack dropped into a chair so that he'd be closer to eye level with them. "Boys, you've got to listen to me. I went and looked at all the paperwork this week. There were some problems with August's custody."

Her gaze flew to his. "Zack."

"They need to know," he assured her.

"Don't scare them."

"What kinda problems?" Jeff asked, pushing his glasses up the bridge of his nose. Sam sneezed.

"Easy-to-fix problems. I filed the papers, talked to the judge. Everything should be straightened out by next week."

Across the room he felt August's tension. One hand stroked Teddy's back, but the other held the arm of the sofa so tightly, Zack could see the veins on her wrist. He held her gaze as he spoke. "In the meantime, George Snopes has no claim on Teddy. If he comes back, I'll get a restraining order."

Josh's nose wrinkled in confusion. "What's that?"

"It means they can't come near ya," Lucas explained. "But it doesn't work. If they wanna hit you, they do."

Zack gave Lucas's shoulder a brief shake. "Nobody's hitting anybody."

"He hit August," Bo said.

"You hit him," Jeff added.

"Grandma hit him, too," Josh supplied.

Zack wiped a hand over his face in frustration. "That was different."

"Boys," August shifted on the couch. Six heads swiveled in her direction. "What Zack is trying to say is that we're going to make sure you're all right. Between Zack and me, nothing is going to happen to any of you. Do you understand?''

Chip shook his head. "But what if he comes back?"

"Then you have to promise to let me handle him," Zack said. "I don't want any of you being alone with him. Agreed?" They nodded. "All right," he said. "Has anyone got questions?"

Bo raised his hand. "What's wrong with our paperwork?"

Zack considered how best to explain the bureaucratic mess Kaitlin Price had created. "Some things weren't filled out right on the forms. Do you remember Miss Price?"

"Sure," Lucas said. "She brought us here."

"That's right. She was in a hurry to get you settled with August, and she forgot to fill out a few forms."

"Are they filled out now?" Chip asked.

"Yes," Zack assured them.

Josh leaned forward to balance his chin in his hands. "Did you have to talk to the judge?"

"Yes."

"Did he say we could stay?" asked Bo.

Zack carefully weighed his answer. "He said he'd look everything over and make a decision next week."

Lucas frowned. "That means maybe not."

"What about Ms. Keegan's lawyer?" Bo said. "He called today."

"Yeah." Jeff shifted to his knees. "He yelled at August."

August shook her head. "He's not going to take you away from me."

Zack concurred. "That's right."

"How about that man?" Chip asked. "He says he can take Teddy no matter what the judge says."

"He can't." Zack leaned back in his chair and studied the worried faces around him. How well he remembered these questions. His brothers and sisters had turned to him so often for this kind of comfort. Then, he'd given it glibly, all the while terrified that he might be wrong. Some things, he supposed, never changed. "If he wants to try and take Teddy away, he'll have to go to court. We'll talk to the judge, and the judge will ask Teddy what he wants. If Teddy doesn't want to go, he won't have to."

"But he can't talk!" Bo wailed. "How's he 'posed to tell the judge what he wants if he can't talk?"

Zack rubbed a hand on Bo's head. "Don't worry. The judge will figure it out."

"Maybe we should all talk to the judge," Jeff suggested. "We could tell him how mean that man is."

"Yeah." Sam wiped his nose on his sleeve. "And that he hit August."

"And that you hit him," Chip said.

"And so did Grandma," Josh said again.

"I'd leave that part out," August supplied.

Lucas snorted. "I wish I'd hit him."

"Me too," said Jeff.

"Boys." Zack injected enough sternness into his voice to guarantee their attention. "I meant what I said earlier. This is over. Nobody's going to hit anybody. He's gone, and he's not coming back. Before you know it, we'll even forget what he looks like."

They looked at him skeptically, but no one argued. Zack exhaled a long, relieved breath. This time, they'd escaped unscathed, but unless he missed his guess, Odelia was behind Snopes's sudden appearance. It was past time he found out what was going on, but tonight, the boys needed comfort. There'd be plenty of time to investigate tomorrow. "Now," he said, as he stood, "what do you say we go out for pizza?"

Josh looked at him in amazement. "All of us?"

"All of us," Zack said, and tried to ignore what the grateful look in August's eyes did to his insides.

By the time they returned home that night, Zack was seriously concerned about August. With typical resilience, the boys had rebounded from the afternoon's events. Even Teddy had allowed Jeff to coax him into a pinball game at Manny Simmerman's Pizza Palace.

August, on the other hand, was tight as a drum. Without asking, he knew that she, too, suspected that Odelia was behind George Snopes's appearance. Continental Motors or no Continental Motors, Odelia was after more than Enid Keegan's property. She'd launched a personal war against August Trent.

In the back of his mind, a missing piece of the convoluted story tickled his subconscious. While August watched the boys, he replayed each conversation he'd had with Jansen, trying to pin down the elusive bit of information. Nobody could hate as strongly as Odelia Keegan without having something to fuel the anger.

On the way back to August's house, they dropped an exhausted Jeff and Sam at their father's. The afternoon's events had exacted a physical toll on the boys. In the front seat of August's truck, Zack held Teddy, who slept heavily against his shoulder. Chip's head lay in his lap, where he'd toppled soon after crawling into the car. From what he could see in the rearview mirror, Lucas's shoulders seemed to be the only thing that kept Bo and Josh from sliding onto the floorboards.

August pulled into her driveway with a quiet sigh. "Home," she whispered.

Zack looked at her over Teddy's head. "You all right?"

"A little sore. That's all."

He shook his head. "That's not what I meant."

She turned to meet his gaze. He saw the fear in her eyes. "I wish I had some of your confidence."

With a soft laugh, he shifted Teddy into her arms so that he could lift Chip's solid weight off the seat. "So do I."

Emma Prentiss awaited them inside. She'd begged off the pizza trip with an excuse that the afternoon's events had given her a headache. The older woman had baked at least eighteen dozen cookies in their absence. She collected Josh, assured August that George Snopes hadn't returned, then bid them a quiet good-night.

Together, they made quick work of settling the kids in bed. Even Lucas surrendered without the usual skirmish. As they trudged down the stairs, August lifted worried eyes to his. "Would you like to stay for a while? Have some coffee?"

He gathered her in his arms. "The time's not right. I don't want what happened today to cloud what's between us."

"Me either."

Zack hugged her close. "Besides, I'm feeling a little agitated about something. Something doesn't quite fit, and I can't seem to puzzle it out. I think I need to go home and sleep on it. If I stay here with you, I'll get distracted."

With a slight nod, she stood on her toes to give him a gentle kiss. "Thanks for what you did today."

"I'm sorry I couldn't have prevented it."

"You couldn't have known."

"Neither could you," he told her sternly. "Don't forget that."

"About—" Her gaze dropped to his throat. "About earlier. In my office." She raised her eyes again. "I'm sorry for what I said."

"Don't be." With a tenderness he had thought long forgotten, he rubbed his mouth against her forehead. "I haven't told anyone that story in a long time. Maybe I'd gotten too far away from it to remember what it felt like.''

"I'm still sorry. I misjudged you.''

"Not entirely.'' He tipped her chin so that he could see her expression. "I'm not a hero, August. I'm here to do a job. Let's not lose sight of that.''

Even though she didn't argue, he couldn't forget the way she looked at him as she told him good-night.

He limped his way to Jansen Riley's house, cursing the insistent pain in his leg. The damned wound was beginning to feel more like a weakness than an inconvenience. Had the scar not been healing so well, he might have been inclined to worry, but the surgeon had specifically told him it could take months before the muscles regenerated enough to ease the pain. The worst part of it was, the insistent ache reminded him daily of Joey's betrayal. Zack didn't want to think about all the things that had led up to that day in the courthouse, nor did he want to consider all the reasons why his life had felt so hollow. The pain, however, wouldn't let him forget.

When he finally reached the top of the stairs, he was breathing heavily from the exertion. The ache forced him to sit in the chair by the hall telephone instead of going on to his room. From this spot, the moonlight glinted off the coffee-can phone line that connected Jansen's house with August's. Zack studied the device, as he considered the charming innocence that had led two children to run it between the houses.

Like the sun rising over a blackened sea, the sight of the coffee can worked its way into the puzzle. August had said something about the cans, something that he should have noticed and hadn't. At the time, he remembered, it had seemed unimportant, but now it niggled at his consciousness with the insistence of a toothache. Slowly, he replayed the conversation he'd had with her regarding the phone line.

Someone had strung the wire before she moved in. He remembered now. She'd specifically told him that the boys frequently used the cans, but the wire had already been in place when she took possession of the house. He frowned as he considered that bit of information. Jansen had told him that no one had permanently occupied the house since his family vacated it ten years earlier. Enid, Odelia's first cousin, had lived in the house next door until her death just a few years ago.

Yet the coffee-can phone line suggested children. Unless— He stared at the can. August had said the boys replaced the cans. He hadn't thought to ask how old the existing cans had been when she occupied the house.

He reached for the phone and punched out Jansen's number. He answered on the second ring. In the background, Zack heard the crowd noises.

"Jansen. It's Zack. Did I catch you at a bad time?"

"Zack. No, no. I just have a few people over. How are things in your neck of the woods?"

"Getting worse by the hour."

He heard Jansen shift the phone to his other ear. "What do you mean?"

"Long story. Look, I won't keep you. I just need to know something. When you grew up in this house, was the tin-can phone line here that connected your house with Enid's?"

Jansen released a long breath. "You know, I'd forgotten all about that. Is it still there?"

"Yeah. August's kids play around with it. So it was here?"

"Sure. I ran it between my bedroom and the guest bedroom in Enid's house so I could talk to Katherine."

Zack stilled. "Katherine?"

"Odelia's youngest sister. She was closer to Enid's age than Odelia's. She spent the night there a lot."

"Why didn't you tell me this before, Jansen?"

"I don't suppose I thought it had much to do with why Odelia wants my land. Katherine died a long time ago."

"How long?" Zack's gaze found the warm glow of the light in August's bedroom.

"I was at Fort Bragg, in North Carolina, on my way to Vietnam. She had tuberculosis, and they sent her to live with some relatives in Tennessee so she could receive treatment at the University Clinic. She never recovered."

Zack's stomach turned over. "How do you know that?"

"My mother wrote and told me. Everyone in town knew. Do you think this is important?"

"Yeah. I think it might be." In the distance, Zack heard someone call Jansen's name. "One more question before you go."

"Sure."

"Were you in love with Katherine Keegan?"

Jansen paused so long, Zack thought he might not answer. "She's the reason I never married," Jansen told him. "Katherine was the love of my life. We were going to be married as soon as I returned from the war."

"Did her family know?"

"You said one more question."

"Humor me."

"Yes. They knew, and they didn't like it. What are you driving at, Zack?"

"I'm not sure yet. Give me a couple of days, and I'll try to get an answer for you." He hung up, then dialed a second number, this time for his sister.

"Talk to me," she said when she answered the phone.

"Margarita. It's Zack."

"Zack?" He heard the surprise in her voice. "Is something wrong?"

"No. Why?"

"Because you're calling me. You never call me unless someone is dead or dying. Is your leg all right?"

He had to fight an irrational surge of irritation. His sister Margarita was the reference librarian at Fisk University in Nashville, Tennessee, where she lived alone in the college district, despite his persistent disapproval of her vulnerability. Of all his siblings, Margie was most like him. Her bluntness never ceased to unnerve him. The others generally padded around him, deferring naturally to his position as leader of the family. Not so with Margie. Headstrong and independent, she considered it her duty to keep him humble. "My leg is fine. I just called to talk."

"This is weird, Zack. Connie said you called her the other night to tell Carly and Beth a bedtime story."

"I did."

"Are you having a midlife crisis?"

He managed a slight smile. "I'm only thirty-seven."

"Yeah, well, how many seventy-four-year-old men do you know?"

"A lot. Now quit arguing with me."

"I live to argue with you."

"Don't I know it! So how are things going?"

"You're serious. You called just to talk to me?"

He winced. He wasn't ready to admit that her accusations were true. Did he really ignore his family except in times of crisis? "Sort of," he said, hedging. "I have something to ask you, but it can wait. How are you?"

"I'm doing real good," she told him. "I got a raise last month, but I'm still thinking of moving. I miss you guys a lot. I'd like to work somewhere closer."

"We'd like that, too."

"Rafe came by last week," she told him.

"He did?" Zack frowned at the mention of Rafael. "What did he want?"

"Nothing, really. He's still doing research on the *Del Flores* papers."

"He hasn't found that ship yet?"

"Nope. There was an archived report he wanted me to retrieve for him through the Library of Congress on-line, but he really just came by to visit. Can you believe it? I hear from both of you in two weeks, and nobody wants anything. My luck must be changing."

"Have I really neglected you that much, Margie?"

"Don't be silly, Zack." Her tone turned serious. "You know I can never repay what you did for me, for all of us."

"You don't have to."

"That's not the point. You've never neglected any of us. No one should have to do what you did for this family. I'll always appreciate you for that."

The words had a hollow ring to them. For the first time in a long time, he wanted more. He pictured Teddy clinging to August's neck, and squirmed in his chair. The meltdown he'd begun to fear was now happening at an alarming rate. He was beginning to feel empty inside, where the ice was edging away. "You did a lot of it on your own. You all did. It's not like I carried the burdens of the world on my shoulders."

"Close enough." As if she sensed his discomfort, she changed the subject. "So what did you want to ask me?"

"How's your love life?" he blurted out.

"You called to ask me that?"

"No. I just want to know."

"It's all right. I'm not seeing Steve anymore."

Zack exhaled a slow breath. He supposed he shouldn't feel as relieved as he did, but he'd never trusted the young doctoral student Margie had dated for the past two years. "I'm sorry."

"You are not. You hated him."

"I didn't hate him. I just didn't trust him."

"Well, as usual, you were right. As it turned out, he had a thing for undergrad students."

The glib comment didn't disguise the hurt in her voice. Zack wished he was more prepared to respond to it. Rafael, he reluctantly admitted, was more equipped for younger-sister angst. Zack's methodical, unemotional mind got in the way of offering the right amount of sympathy. Where Rafe would have volunteered to slug the guy, the best Zack could do was offer a few inane words. Cursing himself, he said quietly, "I'm sorry he hurt you."

"It's okay. I had Rafe rough him up a little." Zack's breath came out on a muttered oath. Laughing, Margie said, "Kidding. Kidding. It's a joke, *hermano*. I thought about it real hard, but I didn't do it."

"I wish you'd told me."

"Why? So you could fly down here and sue him?"

The sting her words caused surprised him. Margie had often bantered with him like this. It had never bothered him in the past. "I just wish you'd told me."

"Zack," she said, her voice gentler, "are you sure you're all right?"

"Fine."

She seemed to hesitate. "Was there something else you wanted to ask me?"

"Yes. Do you have access to state records there at the library?"

"Sure. What are you looking for?"

"Death certificates."

"No problem. I can access them on-line. Someone in particular?"

"Her name is Katherine Keegan. I think she was a patient at the University Clinic." He named the year of her death and that it had been supposedly due to tuberculosis.

"Hold on," Margie said, "Let me get a pencil. I'll need

to get some details from you." He listened while she rustled through a couple of drawers. "Okay, shoot."

The following afternoon, August sat next to Zack, nervously clenching her hands in her lap while he handed copies of paperwork to Judge Fulton Cleese. That morning he'd asked her to accompany him to Hampton Roads, where he was actively trying to expedite the approval of her status as a foster parent. They'd spent the better part of the day dealing with the frustrating bureaucracy of social services. To make matters worse, Kaitlin Price was on vacation, and the caseworker filling in for her had not yet been briefed on the special circumstances of August's boys. By the time they finally got in to see the judge, August's nerves were stripped raw.

"Fulton," Zack told the judge, "the problem here is a bureaucratic tangle. Kaitlin Price was trying to expedite the boys' position to a safe environment. She simply neglected to complete all the necessary paperwork. It's been over eight months since the boys have been in Keegan's Bend with August. There's no foundational reason not to simply approve the paperwork and get the matter off the state's docket."

Cleese studied Zack from across the desk. "Why the rush? You told me last week this was routine."

"It was. Until yesterday."

Cleese's eyebrows rose. "Is there something I should be aware of?"

August glanced from Zack to the judge. On the way into the city, Zack had explained his relationship with Cleese. They'd graduated together from Columbia Law School, and Zack had assured her that Cleese would understand the urgency of the case. "A man who claims to be the father of one of my kids showed up at my home yesterday afternoon. He threatened the boys. I'm afraid that if the paperwork isn't settled, he might have cause to remove the child from my home."

"Which child?" Cleese asked.

"Teddy Donalds," Zack supplied.

The judge referred to the papers on his desk. "Donalds." He pulled a sheet from the center of the stack. "This is the one that doesn't talk?"

"He's made significant improvements since he's been with me, Your Honor," August insisted. "He's still not talking, but he's showing signs of trust. He interacts well with the other children, and he seems to be adjusting to the environment."

"Ms. Trent—" Cleese leaned back in his chair "—no one is questioning your commitment to these children. From what I've seen, and from what Zack's told me, you've done an admirable job with them. The state of Virginia could use more foster parents who cared about kids the way you do."

"If I could," she said, "I'd adopt them."

"You're single?"

"Yes."

"Hmm." He studied the papers on his desk. "That would be difficult to manage. You're employed?"

"I'm self-employed. I'm a veterinarian."

Cleese's gaze dropped to the papers once more. "And the mayor?"

"Yes."

"Admirable."

"But not time consuming," August insisted. "The boys get most of my attention."

"What do you do about child care when you aren't with them?"

"I have a sitter."

"Adult?"

"Older woman," Zack said. "She's a combination nanny-housekeeper."

The judge nodded. "It certainly appears you've provided well for the children, Ms. Trent, but even though these kids, especially with their problems, are the kind who could easily fall through the cracks, the state's adoption laws are antiquated. It's tough for anyone other than a middle-class couple to get approval for a permanent location."

"I know that," she told him. "But Kaitlin assured me that the boys couldn't be taken from my home unless a suitable permanent location was found for them."

"And nobody wants to adopt an emotionally disturbed eight-year-old. Is that it?" Cleese asked.

"Something like that," August said.

The judge looked at Zack. "This goes a little beyond issuing a restraining order against some old woman with a personal grudge, Zack. We're talking about intervention of the boy's legal guardian."

"A step-father who surrendered custody of the child three years ago. I'd bet you real money that Odelia Keegan is responsible for his sudden interest in his son."

"Can you prove that?"

"No."

"Do you think she offered to pay him if he tried to retrieve the child?"

August gave Zack a sharp look. She hadn't even considered the possibility. "Do you?"

Zack nodded. "I think it's possible."

Fulton Cleese shook his head. "But until you can prove that, I can't help much. The state takes these things very seriously. If a child's natural parents want him returned to the home, we like to consider the possibility. It may be in the best interest of the child."

"This time it's not," August insisted. "Teddy is terrified of him. He's violent."

"Are you sure?" Cleese asked.

"He hit August yesterday," Zack said quietly. "In front of the boys."

Cleese's answer was a low, angry curse. He picked up the pen on his desk. "I'll give you another restraining order. And I'll go ahead and sign off on the fostership papers, but if George Snopes is the boy's guardian, you're going to have to plan on a court appearance."

August's mind traveled to a day when she'd sat, wearing her best dress, on the bench outside a judge's chambers. Her feet hadn't reached the floor, and she'd entertained herself during the long wait by swinging her feet back and forth under the hard wooden seat. She didn't even recall the outcome of that interview; she remembered only that the imposing inside of the judge's office had scared her to death. She pictured Teddy waiting for a similar interview and shivered. "When?" she asked.

"Soon," Cleese said. "I wouldn't put it off."

Zack shifted in his chair. "Odelia Keegan's lawyer claims that he's already arranged a court hearing challenging August's custody."

"He may have."

"Who'll hear the case?"

"I'd have to recuse myself if you remained on the case," the judge told Zack. "If I didn't, my objectivity could be questioned, and that would hurt you in the long run."

"I understand."

"So you'd have to deal with Sam Laden."

"Is he tough?"

"*Samantha* Laden is a great judge, with a heart the size of Texas. I'm not sure she'd be able to see the forest for the trees in a case like this. It would depend on how good an actor Snopes is. If he convinced her that he's heartbroken at the loss of his kid, she'd be tough to handle." With a quick economy of motion, he signed the stack of papers on his desk, then handed them to Zack. When he turned back to August, his pale blue eyes held a look of compassion that eased the ache in her heart. "Don't worry, Ms. Trent. The state is going to do everything it can to make sure your kids are well cared for. If what you've told me is true, you shouldn't have any problem maintaining custody."

Zack dropped the paperwork in his briefcase. "Thanks, Fulton. We'll be in touch."

"Any leads on what's got this Odelia character in such a twist?"

"Maybe. I hope to know something in a couple of days."

"Hmm." Cleese leaned back in his chair to prop his feet on his desk. "Considering that you're used to staving off clients like Joey Palfitano, she must be quite a battle-ax to have held you off so long."

"She is." He snapped his briefcase shut. "But she's got nothing on Joey." Holding out his hand to August, he asked, "Ready?"

She slid cold fingers into his, and tried to cling to Fulton Cleese's promise as Zack led her from his chambers.

Chapter Nine

He slanted his third look at her on the way home from Hampton Roads. August hadn't spoken in the three hours since they left Fulton's office. Her hands remained clamped in her lap. Her gaze focused on a spot far beyond the scenery. Twice he'd opened his mouth to offer words of comfort, then changed his mind. She was lost to him now. Her body sat next to his in the passenger seat, but her mind was miles, or years, away.

He hadn't missed the panicked look on her face when Fulton suggested a court appearance. The demons of her past were hot on her heels, and Zack had discovered an anger burning in his gut as he watched her battle them in silence. Someone had done this to her. If his hunch was correct, it hadn't been parents who didn't want her.

It had been Odelia Keegan.

He'd built his reputation based on his hunches. They rarely failed him. Grimly he thought of Joey Palfitano. Until recently, he'd been batting a thousand. Joey had deceived him, true, but he had an unshakable conviction that Odelia was somehow behind the tragic circumstances of August's life.

His hands tightened on the leather-covered steering wheel as he entered the outskirts of Keegan's Bend, where a sign read Keegan's Bend, Virginia, Welcomes You. Welcomes you, he thought, unless you happen to threaten Odelia's corner of the universe. The thought of the old woman finding a man like Snopes to terrify an eight-year-old child was enough to send Zack's temper into the danger zone. For August's sake, he managed—barely—to keep his anger in check. He needed proof before he'd have Odelia where he wanted her. And when he did—his gaze slid to August's pale profile—he'd hold nothing back.

They'd just turned into the driveway of her large Victorian-style house when August mumbled, "Thank you," beneath her breath, then hurried from the car. With a worried frown, Zack followed her up the steps.

The door opened on bedlam.

Bo sat crying on the couch. Jeff was yelling at him to shut up, while Lucas held a flailing Chip away from Josh. Josh stood on the coffee table, precariously balancing a jar of colored rocks that he was threatening to drop. Teddy was attempting to wrest the jar away from him, while Sam had hold of Josh's feet as he tried to topple him off the table.

Zack watched as August's blank gaze traveled the scene in the room. Emma rushed from the kitchen, wiping her hands on her apron. "Thank goodness you're home, August. I told them there'd be hell to pay when you got here."

Sam noticed August's presence first. As if by silent command, the noise stopped, except for the soft sound of

Bo's muffled sobs. August whispered. "Have they been like this all day?"

Emma wiped a plump hand on her forehead. "'Fraid so. I've threatened 'em with everything I could think of. I swatted Josh's behind a time or two. Lucas's, too. But they've done nothing but bicker and fight since you left this morning."

A tear formed in the corner of August's eyes. Zack watched its slow progress over the rim, and down her cheek. Two more welled over, then plopped onto the blue linen of her suit. "I'm sorry," she told Emma, then fled up the stairs to her room.

Zack's gaze followed her retreat. When he turned back to the boys, they were still frozen, watching in comic horror as his gaze narrowed on them. "Josh," he said. "Off the table. Lucas, let go of Chip. Everybody separate. Now."

Lucas gave him a belligerent look. "But he—"

"Now."

The authority in his tone sent bodies fleeing to the far corners of the room. Zack turned to Emma. "Thank you for staying with them today. I'm sorry they gave you a hard time."

"Is August all right?" Emma asked.

"She will be."

Emma shook her head as she reached for Josh. When her fingers closed on his earlobe, she yanked him over to stand with her. "I'll be taking Josh home now." With a firm grip, she pulled the jar of rocks from his hand. She set it on the television.

Josh kept wiggling, trying to break free of her tenacious hold on her ear. "You're hurting me."

"That's not all I'm going to do to you," she warned him. "Out in the car. Scoot. It'll give you time to think about what's going to happen when we get home."

Josh fled the house. Emma scooped up her purse, then gave the boys one last blistering look. "I hope you're proud of yourselves," she told them. "August needed your support today, and instead, you've all acted like a bunch of hooligans." She turned back to Zack. "You're sure you don't need me to stay?" she asked. "I'm good at swatting butts."

"I'm sure. It's nothing I can't handle."

"I'll be going, then. Dinner's in the oven, if you're hungry."

"Thanks." He held open the door. "Sorry again for the trouble."

On her way out, she laid a hand on Zack's sleeve. "I do think it has a lot to do with yesterday's episode. They're a bit upset."

"It's no excuse for bad behavior," Zack told her. "I think August forgives them too much sometimes."

"They've had a rough time of it," she said beneath her breath.

"They don't know the half of it."

When Emma left, he pushed the door shut with a carefully precise click.

Six sets of eyes watched him with varying degrees of wariness as he turned to face them. "Is everybody proud of himself?" he asked.

They all started talking at once. Zack held up a hand. "Nothing," he said. "Don't say anything."

Jeff took a step forward. "But—"

"I don't want to hear it," Zack told them. "There's no excuse for any of this. You were rude to Emma, you upset August, and now you get to deal with me."

"What are you going to do to us?" Chip asked, his eyes wide.

"I'm going to do something August should have done a long time ago."

Bo momentarily stopped crying. "What?"

"I'm going to teach you that you can't go around acting like a bunch of delinquents, then expect people to forgive you for it because your lives are hard."

"What do you know about it?" Lucas demanded.

"More than you think," Zack told them. "And if I wasn't so angry, I might tell you."

Lucas snorted. "Man, you don't know nothing. You got no clue what it's like to grow up when nobody wants you."

"I'm not getting into this," Zack said. "It's not about me. It's about the fact that August has given you everything, all of you, and right now, when she needs to know she can count on you, you pull a stunt like this."

Sam sneezed. "We didn't do nothing. We were just trying to get Chip's rocks back from Josh."

"I don't want to hear it. This had nothing to do with that little episode when we walked in, and everything to do with the way you've been behaving all day. Sam and Jeff," he said, "is your father home?"

"Yeah," Jeff said, wary.

"Then go there," Zack said. "And don't think you're off the hook. I'll be calling him tonight." Recognizing that this could be their last chance to flee, they hurried out the door, leaving Zack with August's four kids, one in each corner of the room. "Now. I want everybody upstairs, in bed, lights off, mouths shut, eyes closed, in five minutes."

"It's not our bedtime," Chip told him.

"Tonight it is."

"August always lets us stay up until nine-thirty," Lucas said. "It's only eight."

"And tonight, I'm in charge. Bedtime is now."

"We haven't eaten yet," Bo said. "Mrs. Prentiss made us wait for you."

"Then I guess you'll be extra hungry at breakfast, won't you?"

Lucas glared at him. "You can't make us go to bed without eating."

"Watch me." Teddy's eyes grew huge in his small face. Zack pointed to the stairs. "Go. Now."

Teddy and Bo cracked first. They tumbled over each other in their rush for the stairs. Chip stalked by Zack, frowning. "I want my blue rock back," he told him. "You can't keep it."

"Tough," Zack said. "You gave it to me. I'm keeping it."

"I didn't know you were gonna be so mean."

"Now you do."

With a disgruntled frown, Chip stomped up the stairs. Zack faced off with Lucas. The boy's face was set in a rebellious pout. "You're not in charge of me."

"Tonight I am."

"Yeah? Who says?"

"I do."

"What if I don't go? What are you gonna do? Hit me?"

Zack exhaled a long breath. "You know, Lucas, one of these days you're going to learn that if you treat the whole world like dirt, they're going to do the same thing to you."

"What's that supposed to mean?"

"Just that maybe your life would be a little easier if you didn't walk around with that chip on your shoulder."

"Well, if people like you wouldn't try to boss me around, maybe I wouldn't have to."

Zack recognized the bravado. "Listen, I know how you feel."

"Sure you do."

"I do."

"You got no idea how I feel. You ever been dumped

out on the street by some woman who wants to knock you around all the time?''

"You ever been abandoned by some old man who wants you to raise his twelve kids?" Zack shot back. Lucas stared at him. "That's right," Zack continued. "When I was a little older than you, my father left us. I was the oldest of thirteen children. My mother died three years later. Taking care of the family was my job."

The tough set of Lucas's face began to fade. "What a jerk," he muttered.

"First-class."

"My father left, too."

"What about your mother?"

Lucas shrugged. "She couldn't handle taking care of me, so she gave me to the state."

Zack's heart twisted around in his chest. Three months ago, he'd been questioning whether or not he even had a heart. Now, it was doing somersaults inside his body every time he walked in August's house. "I'm sorry. How old where you?"

"Six."

"You been mad at the world ever since?"

He saw Lucas's expression falter. "What do you mean?"

"I mean that your mother abandoned you, and it made you angry. How long have you been angry?"

Lucas frowned. "I don't know."

"Are you angry at August?"

"Hell, no."

"Sure about that?"

"Sure I'm sure. Why would I be mad?"

"She's keeping you here, isn't she? If it wasn't for August, if you didn't have a place to stay, your mother would have come back for you by now. Isn't that right?"

"You're wrong." Lucas's lips had begun to tremble.

"Come on, Lucas. When is she coming back?"

"You don't know nothing about this."

"When? She is coming back, isn't she?"

"'Course she is."

"As soon as she gets enough money. Is that the story?"

"My mother is gonna come get me. And it ain't gonna be like that Snopes guy, either. She wants me." His expression started to crumble. "She does," he insisted.

Zack crossed the room in three quick strides. The grown-up facade Lucas carried like armor had begun to crumble. A frightened, lonely ten-year-old child lay beneath, wanting desperately to be comforted. Without waiting for permission, Zack hugged him.

He'd had this exact conversation with Rafael, who'd spent weeks with his nose pressed to the window, waiting for a sign of their father. At the time, Zack had been too angry, too betrayed, to offer the comfort his brother needed. He'd failed Rafael. He knew better now.

"Lucas—" he ruffled his fingers in the boy's blue-black hair "—no matter what your mother does or doesn't do, it's not your fault. She didn't leave you because of anything you did."

Lucas's head wagged back and forth in a miserable denial. "If I'd been better, she wouldn't have sent me away."

"That's not true." Zack painfully lowered himself to one knee. He waited until Lucas's gaze met his. "That is not true."

Lucas wiped his eyes with his sleeve. "What if she ain't coming back?" he whispered.

"Then you've got August, and Chip, and Teddy, and Bo, and Emma, and Jeff, and Sam, and Josh, who care about you. When you have people who care about you, you can handle anything."

"What about you?" Lucas asked, holding his gaze with frightening intensity. "Do you care?"

"Yeah," Zack told him. He refused to think about the funny pain that seemed to have taken up permanent residence in his chest. August and her kids were tearing down his carefully constructed reserve, and he couldn't seem to do a damned thing about it. "Yeah, I care."

Lucas studied him for several more seconds, then broke free of his embrace with an awkward shrug. "I better go upstairs," he told Zack. "Chip always has trouble putting on his pajamas."

"Why don't you go help him?" Zack said. "I'm going to check on August."

"All right." He made it halfway to the stairs before he turned back. "Tell her we're sorry, will ya? She doesn't like it when we fight."

"I'll tell her."

Lucas hurried up the stairs, leaving Zack in the darkening interior of August's den. He checked the locks, switched out the lights, then headed for the kitchen. The smell of Emma's lasagna made his mouth water. Belatedly he realized he and August hadn't eaten since the stale sandwiches they had in the courthouse cafeteria. He prepared two plates, grabbed a bottle of wine, a glass and flatware, then headed for the stairs.

As he passed by the boys' room, he heard softly whispered admonitions through the door.

"I want to wear the Superman ones," Chip was saying.

"Wear mine, then," Lucas told him. "Yours are dirty."

"But I don't—" Chip's voice was muffled as Lucas pulled the pajama shirt over his head. Next door, Bo spoke in quiet reassurance to Teddy. "I'm sure he's not really mad. He just looked mad. I'll bet he won't even 'member by tomorrow."

Zack squelched a surge of guilt as he looked at the two

plates of food. He felt strange about sending them to bed hungry, but remembered that nothing got the attention of a little boy like an empty stomach. He'd make it up to them in the morning with his mother's recipe for French toast.

August's room, he knew, was at the end of the hall, where the coffee-can phone line connected with his bedroom in Jansen's house. He hurried down the hall before the muffled conversations could weaken his resolve.

The door was shut, but a light shone beneath. He kicked lightly with his foot. "August?" She didn't answer. "Honey, let me in."

"You can go home now," came the reply. "I'll handle everything."

"There's nothing to handle," he assured her. "The boys are in bed. Can you let me in? My hands are full."

He heard her shuffling around inside the room. When the door finally opened, she gave him a disgruntled look. "What do you mean, they're in bed?"

He nodded in the direction of their closed doors. "In bed. I told them to quit acting like delinquents and go to sleep."

"It's not their bedtime."

"It is tonight." He shouldered his way past her. Her bedroom looked as he'd imagined. Sparse except for a few pictures on the wall, August's room was filled with little tangible evidence of permanence. He half expected to find a packed suitcase in one of the corners. The small room was immaculate, the only homey touch a large handmade quilt on the four-poster bed. The quilt, he was willing to bet, had been left by Enid.

August's few cosmetics stood in perfectly neat rows on the vanity. Her shoes lay in excruciatingly straight lines in the bottom of the closet. Except for the navy linen suit jacket lying across the arm of a rocking chair, the room was in perfect order. Like a hotel, he thought. Years of practice had evidently taught her not to plan on longevity.

"I brought you some food," he said over his shoulder. "Thought you might be hungry."

"I'm not." She pushed the door shut. "Why are you doing this?"

Zack struggled. He wanted to tell her that he was doing it because she'd been scaring the wits out of him since that afternoon, but he sensed the delicacy of her mood. The look of defeat on her face when they entered the house had all but undone him. Now that the crisis with the boys was settled, his reactions were starting to kick in. She'd looked so hopeless, so destroyed, he'd wanted to smash something when he realized the powerless feeling her hurt had given him. "I'm hungry," he finally said by way of explanation. Setting her plate on the small lamp table, he dropped into the comfortably padded chair. "Emma had already made dinner. I didn't see why I should go home and eat a peanut butter and jelly sandwich."

Warily she approached him. "Why did you send the boys to bed? I could have handled it."

"I'm sure you could, but they were acting like little demons. You were up here, and I was downstairs. So I handled it. No sweat."

August had shed her suit jacket and shoes, and now wore only the cream silk blouse and narrow navy skirt. Zack's hunger took on a new edge as he studied the shadow of lace just visible beneath the smooth fabric of her blouse. Slowly she walked toward him. "That's not what I meant," she said.

"It isn't?" He set his own plate down so that he could pry the cork from the wine bottle.

"No." She now stood in front of him. If he spread his knees a fraction of an inch, she could step between his thighs. "No," she said again. "I meant, why are you taking care of us?"

The cork slipped from the bottle with a loud pop. Zack met her gaze. "Because somebody has to," he told her.

August frowned at him. "Is that why—"

Before she could finish the question, Zack's arm snaked out to catch her around the waist. "No more questions tonight," he said. "I think you got scared today, and I want to be here for you. Agreed?"

She paused for long, nerve-racking seconds.

"Do you want me to leave?" he asked.

Finally, she shook her head. "No. I don't."

Zack's blood heated several degrees. With a firm, insistent pressure, he guided her onto his lap, taking care to position her on his good leg. "Fine. I don't want to. I'm hungry."

"I'm too upset to be hungry."

With a slow, breathtaking precision, he kissed her. "Not that kind of hunger, *querida,*" he whispered against her lips. When he lifted his head, she made that funny little sound in the back of her throat, the one that drove him nuts. Her full mouth was soft and moist, and he had to summon what little control he possessed to keep from kissing her again. "In good time," he whispered.

Her eyes drifted open. In their bourbon-colored depths, he saw her confusion. With a slight smile, he pressed a forkful of lasagna between her still-parted lips. "Taste this and tell me if it's spicy."

The way her mouth closed around the fork sent all the blood in his body rushing to his groin. Momentarily, his breathing stopped. His pulse shot through the roof. She licked her lips when he slid the fork free. "Not too much," she told him.

"Sure?" He pressed another forkful against her mouth. "I don't like it if it's too spicy."

She accepted the bite. "I thought you said your father was Italian," she said when she'd swallowed.

"I did." He fed her another bite.

"Then why don't you like spicy food?"

Zack shrugged. "Call me weird." He lifted another forkful.

This time, August plucked the fork from his hand. "Is this a ruse to force me to eat?"

"Sort of," he conceded. "Actually, it's a ruse so I can watch you eat. It's turning me on."

With a sly smile that sent his already heated hormones into overdrive, she shifted her leg against the pressure in his groin. "I noticed."

"Want to feed me now?" he asked, deliberately provocative.

August reached for her plate. "I don't think my hormones could take it."

"That's the point."

She stuffed a forkful of lasagna in his mouth. "Shut up and chew, Counselor."

As they ate, Zack occasionally tipped the wineglass to her lips. The sensation of the shared wine, coupled with the intimate heat of her pressed against his pelvis, had his body aching for her by the time she finally put her plate aside. She took his plate, and placed it on the lamp table, then threaded her arms around his neck. "Thank you for what you're doing, Zack."

He settled her more comfortably against his chest. "What do you mean?"

"I know you didn't have to take on my woes, or my kids. I'm not sure what I'd do if I didn't have you on my side."

He smoothed his hands over her back and hips. The fabric of her blouse bunched, whisper-soft, between his fingers. "I don't want your gratitude."

"I know." She pressed a kiss to his throat. Her fingers found, and loosened, the knot of his tie. "I just wanted to say thank you."

When she slid the tie loose, Zack's hands tightened at her waist. "Is that why you're doing this?"

"No," she assured him. "It's got nothing to do with gratitude." Slowly, she lifted her head. In the soft light from her bedside lamp, her hair gleamed like copper. A flame seemed to flicker in her gaze as she stared at him. "I just want to be close to you," she whispered.

Zack's breath ebbed from his body in a low, guttural groan. "Sweet heaven." He wrapped his hand around her nape, then held her head immobile as he lowered his mouth to hers. "I'm glad to hear it, *querida*," he said. "The sparks were threatening to burn me alive."

The kiss was everything he'd wanted it to be for weeks. Always before, he'd felt an inexplicable urgency. Each time he held her had been like a stolen privilege. He'd never felt free to learn her shape, her taste, until the scent and feel of her filled him. So he explored the full contours of her mouth with deliberation, taking his time, enjoying the taste of the wine where it lingered on her lips.

August worked open the top three buttons of his shirt as he kissed her. The exotic feel of his mouth on her skin sent shivers racing along her already sensitized flesh. Heat seemed to pool in her stomach as his large hands rubbed the shape of her hips. Yearning for the feel of his body pressed fully to hers, she pressed herself closer to him.

With a gasp of pain, Zack raised his head. "Ah..." he breathed, shifting his left leg from under the weight of hers.

In horror, August realized what she'd done. "Oh, Zack, your leg. Did I hurt you?"

He shook his head. "No."

She frowned at him. "I did." Automatically, her hands reached for his wound. "I didn't think. I was trying to—"

"Querida—" his fingers nudged her chin until she faced him "—I think I'd let you cut my leg off if I could convince you to keep seducing me."

With a slight smile, August pressed a tender hand to his thigh. "I don't think the price is going to be quite that high," she told him.

Chapter Ten

Zack sucked in a desperately needed breath. In the dim glow of her bedside lamp, August's skin gleamed like polished ivory. Its softness beckoned to him to touch. He glided trembling fingertips along the velvet-smooth curve of her cheekbone. "Do you have any idea how much I want to make love to you?"

A tiny crease formed on her forehead. "Zack—"

He caressed the wrinkle away with his thumb. "I want you," he said again, "in a thousand different ways. There's a fire in you that I want to feel." His lips rubbed one of her eyebrows. "There's a passion I want to know. When I touch you, I feel it."

August's body swayed against him. "I'm not sure—" she paused when his teeth found her earlobe "—not sure I'm ready for this."

Zack raised his head to capture her gaze. "Are you afraid?"

Color tinted her cheeks—the same peach flush he'd been aching to see on the rest of her body. "Yes," she whispered. "I'm not in your league, you know. I'm just not sure I can pull this off."

His hand tightened on the curve of her waist. "*Querida,* if you were any better at driving me crazy, I'd have to be committed."

"That's not what I mean." When his thumb flicked across the lace-covered tip of her nipple, she squirmed in his lap. "I mean, you're experienced. You—"

With a half groan, Zack covered her mouth with his. When she favored him with a moan, he lifted his head. "I'm not experienced with you," he told her. "With you it's the first time."

Her resistance seemed to melt away like snow beneath the sun. August flowed against him. The fingers of her left hand threaded into his dark hair. She pressed her other hand flat against his chest. Through the fabric of his dress shirt, her palm felt exquisitely warm.

He kissed her again. This time, he teased her lips with his tongue until she opened for him. The inside of her mouth was as hot and soft as he'd imagined. With a gentle suction, she pulled at his tongue. The erotic images that played through his mind had his body screaming for release.

The need to feel more of her, for the press of her bare flesh against his, consumed him. His fingers drifted to the front of her blouse, where he gently pried loose the buttons. The skin beneath was as soft as the silk that covered it. A spray of freckles, as delightfully tempting as fairy dust, spread across the rounded top of each generous breast. With a sigh of utter pleasure, he wiped his tongue across the trail of cinnamon-colored flecks.

Her fingers tightened on his scalp. "Zack."

"I love the taste of you," he said, then kissed the valley

between her full breasts. Above the ivory lace of her bra, the rounded edge of her peaked nipples taunted him. He flicked his tongue on one turgid peak. "You taste like brandy. It's intoxicating."

His hand cupped her left breast while he continued to kiss the other. August clasped his large, tan hand in her smaller one, and pressed it hard against the full mound. The sight of his brown fingers on her pale flesh enflamed him. With a quick economy of motion, he tugged her blouse free of her waistband, only to find himself frustrated by the presence of another layer of silk. He grumbled something beneath his breath.

With a slight laugh, August pulled the teddy up to give him access to her bare skin. "Don't tell me women don't wear teddies in New York."

"They wear them," he muttered, shoving the fabric aside so that he could cup her naked breast in his hand. "I've just never seen them on a woman who's so—" he paused as he squeezed the ripe weight of her breast "—generous."

August pinched his earlobe. "I thought we weren't going to talk about other women."

He heard the touch of pique in her voice, and couldn't resist the urge to taunt her. "I didn't bring it up." With the silk teddy now bunched above her breasts, they quivered in tantalizing proximity to his lips. "But now that you mention it, you are, undoubtedly, the most beautiful naked woman I've ever seen." His gaze met hers. "Satisfied?"

"I'm not naked," she told him.

His lips twitched. "Wanna be?"

"Shut up and kiss me, Counselor."

Zack complied with a delighted laugh. He couldn't remember the last time he'd had a partner who made him laugh, a partner who felt real, who made him feel real.

August's heated response had him levering her off his lap as he maneuvered them both to the bed.

His suit jacket and shirt fell away beneath her hands as he walked her backward. He had stripped away her blouse and teddy, and his hands had found the button of her skirt when the back of her knees bumped against the edge of the bed. With a steadying hand at the small of her back, he braced their fall with his knee. Finally, she lay full-length on the soft quilt. He spread his body over her in an enveloping blanket of warmth. Nothing, his fevered brain realized, had ever felt quite as good as having August's welcoming length cushioned beneath his body. A guttural groan tore from his chest. "You feel so good," he said. "I can't breathe, you feel so good." Her hands skimmed the naked expanse of his chest, twining in the curling hairs, rubbing against the hard male nipples. "Touch me." God, was that his voice? "Keep touching me."

August's mouth pressed against his ear. "I want your lips," she said. "Taste me."

A current of passion snaked through him, tensing and bunching his muscles into aching knots as he felt her guide his head to her breasts. His mouth had just fastened on the elongated bud of a dusky, peach-tinted nipple when he heard the soft knock on her door.

"August?" came the small voice from the hall.

A moment to absorb the incredible. He raised his head. The sound of her raspy breathing mingled with his own.

"August?" It was Chip, he now realized.

Zack sucked air into his lungs as August's confused gaze met his. "It's Chip," he mouthed.

"Oh, God." Reality began to seep into her gaze. She pushed at his chest.

Zack looked over his shoulder at the door. "What's wrong, Chip?"

"I wanna talk to August."

She pushed at Zack until he rolled onto his back. "What's the matter, sweetie?" she asked.

"Can I come in?" He rattled the latch.

"Just a minute," she said. "The door's locked. I'm coming."

Zack frowned at her. "He's supposed to be in bed."

"Yeah, well—" she reached for his shirt "—children don't always keep adult schedules."

"How do married couples ever manage to have more than one kid?"

"Your parents had thirteen, didn't they?" Slipping his shirt on, she buttoned it to her throat.

She would have rolled off the bed, but he grabbed her arm. "We're not through."

Chip knocked again. "August?" His voice had taken on a desperate edge.

"Make a bet?"

"How can you switch it off like this?" he asked, growing irritated. "I'm on fire."

Grabbing his hand, she pressed it to her chest. Beneath his fingers, he felt the erratic, racing beat of her heart. "So am I," she whispered.

He would have kissed her again, but Chip rattled the door latch once more. With a groan, August rolled from the bed to pad to the door.

Zack glared at her retreating back. A part of him realized he needed to put this in perspective, that he wouldn't die if he didn't have her. But another part, the part that had been screaming warnings at him since the first day he saw her across the fence, was telling him that this was exactly the reason he couldn't get involved with her. August needed a man who could make her and her kids a priority in his life. He'd sworn to himself years ago that no one would own him like that again.

She unlocked the door, then opened it to find Chip,

clutching the bear he'd won at the Fourth of July picnic, staring at her.

"How come the door's locked?"

"Zack and I were having a private discussion," she told him.

Zack snorted. Chip glanced curiously from August to Zack, then back again. "You got on his shirt."

"You got on Lucas's pajamas," she retorted with an unflappable logic even Zack had to admire.

Chip seemed to accept the explanation. "Can I come in?" he asked.

August didn't budge from the doorway. "What do you want? I thought Zack told you guys to go to bed."

"I'm scared," Chip whispered.

Perhaps it was the way his arms clung to the bear, or maybe it was the uncertain look in the wide blue eyes, but Zack knew as surely as he knew his own name that August couldn't send the child back to bed. With a frustrated groan, he surged to his feet. "I guess I'll go home," he said. "I need a shower."

She barely seemed to notice him as she waved absently in his direction. She was already dropping to her knees in front of Chip. "Honey, what's wrong?" she asked him.

"Are you mad at us?" The question fell just short of a wail.

"I'm disappointed," Zack heard her say as he slipped on his shoes.

August lay in her queen size bed, surrounded by four small bodies, watching Zack's shadow as he moved about in Jansen's house. Her pulse had finally begun to return to normal. Had it not been for Chip's untimely visit, she would have made love with Zack. The belated fear she felt at the realization had her trembling.

Once Teddy and Bo realized that Chip hadn't been sent

back to bed, they'd been quick to follow. Even Lucas had made his way down the hall. A part of her had known that their behavior today was an outward expression of the inner anxiety they felt about her trip to Hampton Roads. They'd known she and Zack were going to see the judge. The stress had manifested itself in the scene she and Zack had found when they entered the house.

It wouldn't be fair not to tell them all that had happened. They had a right to know what had been discussed about their future. As methodically and nondramatically as possible, she told them about her meeting with Fulton Cleese.

Within minutes, she had them comfortably asleep in her bed. One more dragon slain, one more night of peace.

But while they slept, her mind continued to twirl about in anxious indecision. She wasn't sure why she'd allowed them to sleep in her bed that night. Under normal circumstances, she worked hard to help them feel independent. While she had no intention of letting anyone, including George Snopes, take them away from her, she knew from experience that a feeling of self-sufficiency added another layer of security to an otherwise unsettled life. Allowing them into her bed was an unprecedented decision, one they'd taken to like ducks to water. The slightest indication from her had had them scrambling between the sheets, where they'd lain quietly, waiting for her to tell them about the judge.

She hadn't had the heart to send them away. Resigned, she'd stepped into the walk-in closet to pull on a pair of pajamas while she told them what Fulton Cleese had said about Teddy's case. When she emerged, they had been sleeping soundly, leaving her to wonder what had caused the rash decision.

Perhaps the fear she'd felt when Cleese told her they'd probably end up in court fueled her restlessness. Perhaps it was the look of utter devastation on the boys' faces when she'd fled the den that evening. More likely, she admitted, it was the notion that they'd serve as a safety net between her and Zack. The look he gave her as he walked, shirtless, from her room had been hot enough to send her shivering beneath the covers, despite the warm night.

In seconds, he'd stripped away her every defense, and half her clothes, and had her clinging to him with a desperate yearning need that scared her witless.

She could not afford to fall in love with Zack Adriano, she told herself as she slipped beneath the quilt. He'd leave. He'd told her he would. Even knowing that he'd walk out of her life, leave her feeling like an abandoned child with a shopping bag full of meager clothes, hadn't been enough to stop her from making a physical commitment to him that was only the outward expression of a deep emotional attachment. Zack might be able to manage a no-strings-attached casual affair, but she couldn't. If she'd made love with him, she'd have given him the power to destroy her.

How close, too close, she had come to initiating her own destruction. And how—she glanced at the small heads sleeping peacefully in her bed—was she going to keep it from happening again? Chip couldn't be counted on as a knight in shining armor, that much was certain.

As if on cue, the tin can by her bed rattled. She pulled it to her with a sense of anticipation and dread. "Hi."

"Hi." His voice sounded rumbly and soft. "Everybody asleep?"

"Except for me."

"Sorry I left without saying good-night."

"Sorry you had to," she said.

"Maybe it's better this way. You weren't yourself tonight. I wouldn't have wanted you to feel like I took advantage of that."

"You didn't," she insisted. "I needed to be close to you."

"Keep saying things like that, and I'm coming back over."

"I have a bed full of kids."

"And mine's empty."

She sank into the pillows with a slight smile. "I don't suppose you'd like to come join the slumber party."

His laugh made her skin tingle. "When I finally get to sleep in a bed with you, there aren't going to be any kids involved."

"Do you have any idea what you'd have to do to arrange an uninterrupted night?"

"Believe me, I've got plenty of ideas."

"None of that, Counselor," she quipped. "I'm here and you're there. No teasing allowed."

"What if I tell you I can't keep my mind out of your sheets?"

"I'd tell you to let your imagination run wild."

"Trust me. It already is."

Whistling, Zack cracked fifteen eggs into the French toast batter. He stood, barefoot and content, in the sunny expanse of August's kitchen. His remarkably good mood amazed him. Most men, he figured, didn't awaken feeling quite this fine after having their plans effectively squelched. He'd been awake most of the night. August's scent had clung to his bare skin. He'd been reluctant to take a much-needed cold shower, lest he lose the memory of it. The thought of her so tantalizingly close, and yet so completely untouchable, had kept him in an almost constant state of unfulfilled arousal. He had only to picture her lying beneath him on the bed to feel his body grow heavy and warm.

With a brief economy of motion, he scrambled the egg-

and-milk mixture. By rights, he should be feeling frustrated and annoyed.

Had he not come to some conclusions during the night, he thought as he slung three drops of grease onto the griddle to test the heat, he probably would be. Lying alone in Jansen's house, he'd had plenty of time to think. He felt like a fool for not realizing sooner what was going on. He'd let August's commitment to her kids drive her from him, instead of using it to his advantage. There was no reason why everyone shouldn't get what they wanted. He could give her the security she needed. He could keep his promise to the boys. And August's warmth could still belong to him. He just had to convince August that he was right.

For the first time in months—for the first time, he admitted, since Joey Palfitano lied to him—he'd felt a sense of purpose. His whole life, he'd been needed by someone. First his mother, then his brothers and sisters, had depended on him to be reliable, decisive, just. For the past several years, he'd felt that need slipping away.

Despite the effort he'd made to deny how important that need was to him, he felt lost without it.

Perhaps that explained the decisions he'd made in the early hours of the morning. As the sun crept over the trees, he'd thought of the small family sleeping in August's bed, and made several rapid decisions. The feeling of being needed had seemed as comfortable as an old sweater. Ruthlessly he'd crushed the inner voice that insisted that August didn't need him. August was the strongest woman he knew. She didn't need anyone.

Determined, almost desperate, Zack had pictured her staring in horror at Fulton Cleese, and clung to the image as if it were a lifeline. Here, he was needed. He felt like a man too long deprived of oxygen, suddenly surfacing for air. Immediately, his weary soul had responded to the challenge. This, he knew how to handle. This was what he did best.

With a few strategically placed phone calls, he'd managed to turn his life upside down. And he felt great about it.

"Whatcha doing?"

Zack glanced over his shoulder and found Bo looking at him with a curious expression. His Batman pajamas had that faded look of too much wear and too many washings. "Making breakfast. You hungry?"

"Sure. Are you still mad at us?"

"Nope." He handed Bo a handful of flatware. "You want to set the table?"

"What are we eating?" Bo took the pile of forks and knives in both hands.

"French toast." He dropped three more drops of grease on the griddle. They sizzled and danced about on the hot surface until they disappeared in tiny brown puffs of smoke. Satisfied, Zack dipped twelve pieces of bread in the egg and milk mixture, sprinkled them liberally with cinnamon, then spread them on the large surface of the heated griddle.

Immediately, the pleasant smell permeated the kitchen. Chip appeared in the doorway, still clutching his bear. "What's that?" he asked Zack.

"French toast."

"I'm hungry." He hurried across the kitchen to peer over the counter at the griddle. "Is it ready?"

"Not yet. A few more minutes."

"Mr. Adriano?" Bo tugged on the leg of Zack's jeans. He held two forks and knives in his hand. "You got extras."

"I know." Zack handed Chip a bowl with cinnamon and sugar, and a large wooden spoon. "We got company coming."

"Company?" Chip juggled the bowl and the bear until he'd set them down on the counter.

"Yep." He pointed to the bowl. "Stir that, would ya?"

Scrambling onto one of the high stools, Chip peered into the sugar mixture. "What is it?"

"Cinnamon and sugar. You eat it on French toast."

"August just gives us syrup," Bo said.

"Then August doesn't know what she's missing."

Lucas and Teddy entered the kitchen together. Teddy was rubbing one fist in his eye, while Lucas watched Zack with a wary expression. "Hi," he said.

Zack glanced at him as he flipped the toast. "Morning."

A lock of Teddy's hair stood straight up on his head. He yawned as he padded across the kitchen to Chip's place at the counter.

"Cimmanon sugar." Chip tipped the bowl so that Teddy could see the tan mixture.

Zack felt Lucas's approach. "Teddy," he said over his shoulder, "would you get glasses out and pour milk and juice?" With a quick nod, Teddy scrambled for the cabinet under the sink. Lucas took another step closer to the griddle. Zack flipped three more pieces of toast as the boy watched.

"What are you doing here?" Lucas asked.

"I thought you guys might be hungry after last night."

"So how come you're cooking us breakfast?"

He handed him the plate. "I'm trying to impress August."

Lucas had just opened his mouth to respond when August came into the room. She looked warm and tousled, and Zack had to fight back an urge to take her back to bed. She wore baggy yellow-and-green men's pajamas. Her red curls lay in a riotous mass around her face. Her eyes, still blurred from sleep, swept the tranquil scene in the kitchen with quiet bewilderment. "What's going on?" she asked.

"French toast," Bo said.

Chip showed her the bowl. "With cimmanon sugar."

She raised an eyebrow at Zack. "How domestic."

"It's the only thing I know how to make besides peanut butter and jelly."

"So you're doing it in my kitchen."

"My recipe feeds fifteen. I figured I probably couldn't handle it all myself."

"Just how I like a man," she quipped. "Barefoot and cooking."

He decided he didn't care if the boys were watching. Strolling across the kitchen, he tugged the dishtowel from his bare shoulder. In a quick move, he looped it around her waist, then pulled her against him. "I can show you a few other things you'll like, too," he whispered.

Her hands were sandwiched against his chest. She gave him a warning look. "We have an audience."

"Who cares?" he mouthed, then claimed her lips for a leisurely kiss. Her lips were slightly swollen and warm. The taste of her toothpaste mingled with the musky scent of her to send an unexpected burst of passion flaring through him. August's hands slid up his chest to wind around his neck.

Beneath his hands, her curves fit against him like a second skin. He pressed her to him with one hand at the small of her back, while the other roamed her neck and shoulders. When his fingers tickled the nape of her neck, she gifted him with a slight moan.

Zack finally ended the kiss when the giggling in the room drowned out the passion roaring in his ears.

August nearly collapsed in a pile on the floor when he released her. The man was creating serious havoc with her equilibrium. The boys were looking at her in amazement, as she struggled to regain what little bit was left of her composure.

"Coffee?" Zack asked, pushing a mug into her hand.

She gave him a disgruntled look. "My hero."

His laugh was warm and rumbly, and it set off a flurry of butterflies in her stomach. "I hope so."

She took a grateful sip of the coffee, forcing her gaze from him to the boys. The sight of him barefoot and comfortable in her kitchen was entirely too pleasant for her peace of mind. There was something too homey, too right, about the domestic happiness of this scene, and it was sending little panicky flutters down her spine.

"Lucas," Zack called over his shoulder, "will you bring me the butter from the refrigerator?"

"Sure." Lucas eased past August. When he returned with the tub of butter, he pressed it into Zack's hands without comment.

"Thanks," Zack told him. "Why don't you help Bo finish setting the table?"

August's eyebrows lifted in surprise when Lucas padded off across the kitchen with an amiable "Okay."

"You two certainly are chummy this morning," she whispered to Zack.

"We had a chat last night," he told her.

She opened her mouth to respond, but he pressed a warm crumb of the French toast between her lips. "How's it taste?" he asked, rubbing away the cinnamon from her lips with the pad of his thumb.

Decadent, she thought. It tasted decadent. She just barely refrained from licking his thumb. "Fine." At her mumbled answer, he gave her an amused, slightly heated look. Mentally chiding herself to get a grip, she forced herself to walk away. Studying the mixture in Chip's bowl, she asked, in what she hoped was a halfway-normal tone, "Whatcha got there, buddy?"

He beamed at her, his grin saying that he, at least, had completely recovered from the previous night's trauma. She should be so lucky. "Cimmanon sugar," he explained. "Zack says you eat it with French toast."

"Some people do," she said, reaching to steady a glass as Teddy sloshed milk into it.

Across the room, Zack gave her a look that threatened to melt her insides. "Some people know what's good," he drawled.

A firm knock on the front door saved her from responding.

Bo finished setting the last of the plates on the table. "I'll get it."

"Me too." Chip jumped down from his stool.

August took a calming sip of her coffee. "Must be Sam and Jeff." She glanced at the clock. "Henry's a little late dropping them off today. I don't know where Emma is, either. I've got to go out to Bruce Duggs's place this morning. He thinks he's got a few hens with fowl cholera."

Zack frowned. "Ugh."

August shrugged. "You don't have to watch, you know. It's going to take me a couple of hours to run the tests, and I need Emma to watch the boys today. I'd like to go ahead and get out there so I can make a council meeting at three." She glanced at the clock above the sink. "We're voting on that Continental Motors plant today."

"You won't have time," Zack started to say, but then the kitchen door swung open with a loud bang.

Chip skidded into the room on the rubberized bottoms of his pajamas. "August. There's a pirate in our den."

When Bo ran through the swinging door, it bumped Chip in the back. "And he's got friends."

"That," Zack said, plunking another plate of French toast on the table, "would be my brothers."

Chapter Eleven

Before August could question him, the kitchen door swung open. Three men who did, to Chip's credit, look like pirates strolled into her kitchen and suddenly took up all the available space. In the back of her mind, she remembered that she'd first thought that about Zack. The dark hair, the brooding features, had all reminded her of some fantastical drawing of Long John Silver, or Blackbeard. In comparison with these three, however, Zack looked alarmingly normal.

The one in the middle, the tallest of the three, had the widest shoulders she'd ever seen. Dressed in black jeans that hung just right on lean hips, he wore a full white shirt that emphasized the breadth. His long hair, as dark as Zack's, was clipped at his nape. A black patch over his left eye completed the look. All he needed, she thought a little wildly, was a swirling black cape and a peg leg.

"You must be August," he told her, swooping down on

her with an astounding grace for a man his size. "I'm Rafael. Welcome to the family."

She felt Zack's hands close on her shoulders. "I didn't know you were coming," Zack said quietly. She heard the steely note in his voice.

"The family?" August asked.

Another of Zack's brothers, this one with a military-style haircut, stepped forward. August noticed the way her boys seemed transfixed by the presence of the three men. She couldn't blame them. Zack alone was a daunting man. Flanked by his siblings, he was downright intimidating. "I'm Miguel," the stranger said. Vaguely August remembered Zack telling her one that one of his brother's was in the navy. "I'm sorry we've barged in on you like this. Zack made it sound urgent."

She glanced at Zack. "Urgent?"

His hands tightened on her shoulders. "Miguel, what's the meaning of this?"

Rafael held up his hand. "I was visiting with Miguel when you called. I decided if you were getting married, I was coming along."

August's eyebrows rose. "Marriage?"

The third brother eased his way forward. He extended his hand to August. She took it reflexively. The callused feel of his flesh was oddly comforting amid the chaos. "I'm Sebastiano," he said. "And we're being rude." He muttered a few phrases in Spanish that had his brothers easing away from the tight circle they'd formed around August. Zack's fingers remained like steel manacles on her shoulders.

"Would someone like to explain to me what's going on?" August asked.

Sebastiano smiled at her—a wicked grin that, had she not been able to compare it to Zack's oh-so-tempting smile, might have given her heart palpitations. Any of the three men, she imagined, could set half the female population on its ear. Still, they paled in the face of Zack's commanding presence. Even with his body pressed to her back, she could feel the determination in him. He spoke in Spanish to his three brothers. A few short phrases seemed to ease the tension. Miguel held up his hand. He glanced sharply from Zack to Rafe. "Both of you, cut it out," he said in English. "Act like grown-ups for a change."

"We're perfectly capable of getting along," Zack said.

"Of course." Rafe nodded, then slanted a look at Miguel. "We're not going to fight."

"That would be a switch," Sebastiano drawled.

August pulled free of Zack's grip. "Any time you want to explain this…" she said, prompting him.

"Mierda, hermano," Rafael said. "Don't tell me you haven't told her yet."

"I'm getting to that." Zack gritted the words out. "And watch your language."

Chip was actively tugging on Rafael's pant leg. Rafe bent to bring his face eye level with Chip's. "What is it, *amigo?*"

"I'm not *amigo*. I'm Chip."

Rafe smiled a rascal's smile over Chip's head at Zack and August. "So you are," he said. "What do you want?"

"Are you a pirate?"

With a slight laugh, Rafe dropped into one of the kitchen chairs. "Do you think I am?" he asked.

"Don't scare him," Zack snapped.

Chip looked at Zack. "I'm not scared." He advanced a few steps so that he could examine Rafe at close proximity. "You look like a pirate."

Teddy and Bo crowded near. "Are you?" Bo asked him.

Sebastiano leaned one broad shoulder against the door frame. "Get out of this one, Rafael."

Rafael thoughtfully stroked his chin. "No. I'm not a pirate. I'm Zack's *padrino de boda.*"

Teddy's face wrinkled in confusion. Bo frowned at Rafe. "His what?"

"Best man," Miguel translated. "He's Zack's best man."

"That's it." August gave Zack a disgruntled look. "What is going on here?"

He pressed a hand to the small of her back. "Come outside with me," he urged. "We'll talk."

"Why can't we talk here? Everyone else seems to know what's going on."

His gaze scanned the crowded room. "What I've got to say to you," he said in a dark, rumbly voice that made her knees feel weak, "I'm going to say without an audience."

Zack wondered if she had any idea how appealing she looked standing in the morning sunlight. Her tousled curls, the baggy pajamas, the still-sleepy look in her eyes, waged war on his senses. He already felt his body growing heavy. Dear God, but he wanted this woman.

And it went a whole hell of a lot deeper than some physical ache. August Trent made his soul yearn for her. In the deep recesses of his mind, he admitted to a yawning fear that she'd slip away from him. She was too independent, too sure. In the dark night, he'd realized that if he didn't move quickly to bind her to him, she might easily slip away. To be needed. His fingers flexed on the worn wood of her porch railing. He would tie her to him so tightly, she'd forget that she'd never really needed him at all. Then this terrible, tearing fear would subside. He was sure of it.

"Zack, what's going on?" She watched him through bright bourbon-colored eyes.

What was needed here, he knew, was a certain level of verbal persuasion. If he rushed her, she'd flee. "I've decided we should get married," he blurted out, before he could stop himself.

August's body stilled like the air before a storm. "I beg your pardon?"

He drew a deep breath. "Last night, while you were sleeping, I decided that the best thing for the boys would be if you and I got married."

"Married?" Her expression didn't flicker. "For the boys?"

"That's right."

"Just like that. You decided we should make a lifetime commitment."

"I didn't say it had to be a lifetime commitment."

"Oh, excuse me. I thought marriage was sort of a permanent thing."

Frustrated, Zack wiped a hand over his face. He was handling this badly. "Think of it as a business arrangement."

Her quick laugh fell just short of hysterical. "A business arrangement? Are you nuts?"

"Maybe." Zack turned to look at her. Propping one hip against the porch railing, he studied her taut features. "Just listen to me for a minute. I can explain."

"This should be rich."

Because he couldn't resist the need to touch her, as if the tangible proof of her presence would help fend off the clawing fear that she was slipping away from him, he straightened the collar of her pajama top with his fingers. "You heard what Fulton said," he told her. He needed the best ammunition he had. "We're going to end up in court with Snopes. If you want the judge to believe you should have permanent custody of Teddy, you've got to prove you can provide a stable environment.''

"I *can* provide a stable environment.''

"You said yourself that the court's approach to adoption laws is archaic. If you're married, you'll have a much better chance of gaining permanent custody. Not just of Teddy,'' he added, "of all of them.''

"And just who is going to believe that you and I are a stable couple? I've only known you a few weeks.''

"August.'' He closed the distance between them so that he could press her against his body. "I'm handling this badly. I'm sorry. If you'd just think this through, you'd understand why it's a good strategy.''

"Oh, it's a strategy now? Funny, I thought it was intimidation.''

"I'm not trying to intimidate you,'' he insisted, despite the twinge of guilt he felt.

"You don't call summoning the troika—'' she indicated his three brothers, entertaining the boys in the kitchen "—an act of intimidation.''

"It wasn't meant that way. I talked with Fulton this morning. He agreed to perform the ceremony this afternoon.''

She gasped. "This afternoon?''

Zack rubbed a calming hand on her spine. "He thinks he can get us in to talk with Judge Laden first thing next week.''

"I can't marry you today.''

He ignored her. "I wanted Miguel and Sebastiano here to watch the boys while we're in Hampton Roads. After the stunt Snopes pulled the other day, I'm not taking any chances.'' His lips thinned as he watched Rafael telling an animated story to a fascinated Chip and Teddy. "Face it, Emma's no match for him, and we can't rely on the police.

Rafe was an extra bonus. We won't have to worry about their safety this way."

"Zack—" she poked his chest "—will you listen to yourself? We're not talking about a trip to the grocery store here, we're talking about marriage. You can't possibly expect me to marry you this afternoon."

"Odelia's closing in, August. I'd bet real money that she was behind Snopes's arrival."

"You think so?"

"Definitely. She's declared war on you. It's only a matter of time before she has you in court, anyway. If Laden can see us at the beginning of the week, we can get a decision from her. I think we should have this marriage business out of the way by then."

"Like a vaccination," she mumbled.

Zack moved both hands to her hips. "I'm not suggesting that I'm not pleased by the idea."

"This from a man who told me he doesn't make long-term commitments. You're awfully chipper about this marriage business."

He bit back an oath of frustration. Her insistence on the temporary should have given him a sense of security, but he found himself increasingly agitated by her insistence that their relationship would eventually implode. "I gave my word to the boys that I'd help them," he told her. "I thought you wanted to help them, too."

"That's playing dirty. How dare you accuse me of that!"

"Then marry me." He pressed his face to the curve of her neck. "I don't know how long it'll last," he said, "but I'd never abandon you. As long as you need me, I'll be here."

He felt the tenseness in her body. After long, agonizing seconds, she asked, "What do you think the chances are of winning against George Snopes if I refuse?"

Zack met her gaze. "Fulton thinks you have a better-than-average shot at getting custody," he admitted.

"But not great?"

"Not great."

August glanced at the boys. "I can't lose them."

"You don't have to. If we go to Laden, show her we're married, prove to her that we'll provide them with a stable, healthy environment, she'll not only award you custody, she'll probably let you proceed with the adoption." The last was a cheap trick. He knew it. He could still feel August's resistance, however, and wasn't above stooping to emotional blackmail.

She drummed agitated fingers on his chest. "Still," she said, hedging. "Marriage."

"August." He moved against her. "Don't you trust me?"

She worried her lower lip between her teeth. When her gaze met his again, he saw the resolve in their depths. "Of course I do," she muttered.

"Then marry me. Let me help you." He nodded his head toward the kitchen. "Let me help them."

He sensed her surrender in the way her body relaxed against him. "I'll marry you, Zack," she whispered, "but on one condition."

"Name it."

"Swear to me that you won't hurt my kids. I'll never forgive you if you hurt them."

His hand trembled as he rubbed the back of her head. "I won't. You have my word."

August stared at herself in the bathroom mirror of Jansen Riley's house as she contemplated the enormity of what she'd just done. She was married to Zack Adriano. A few minutes in front of Fulton Cleese, her signature on an embossed piece of paper, and it was over. What had she been thinking?

She frowned as she looked at her pale face. She looked more like a widow than a bride. As if he feared she'd change her mind, Zack had hurried her through the day. He'd spent most of the morning on the phone, while she made her trip out to the Duggs's farm, presided at the council meeting and completed her usual rounds. By the time she walked in the door, he'd been dressed in a dark suit, waiting for her with a look that was almost predatory.

She'd barely had time to dress in a cream-colored suit and leave instructions with his three brothers before Zack swiftly ushered her to the car. They'd made the trip to Hampton Roads in silence. In the close confines of his car, she'd sensed the tension in him. He'd seemed driven by an inexplicable urgency. Only his strong grip on her hand had seemed real during the long drive.

At least a dozen times that day, she'd contemplated telling him she'd changed her mind. But the memory of George Snopes's face, menacing and cold, would spring to mind, and she'd forcibly bite back the words.

By the time they reached Fulton Cleese's office, August had been a mass of nerves. Zack had dispatched the paperwork with his usual efficiency. Nothing in his manner had given her even the slightest hint that he was suffering the same turmoil as she. Why, she'd been left to wonder, was he doing this? She'd never found the courage to ask.

It had been over, it seemed, before it began. In the span of a few short minutes, Zack had been assisting her into his car, and they'd been on the road back to Keegan's Bend. During the trip home, they'd again lapsed into silence. Zack's hand rested casually on her knee. His fingers occasionally flexed. Once or twice, she'd felt his gaze travel from the road to her face, but as they approached the outskirts of Keegan's Bend, she'd realized they hadn't

spoken since they left Cleese's office. Briefly she'd tried
to make conversation, offering some inane comment about
how Keegan's Bend hadn't changed in the hours they were
gone. His only response had been the tightening of his
fingers on her knee.

Now, she stood alone in his bathroom, on a wedding
night far different from any she'd ever imagined. She
hadn't even bothered to express her surprise when Zack
turned into Jansen's driveway. Instead, she'd fled into the
house, into this bathroom, with a muttered apology. Staring at the cold reality of her reflection, and the ring on the
third finger of her left hand, she made herself admit why
she'd married Zack. It had been easy to hide behind her
boys as an excuse, but the simple truth was, she'd married
him because she wanted to. Despite all her best intentions
and determination, she'd allowed herself to fall in love
with Zack Adriano.

The realization gave her an odd sort of strength. So he'd
taken her heart. So he'd probably break it. She harbored
no illusions that a man who claimed he'd already raised
all the family he'd ever wanted could have a permanent
place in her life. But how many times had she turned her
back on intimacy, simply to avoid being hurt? More than
she could remember. For the first time, the price of the
pain was outweighed by the potential pleasure. She would
revel in her feelings for him as long as she could, and
when he left, she'd simply have to find a way to survive.
"No sense in being a coward, August," she told her reflection. "What's done is done." Gathering her wits
around her, she reached for the door handle.

Zack stood with his back to her, facing out the window
of his bedroom. He'd stripped off his dress shirt, but still
wore the pants from his suit. The stifling afternoon sun
had left the upstairs bedroom stuffy and close, but the hu-

mid warmth paled in comparison to the heat that seemed to radiate from his skin. "Zack," she said.

His shoulders visibly tensed. "Yes?"

"Are you—" she paused "—all right?"

He slowly turned from the window. At the intense look in his dark eyes, her stomach fluttered. "Are you?" he asked.

"I don't know," she said.

"Thank you for being honest."

"Are you sorry we did this?"

"No."

She had to fight the urge to fidget beneath his gaze. His eyes seemed to be probing her thoughts, her soul. "You seem tense."

"I want you, *querida,*" he breathed. "More than you know."

Something like lava poured through her blood. Her limbs grew warm and heavy as she watched him advance across the room.

"But I will not," he continued, "use that as an excuse. That's not why I married you." He stopped, inches from her. "You may go home tonight, if you wish."

"Is that what you want?" she asked.

His laugh was almost a groan. "No. I went to extraordinary lengths to ensure you wouldn't have to. I have a security force staying with the boys." With a look that threatened to wilt her eyelashes, he studied her in the dim light. "I had planned a flawless seduction."

The words resonated in her head. "What changed your mind?"

"The way you looked at me in Fulton's office," he admitted. "Like you were sacrificing yourself. That's not what I want from you."

August exhaled a long breath. "This *is* a bit sudden,"

she said. "I think you can understand why I'm feeling overwhelmed."

"Of course. That's why I want you to know you're free to leave. I'll keep my end of the bargain, regardless of your decision."

In the soft glow of the lamp, August studied the determined set of his jaw. All at once, she knew just why she'd fallen for him. For twelve dollars and thirty-seven cents and a rock, her boys had hired themselves a champion. Nothing in the world could make her turn away from a man who cared for her kids as Zack did.

It was her responsibility to keep her feet firmly grounded in reality. One day, Zack would leave her. When he did, she'd be as she'd always been: alone. But she'd have her kids. And she'd have the memories. Tonight, that was all she needed.

Behind Zack's implacable facade, she pictured a fourteen-year-old boy waiting in vain for the return of his missing father. On the strong width of his shoulders she imagined the remembered burdens of caring for his brothers and sisters. In his lifetime, she realized, he'd stood always surrounded by family, yet always alone. Hauntingly, achingly alone. That thought reached her as no other could have. Zack Adriano, she realized, had once again shouldered a burden, only to find himself terrified of carrying it alone. With a soft smile, she closed the distance between them. "You know," she said, "if I didn't know any better, I'd think you were trying to get rid of me."

His body tensed when she laid her palms on his bare chest. "But then—" August rubbed her fingers on the lines of his ribs "—I have a feeling you're sparking like a firecracker."

"August—" he captured her hands when they skimmed over his stomach "—be sure about this."

She raised laughing eyes to his. "Oh, I'm sure. I'm not sure about much else, I'll admit. But I'm sure about this."

With a groan, Zack encircled her waist with one strong arm. He lifted her against the length of his body. *"Dios, querida,"* he whispered. "What you do to me."

His accent had thickened to an exotic burr. August felt an answering quiver in the pit of her stomach. "Tell me," she said. "You can't even imagine how much I love the way you talk to me."

With a joyous laugh, Zack eased her back toward the bed. His fingers found the lapels of her suit as he lowered her onto the mattress. "What do you want to hear?" He nipped at the sensitive skin behind her ear.

The shrill ring of the telephone broke the spell. "Not that," August muttered.

"Ignore it," Zack urged her. "They'll go away."

She shook her head as she reached for the receiver. "Welcome to parenthood. Never ignore a ringing telephone. One of your kids could be on the way to the emergency—" she gasped when Zack's mouth found the line of her skin above the green silk of her bodysuit "—room." She pushed at his head, to no avail, as she lifted the receiver to her ear. "Hello." Her breathing was so shallow, she sounded as if she'd just run a marathon.

"August?" It was Chip.

"What's the matter?" she asked him. Zack's tongue traced a wet path along the line of her collarbone.

"Lucas won't give me back my bear."

August's eyes drifted shut. "Tell him I said to."

"Are you coming home?"

"Not tonight." Her back arched when Zack gently bit her shoulder.

"But why?"

"Because—" Zack's fingers began prying the receiver

from her hand. "Because I'm spending the night at Zack's."

"Can we come over?"

She would have laughed, except that Zack's hand had closed over her breast. He wrested the phone from her. "Go to bed," he said into the receiver.

"But I want my bear." August heard Chip's whine. She gave Zack a skeptical look.

"Then tell Rafe to get it for you. He's good at that." He hung up before Chip could ask another question.

With a playful smile, he pushed her jacket from her shoulders. Trapped as she was against the bed, the jacket held her arms tightly against her sides. "Think we'll get through the night without another crisis?"

"I wouldn't bet on it. I thought you said your brothers could handle it." His eyes, she noted with a little shiver of pure anticipation, were studying her with definite calculation.

"They can," he muttered, as he bent his head to rub his lips on one of her eyebrows. "They're just a little out of practice."

As if on cue, the phone rang again. August gave him a disgruntled look as she wiggled her arm free. "Promises, promises." She picked up the receiver. "Yes?"

"August?" This time, it was Bo.

"Yes, Bo?"

Zack gave her a wicked smile as he levered off the bed. "Be right back," he muttered.

She watched him retreat from the bedroom as she told Bo there was nothing she could do about the fact that his cartoon sheets weren't clean. Tonight, he'd have to sleep on white ones.

Zack wandered down the hall, snapping off lights with a strange sense of contentment. His body felt deliciously heavy and warm as he contemplated the night ahead. Despite his misgivings that he'd manipulated August, he felt better than he had in years. Even the ever-present pain in his leg seemed to have subsided.

He paused en route to the kitchen to check the fax machine he'd brought with him from New York. Quickly, he scanned the fax Margie had sent him that afternoon. The contents confirmed his suspicions. A stab of guilt told him he should discuss it with August tonight, but he pushed aside the notion. He wouldn't muddy the waters tonight with unnecessary explanations. Once she was securely bound to him, then they would talk, but now, he needed her the way he needed oxygen.

It wasn't as if he'd failed to give her ample opportunity to leave, his conscience argued. No, she'd come to him, willingly. She'd agreed to be his wife. The idea left him feeling a strange sense of undeniable security. His wife. He contemplated the words as he moved through the house. For the first time in months, years, maybe, the yearning in his soul seemed to have eased. The cloying feeling of panic that had threatened to overwhelm him since the day he saw Joey Palfitano nearly let his own child be killed had abated. In its place was a bone deep satisfaction. August Trent needed him, enough to become his wife.

Instinctively, he sensed that the physical commitment they'd share tonight would hold deep meaning for her. She wouldn't give it lightly. Tonight he'd ensure that she was fully and completely his. Then nothing else would seem as threatening.

Zack proceeded to the kitchen, where he fetched a glass of ice water, checked the locks, then switched out the porch lights. He heard the phone ring twice more as he completed his rounds. With a quiet sense of elation, he climbed the stairs as he listened to the rich sound of her voice instructing Lucas to give Chip his bear.

He found her seated on the side of the bed, looking flustered. "Problems?" he asked as he set the glass of ice water down on the bed stand.

"They're wild," she told him. "They're going to give your brothers fits." The troubled look in her eyes was echoed in her frown. "I think I'm going to have to go over there."

Zack shook his head. With a firm hand at her shoulder, he pressed her back against the pillows. "No way."

"Zack, they're going nuts. What are we—"

He cut off the question with a hard kiss. When the phone rang again, she pushed at his chest. "Told you."

His fingers snatched the receiver from her. "What?" he snapped at the caller.

Miguel's rich baritone laugh echoed on the phone line. "Problems, *amigo*?"

Zack smoothed the crease from August's forehead with his thumb. "Interruptions," he told his brother. "The only problem I've got is that my three brothers can't control four little boys."

"We can control 'em. We just thought maybe you needed a little help."

"I'm unplugging the phone," Zack said.

"What if we have an emergency?"

"Yell out the window." He gave the phone cord a hard jerk, and it snapped from the wall outlet. "There. Free at last."

"Don't you think—" August started to say.

Zack covered her mouth with his hand. "No. They're going to be fine. Nothing is going to ruin this night." Briefly, he thought of the fax in his back pocket, and then he muttered, "Nothing," as he lowered his head to kiss her again.

August allowed herself to slip back into the sensual haze he so swiftly created. Zack's big body moved over hers with an unexpected grace. Every touch left her skin tingling, wanting more. He stripped off her suit jacket, and the feel of her silk bodysuit suddenly seemed too confining against her breasts. "Zack," she whispered. "Please touch me."

With a low growl, he lowered his head to her breasts. The feel of his mouth through the silky fabric had her clinging to his wide shoulders. He laved at her nipples until they ached. With long, bronzed fingers, he rolled one stiff peak to a diamond-hard tip, while his mouth and tongue played with the other. When she felt close to bursting, he switched his attentions. On and on the playful caress went, until her body yearned for a stronger pressure. "Zack..." she pleaded.

"Tell me what you want, *querida?*" he whispered against her flesh.

"Suck them," she said. The words shocked her. Never had she felt so bold. In her limited experience with men, she'd never felt this driving, urgent need. But Zack brought out a side of her that August didn't even know existed. Her bodysuit clung to her breasts like a glove of wet silk. Her too-narrow skirt kept her thighs pressed together, heightening the pressure that was building there. Through the silk of her panty hose, she could feel the dampness. Zack made her feel at once feminine and powerful. His pirate's eyes gleamed in the soft light as he met her gaze.

"Ah, August," he said. "Have you got any idea what you do to me?"

She guided his head to her breast. Seconds before his lips closed on her, he murmured, "Close your eyes, sweetheart. Just feel this."

Her eyes drifted shut on a sigh as he took her nipple in his mouth. The gentle pressure wrung a moan from her throat. Zack's husky growl tripped across her nerve endings. "The siren's song," he said. His lips skated across the rounded curve of her breast, nipped the valley between, then found her other nipple. "I think I'm addicted to that sound."

August clung to his dark hair. She'd never felt this engulfing, driving passion. There was something erotic and forbidden about lying on his bed, eyes closed, still partially dressed, while Zack visited this incredible pleasure on her heated flesh.

"It's grown warm in here," he said.

She wouldn't be surprised if the windows were fogged. All she could manage was a slight nod. Vaguely, she heard the rattling of a glass beside the bed. Her fevered mind tuned out the sound. Zack's hand had found the button of her waistband. With an expert twitch of his fingers, he released it, then slid down the short zipper. She arched her hips so that he could slide the skirt free.

When a startling cold touched the tip of her breast, her eyes flew open. "What—what are you doing?"

He was rolling an ice cube between his thumb and index finger. "You looked hot."

August gasped when he touched the ice cube to her throat. "Oh, Zack."

"Is that—" he sucked away the ice cold residue "—a yes?"

"Yes," she muttered, raking her hands down his back. "Yes."

Zack looked at her flushed face, the rapid rise and fall of her full breasts, and almost exploded. There had never been a woman, he was sure, not in the history of the universe, as absolutely desirable as August Trent. Had she lived in another age, she'd have had empires at her feet. Dressed in an emerald green silk teddy and white stockings, she lay stretched on his bed in a display of feminine luxury that had him hurting. His trousers had grown unbearably tight. His flesh felt sensitized. His mouth went dry. "Tell me what you like," he said, wanting to hear the exquisite sound of her voice, that voice that ripped away his long-practiced civility and made him feel so wild. "Tell me exactly what pleases you."

"You do," she said, pressing a kiss to his naked chest. "Everything about you pleases me."

With a low chuckle, Zack ran his hand along the length of her body. "The feeling is mutual, *querida*." He held the ice cube over her stomach. "Now let's see what we can do about this heat problem."

With slow, precise strokes, he pressed the ice cube against her teddy. He moved it over her breasts, groaning when he saw them quiver. A tempting ridge of goose bumps dotted the upper curves. He licked at them while he moved the ice cube down the flat of her stomach.

August's hands moved beneath the waistband of his pants the same instant her stomach retracted at the touch of the ice. "Zack, I'm on fire," she told him.

"Is it cold?" he asked.

"Ah..." Her breath came out in a gasp when he pressed the cube to the nest of curls at the apex of her thighs.

"Cold here?" He slid the cube lower.

"Or here?" The ice brushed the sensitive skin of her thighs. He flicked open the snaps that held her teddy in place so that he could peel away the damp silk. When he rubbed the ice cube against her most sensitive spot through the thin barrier of her panty hose, August's hips jerked against his hand. "Easy," he said. He used his other hand to strip away the silk stockings. "Easy, *querida*. Not yet."

"Zack, I can't stand—"

He silenced her by pressing his lips to the flat of her stomach. Her flesh was cool and damp where the ice cube had traveled. Soft as a butterfly's wing, her skin trembled beneath his lips and hands. In a smooth stroke, he stripped away the silk stockings. With one hand, he bunched her

teddy under her breasts. August's hands had begun clawing at his back. When his tongue stabbed into her navel,
her nails scored his flesh.

Zack slid one hand beneath her buttocks. "Hold still,"
he told her. "Open up for me." When he pressed his hands
to her thighs, they drifted apart. Zack kissed each thigh,
then the wet center of her body.

From his vantage point between her legs, he watched,
entranced, as the peach flush stole up her flesh, flooded
into her face. Her eyes were closed in pleasure, her lips
slightly parted, her body laid bare before him. Never in
his life had he felt this need to own, to possess, a woman.
Gently, he parted her most intimate place with his large
fingers. August moaned when she felt the pressure. Using
one long finger, Zack eased what was left of the ice cube,
now a tiny frozen ball, into her sleek passage.

With the earthy cry of a seductress, she climaxed around
his hand. His head jerked up to watch. With her head
thrown back against the pillows, her hands clenching his
shoulders, her full breasts trembling, her body convulsing
around him, she was the most beautifully feminine thing
he'd ever seen. His body was, at once, aching and rock-
hard.

Her eyes drifted open on a gasp of surprise. "Zack,"
she said. "I want..." Her voice trailed off when an after-
shock rippled through her.

He gave her a quick kiss. "I know." With a quick tug,
he pulled the sodden bodysuit over her head. It dropped
to the carpet with a soft plop. Swiftly he rolled to his feet.
His hands shook as he stripped away his trousers and
briefs.

At the first sight of his bare legs, August rose to her
knees with a soft cry of alarm. Her hands pressed gently
on the ragged scar that striped his left thigh. It snaked

through the dark hair in a menacing path of pink flesh. "Oh, Zack. Your leg."

His eyes fluttered open. "It's not my leg that needs your attention, August. I hurt other places."

She met his gaze, found herself hypnotized by the desire in it. When she reached for him, he groaned as her hands closed around him.

The sound enflamed her. She suddenly couldn't touch him enough, feel him enough. His taste and scent surrounded her. Inside, her body still quaked around the rapidly disappearing ice cube. It created an urgency in her that yearned for him. Her hands encircled his length; whisper-soft skin covered steel. His voice was low and guttural as he murmured endearments. Spanish, English, they mingled on his lips.

When he jerked open the drawer in the nightstand, August reached inside for one of the foil packets.

"*Querida,* I can't stand much more of this."

"Me either." With shaking hands, she rolled the condom onto him.

Zack toppled onto the bed with her, pulling her over him. August's thighs straddled his hips. The strong muscles in his legs tightened beneath her legs. Her fingers threaded through the crisp hair on his chest, found his flat nipples. With a sigh of utter surrender, she sank onto him.

"*Querida,*" he groaned. "Hold tight." His hands clenched at her hips, guiding her up and down in a piercing rhythm. When his teeth closed on her nipple, she cried out as he brought her to the edge. Her name, loud and gruff, ripped from his chest as he pressed into her with a final, mind-stealing stroke.

Chapter Twelve

Long minutes later, as Zack felt his breathing begin to return to normal, he swept a hand up the naked expanse of August's back. She lay sprawled on top of him, her silky red hair tickling his chin, her smooth flesh still pressed intimately to his.

His wife.

The knowledge brought sure, deep satisfaction. Just as he'd expected, she was a deeply passionate woman. And she was his. August needed him.

"Zack?"

He wasn't sure he had the energy to respond. "Hmm?"

Her fingers trailed a featherlight path up his arm. "I didn't know it could be like that."

Primitive satisfaction pounded through his blood. "Me either."

She crossed both hands on his chest, then pillowed her head on their cradle. Passion still clouded her stormy green eyes. Her hair lay in a riot of tempting curls around her flushed face. "Don't tease me," she said. "I'm serious."

"So am I."

August shook her head. "You don't have to say that. I'm sure there have been women who—"

With a heavy sigh, he cupped her face in his hands. "*Querida*, you say the damnedest things, you know that?" His fingers traced the line of her jaw. "The last thing in the world I want to think about is other women. I've got all the woman I want right here."

She gave him a tentative smile. "That's not what I meant. It's just that you have some level of comparison, and I don't."

It took him a long moment to absorb the incredible. "August, are you saying what I think you are?"

"You're the first," she admitted. "You'll be happy to know you made it worth the wait."

Tenderness, and something else, something slightly barbaric, swept through him. He pulled her more fully across his chest. "I wish I'd known," he said.

"Do you mind?"

Didn't she know, he wondered, what the soft admission had done to him, for him? "No, *querida*. I don't mind." He rubbed his dark hands on the curves of her shoulder blades. "In fact, I'd have to say I'm a lot more pleased than any modern male has a right to be."

"Oh." Her gaze dropped to his throat. "I'm glad you weren't disappointed."

He muttered a soft expletive. "You must have known I wasn't disappointed. Any better, and I'd have probably had a heart attack."

August was quiet for long moments. He wished he knew what she was thinking. He had grown accustomed to her ready sense of humor, her quick wit. "August, I didn't hurt you, did I?"

She raised her head too look at him. "No. Of course not."

"You're sure?"

"Yes. Why?"

"You're so quiet." The more serious side of her seemed more volatile to him, more unpredictable.

"I was just wondering why you left New York." she admitted.

His eyebrows lifted in surprise. "I told you. After the accident, I needed the recovery time, and Jansen wanted someone to look into the situation here in Keegan's Bend."

"Hmm." She turned her head to look at him again. "That's not what I meant. You could have gone to your family. You could have just taken time off from your practice. But you didn't. You came to this little remote place on the whim of a client. Why did you do that?"

"Jansen paid me five figures. It wasn't exactly a whim."

"Don't you have any idea why it was so important to him that you come here?"

Unbidden, the memory of the fax he'd received from Margie intruded on his lazy contentment. He tried to justify to his conscience the thought that Jansen had paid for the information, had the right to see it before August. Technically, Zack could face sanctions if he even discussed it with her before giving it to his client. But his conscience wasn't listening. Guilt, as subtle as a locomotive, was threatening to rip a canyon-size hole in him. Ruthlessly, he thrust it aside. Now was not the time. "I have some ideas," he told her, hedging. "Nothing concrete."

"So why—" she pursed her lips in an unconsciously seductive expression "—did you agree to come here? Surely you could have found a vacation spot that offered a little more entertainment than Keegan's Bend."

His hand traced the line of her bottom. "I doubt it."

"That's not what I meant."

He could tell from her expression that she was warming to the conversation. Inwardly squirming, he tried to head her off. "August, it's not a big deal. Jansen wanted my help. I respect the man. In many ways, he's been like a father to me. I needed a place to go, and he had one."

A frown puckered her brow. "I think you should tell me about the day you got shot," she persisted.

"Why do you want to hear about that?"

He saw a softening in her gaze that tugged at his heart. She laid a warm hand against his face. "I'd like to understand why a man like you decided to help my kids."

Zack searched her eyes. There was something, something just beneath the surface, that he couldn't quite define. He sensed a certain danger in the way she was probing him, as if she were looking for something other than the simple explanation. Her clear gaze held his with a steady calm. With something of a shock, he realized that the turmoil he'd felt over Joey's betrayal seemed to have stilled. August made him feel safe from the turbulent frustration that had torn at him for the past few months.

"I was defending Joey Palfitano," he said, testing the words. They came with surprising ease.

"I knew that. He was accused of murdering a police officer."

Zack nodded. "I want you to know that I've never taken a case when I didn't believe the client was innocent."

August tipped her head to one side. "All that evidence, Zack? The press made it sound very incriminating."

"You only heard the public image. There were plenty of extenuating circumstances. I took Joey's case because I believed he'd been framed by a crooked cop in the New York Police Department."

"Jack Garrison," she said.

It didn't surprise him that she'd heard the name. The case had been widely publicized. "Jack Garrison. He's dirty, maybe not in this case, but he's definitely dirty."

"So why did you think he'd fingered Palfitano?"

"Don't get me wrong. I may have believed in Joey's innocence, but that doesn't mean I thought he was a choir-boy. He'd been involved in plenty of shady, if not down-right illegal, stuff before, but this time, Garrison had gone too far." He wiped an agitated hand through his hair. "I took the case because I have a fundamental belief that the law is supposed to protect people. Nobody, even a creep like Joey, should be sent to prison for a murder he didn't commit."

"But he wasn't innocent?" she asked quietly.

Bitterness swamped him as he remembered the report his investigator had handed him just minutes before the verdict. "No. I didn't even know until it was too late to do anything about it. Either because of my own stupidity, or my willingness to overlook the obvious, I helped a guy guilty of killing a twenty-five-year-old police officer walk away a free man." He met August's gaze. "The hell of it is, if I go to the police with what I now know, I could be disbarred for violating Joey's attorney-client privilege. And here's the part you'll love. If it hadn't been for what happened after, I don't even know if I would have cared."

"You would have," she said.

He ruffled his fingers through her hair, gently smoothing it away from her face. "Don't have so much faith in me, *querida*. I don't deserve it."

"Zack, you can't beat yourself up over this. You didn't know he was guilty, did you?"

"No."

"Then all you did was your job."

"I allowed him to deceive me. How do I know I didn't want to be misled?"

She frowned at him. "That's ridiculous. You were betrayed by a client. Anyone would be hurt by that. It wasn't your fault."

"The shooting was," he said quietly, confessing for the first time what he'd told no one, what he'd barely admitted to himself.

August's eyes widened. "What?"

"The shooting. It was my fault."

"I can't believe—"

He shook his head. "No." His voice had grown hoarse. "It was. I was suspicious of Joey from the beginning. I put one of my investigators on the case. During the course of the trial, he turned up incriminating information that implicated one of Joey's former associates in a concurrent case. I had the information relayed to the prosecuting attorney on the other case, because it gave credence to Joey's defense in my own. Garrison's connection to the defendant was concrete. I knew that if news of Garrison's corruption became public, I'd have a better chance of proving his link to the murder. I never even thought about the consequences, never waited for the rest of the evidence. I wanted to win. I was willing to do anything to make it happen."

He shook his head. "It does strange things to a man when he realizes he's lost every ounce of principle he ever possessed."

"Stop it." She shifted so she sat facing him on the bed. "That is not true." As she tucked the sheet under her arms, Zack watched the way her jaw set into the same determined line he'd seen when she defended her kids. August had more goodness in her heart than most of the world put together.

Self-recrimination flooded him as he realized that, once again, he'd pushed aside every shred of decency to get what he wanted. He'd wanted her in his life, in his bed, and he'd pursued her ruthlessly. Even emotional blackmail hadn't been beneath him. He thought again of Margie's fax, and found a perverse pleasure, a sort of self-flagellation, in knowing that August would see him as he really was when he told her the truth.

Her small hand lay in the center of his chest. "You can't keep blaming yourself for this," she urged. "You couldn't possibly have known what was going to happen."

"You don't think so?" He felt the hard edge in his voice. "Because of the information I gave that prosecutor, John Burgesson went to jail. He knew that only Joey could have turned state's evidence on him. I didn't even consider that Joey had deliberately left the information for me to find. I just plowed ahead, determined to win.

"Burgesson wasn't about to take Joey's betrayal lightly. He put out a hit on Joey, and the day we walked out of the courtroom, the day I found out that Joey really had killed that officer, Burgesson's man opened fire in the corridor at the courthouse."

"Oh, Zack."

"You want to hear the worst part?" He wiped a hand over his face. "Joey's family was in the courtroom that day. His daughter, she's beautiful. Looks just like my sisters did at her age. She was running across the corridor toward Joey when this guy fired the first shot. Joey just stood there. His child was between him and the gunman, and he stood there. God." Zack dropped his head back against the headboard with a pained groan. "It sickened me. He'd have let her get killed. And I helped him walk away from a life sentence."

"But you saved her."

"I got shot in the leg when I pulled her out of the way."

August's strong hands cradled his face. "You can't take responsibility for this. It'll eat you alive."

"It already did," he confessed. "I looked at myself that day and realized I hated the person I'd become. I'd turned my back on everyone and everything I ever cared about to build a career that consisted of defending sleazeballs like Joey Palfitano.''

With a soft sigh, August pressed herself to his chest. She seemed to be trying to absorb his hurt. ''So you came to Keegan's Bend to get away from New York.''

''This seemed to be as far away as I could get. August—'' he trailed a hand up her back ''—I want you to know that being here, being with you, has helped me find a center again. I'd forgotten how much my family meant to me.''

''That's why you called your brothers,'' she said. He heard the dawning understanding in her voice.

''Three weeks ago, it never would have occurred to me to ask for their help. I'm glad you helped me find that again.''

''I'm glad, too,'' she whispered. When she met his gaze once more, he saw a deep compassion that affected him as nothing else could. With a slight groan, he pressed a hard kiss to her mouth. ''Don't go looking for heroics where there aren't any, August. You'll just get hurt in the long run.''

''Hmm. Why don't you just let me worry about that?'' She rubbed her breasts against him, and he felt his body stir.

August traced a random pattern on his chest. ''But from a strictly medical perspective,'' she continued, ''I'm wondering how an injury like your leg wound would affect your stamina.''

His fingers tightened on the soft flesh of her bottom. ''Is this leading where I think it's leading?''

''I'm a doctor,'' she insisted. ''I'm concerned.''

''You're a vet. And if I'm not careful, I'm afraid you'll be chasing after me with one of those three-foot needles.''

"What if I just chase?" She moved to press a kiss to the underside of his chin. "No needles."

The breath left his body in a whoosh. "What are you going to do when you catch me?"

She slid along the length of his torso. Her full breasts scored his chest. When she pressed a kiss to his abdomen, his stomach clenched. "I don't know," she whispered, circling his navel with her tongue. "I suppose I'll think of something."

Before she finished, he rolled her onto her back with a low growl. "You're probably going to be the death of me," he muttered.

"What a way to go."

She was still laughing when his lips found hers.

August awoke to the sound of laughter. For long minutes, she savored the gentle breeze that wafted through the open window. There was an unaccustomed warmth at her back, and she shifted against it. A delicious languor steeped through her body as the sounds and sensations of the morning slipped through her veil of sleep.

Her boys, she realized, were playing outside. She heard their voices mingled with other, deeper sounds. Snuggling under the sheet, she felt the tightening of a band at her waist. Her fingers found the rough texture of a man's arm. At the bend of her neck, the warm slide of his mouth tickled her flesh.

Her eyes flew open. Zack.

He sensed her sudden awareness. With a warm chuckle, he whispered, "Good morning."

August leaned into him with a luxurious yawn. "Good morning."

His mouth trailed the top of her shoulder. "Sleep well?" he drawled.

"Hardly." She turned in his arms to align her body with

his hard length. The slight ache in her limbs brought a flood of delicious memories. "Someone kept waking me up."

He nuzzled the curve of her ear. "Must have been damned inconvenient."

August giggled. "You could say that." She gave herself long minutes to enjoy the sensations of waking up with Zack Adriano. In the night, he had proved to be an extraordinary lover. He had learned her body with tender, gentle hands that left her aching for him. Playful when he wanted to be, intense when the sensations created a sensual storm, he had given her an uninhibited passion. His morning kiss was long, thorough. Incredibly, her body still hummed beneath his hands.

She pulled her mouth from his with a soft sigh of regret. "The boys are up," she told them. "Hear them?"

Zack lowered his lips to her neck. "Um. They're playing outside with my brothers. They'll be fine."

"I think we have about five minutes before they storm over here."

"I gave instructions," he insisted. "Nobody's coming over." One of his long legs slipped between hers.

She laughed when he softly bit her shoulder. "Zack." She gave him a slight push. He swiped his tongue in the hollow of her throat. "We can't spend all day in bed."

Finally, he lifted his head. "Why not?"

"Because I—"

"Zack!" Miguel's commanding shout sounded from the yard.

With a groan, Zack rolled from the bed. "This better be good," he mumbled.

August's throat went dry as she watched him stroll, naked, to the window. He gave the shade a hard yank. "What?"

"We got company," Miguel told him.

Zack's shoulders visibly tensed. He glanced over his shoulder at August. "Get dressed, honey. It's Snopes."

Chapter Thirteen

When they reached the yard minutes later, Zack took one look at the terror on Teddy's face and felt his pulse shoot to the moon. "I warned you, Snopes," he snarled, stalking across the yard. He'd paused only to tug on a pair of jeans before hurrying downstairs. August trailed behind him, wearing her skirt and one of his shirts. He ignored the prickly feel of the gravel on his bare feet as he advanced toward George Snopes.

August's fingers curled into his bare arm. "Zack, don't."

"Don't try to stop me," he told her. "I've had enough of this."

George Snopes hooked his thumbs in the belt loops of his dirty work pants. "You can't stop me from taking that boy," he said. "My lawyer said so. He said I could sue you for slugging me."

Zack managed to shake off August's arm. "Is that a

fact?" He took three more long strides, then grabbed Snopes's shirtfront. "Then let's give him something to get worked up about." He would have slammed his fist into Snopes's fleshy face, but Miguel's fingers clamped on his wrist. Zack glared at him. "Move," he ordered.

Miguel stood his ground. With a brief nod of his head in the direction of the boys, he muttered, "They're counting on you. Think with your head."

Zack glanced at the boys. Rafael held a straining Lucas by the shoulder. The boy's dark eyes were determinedly fixed on Snopes. Chip held fast to one of Rafael's legs, while Bo peeked around Sebastiano's thigh. Sebastiano held a hammer in one hand, while the other curved protectively around Bo's head. Scattered pieces of lumber and tools in the yard mapped a trail to a half-finished tree house. Teddy lay on the plank floor, looking down on them with unspeakable fear. With a deep, calming breath, Zack forced the tension out of his arm. He gave Snopes a hard shake before he thrust him back against the fence. "Miguel, please take the boys in the house."

August's hand touched his arm. "Zack—"

"Take them inside," he pleaded. "I'm not going to hurt him."

Snopes muttered a low curse. "It's not me she should be worried about, pretty boy. I should gut you like a fish."

Zack smelled the liquor on him, knew he was unpredictable. He didn't need to look to know his brothers were closing ranks. "I don't think so," Zack told him. "I don't know why you came here this morning, but you're not taking Teddy."

Snopes gave him a menacing look. "You can't stop me."

"The hell I can't." Zack took a step forward. "I'm about an inch from hitting you, Snopes, and if you're smart, you'll get out of here before I lose my temper."

Snopes wiped a forearm across his mouth. "You're not going to stop me from getting my money," he said. "No matter what you do." Before Zack could stop him, his hand shot out and captured August's wrist. "You want the lady and those kids to stay safe, you'd better make sure I get it." He gave August's wrist a hard wrench.

With a muttered curse, she kicked him in the shin. "Let go of me."

He would have slapped her then, but Zack grabbed his fingers in a bone-crushing grip. With a quick twist, he had Snopes's arm hitched behind his back. The man howled in pain. Zack gave his arm a quick yank. "August, take the boys inside," he said. "Snopes is leaving."

Blissfully, she chose not to argue with him. She indicated the back door with a tilt of her head. With a little prodding from Zack's brothers, Lucas, Bo and Chip headed for the door. August made her way across the yard to Teddy's perch in the tree house.

Using his grip on Snopes's arm as leverage, Zack ushered him toward the beat-up truck sitting in the driveway. "Get in," he ordered.

"You can't push me around."

Zack jerked open the door. "Don't count on it."

"I'll tell my lawyer—"

"You do that." He shoved Snopes into the driver's seat. "You tell your lawyer that you violated a restraining order to come over drunk and threaten my kids, and you see what he has to say about that."

Snopes's face twisted into a mask of resentment. "I'm going to get that money."

"And while you're talking to your lawyer," Zack continued, "you tell him that the court doesn't take real well to bribery. Don't think I don't know why you want Teddy."

"He's my kid."

"And somebody's paying you to come after him."

Snopes frowned. "That's not—"

Zack wrapped his fingers in the man's collar so that he could pull his face closer. "I'm on to you, Snopes. And you'd better trust that lawyer a whole damn lot, because if I have my way, I'll have you behind bars."

"I ain't going to prison."

"Then back off my kids." He thrust him back against the seat. "Now get the hell out of here."

Snopes glared at him as he jammed the truck into gear. "This ain't over," he muttered, then squealed out of the driveway. Zack felt the tension pouring through him as he watched the retreating truck. He'd been right. Snopes hadn't actually said Odelia's name, but Zack was willing to bet bad odds that the money he was talking about was coming from Odelia.

She'd had her lawyers locate Snopes, then offered him money if he succeeded in getting Teddy away from August. Anger, hot and blinding, ripped a milewide path through his common sense. Odelia had just played her last card. Nobody screwed around with Zack Adriano's family.

God, he wished he'd hit the bastard.

With his fingers still curled into tight fists, he strode around the house to the backyard. August still stood on the small tree-house ladder, trying to coax Teddy down. From the house, he heard his brothers' voices mingled with the boys' as they offered reassurances. He approached August and Teddy with measured calm.

When he took two steps up the ladder, August's rounded bottom pressed against his waist. He dropped a light kiss on the curve of her neck. "Problems?"

She ignored him. "Teddy, it's all right. He's gone. Zack got rid of him."

Teddy remained pressed against the trunk of the tree. With miserable eyes, he searched Zack's face. "He's gone," Zack assured him. "You don't have to be afraid of him." August glanced at Zack over her shoulder. He saw the pleading look in her eyes. "It's all right," he told her. "Why don't you go inside and change? Teddy and I need to have some guy talk."

She looked unsure. "I don't—"

"August—" he pressed a soft kiss to her forehead "—trust me."

With a slight sigh of surrender, she glanced at Teddy again. "Are you sure you don't want to come in, sweetheart?"

He wagged his head no. August slipped through Zack's arms to the ground. "I'll wait inside then," she said. "Call me if you need anything."

With a reassuring look, Zack nodded her toward the house. "Don't worry. I've got this under control." She searched his expression, but didn't reply as she turned to pick her way across the lawn.

Zack watched until she'd disappeared into the house, then hoisted himself onto the wooden platform so that he could sit next to Teddy. "How you doin', pal?"

Teddy didn't budge from his spot by the trunk.

Zack rubbed his hands on the rough fabric of his jeans. "It was scary, wasn't it?" Wide-eyed, Teddy nodded. "I thought so, too," Zack confessed.

When he saw the skeptical look the child gave him, he nodded. "Really. I was scared like that once. I was a little older than you, but it was still frightening." Teddy eased slightly away from the trunk. Encouraged, Zack continued with the story. "When I was fourteen, my father left me and my mother, and my twelve brothers and sisters. We didn't have any money, and we were all scared that somebody was going to split us up."

He paused as he studied Teddy's face. "Do you have any brothers and sisters?" Teddy shook his head no.

"What about your mother?" The boy's eyes dropped to the plank floor.

"Hmm." Zack leaned back on his hands. "Well, anyway, I don't think I stopped being scared of somebody taking my family away until we were all grown up."

Teddy met his gaze once more. There was a look in his eyes that was years too old for his young life. With a deep sigh, Zack laid a hand on Teddy's head. "But you know what I did when I was the most scared?"

Teddy shook his head.

"I talked to other people about it." Zack waited long seconds while Teddy absorbed the statement. "Teddy, I want to help you. I'm going to help you, but you've got to trust me. I need you to tell me about that man."

With trembling lips, Teddy slid closer to Zack. Zack waited until the boy's thin leg was pressed against his own. "Am I your friend?" he asked him. Teddy nodded. "Then friends trust each other. You can trust me, Teddy."

Long, tension-filled seconds followed. Teddy's hands rubbed nervous circles on the plank floor. Finally, when Zack was ready to give up, Teddy whispered, "Are you going to forget what I look like?"

Breath froze in his lungs. Afraid to talk, afraid to move, lest he startle the child, Zack closed his eyes. In the gentlest voice he could manage, he asked, "What do you mean, Teddy?"

Teddy looked at him. In his gaze, there was an anguished plea for reassurance. "After Pop came last time, you said that after a while, we'd all forget what he looks like." He paused. "If I have to go with him, are you going to forget what I look like?"

The breath drained from his body. With a low groan, he scooped the child into his arm and hauled him onto his lap. Zack leaned back against the tree so that he could cradle Teddy's slender body against his chest. "No," he said, mustering all the authority he possessed. "No, I am not going to forget. I'd never forget. And you're not going with him."

Teddy's small hands crept around Zack's neck. "I'm afraid of him," he whispered.

"I know it. Why don't we just sit here while you tell me why?"

From her vantage point in the kitchen, August had to stifle tears when she saw Teddy clinging to Zack. A large hand settled on her shoulder. "You okay?"

She glanced at Sebastiano. "Yes," she said, her voice breathless. "Yes, I'm fine."

Sebastiano's gaze traveled to Zack and Teddy. "Zack the rock," he said with a slight smile. "He's always been that way. No matter what happened, we all counted on Zack."

August frowned as she considered Zack carrying the world on his young shoulders. "Who did Zack count on?"

His eyes twinkled as he studied her in the morning light. "I think," he said, "he finally found someone he can."

When Zack returned to the house with Teddy, the child's face was tear-streaked. August was nervously pacing the kitchen when they entered the house. She'd watched the interchange from the window and barely restrained the urge to rush toward them. Instead, she dropped a dishtowel on the table, then crossed the room to give him a reassuring hug. "Better?" she asked. Teddy slipped his fingers into Zack's.

Zack gave the small hand a tight squeeze. "It's okay, buddy. Why don't you go in with the guys? I think Sebastiano is probably helping them design a fortress for the tree house."

Teddy glanced at August. She gave him a slight nod of

approval, and he raced from the kitchen. Her gaze collided with Zack's. "He talked to you," she whispered. "My God, do you know what that means?"

Zack pulled her into his arms. Gratefully, August wrapped her arms around his waist. "Yeah, I know what it means," he said. Turmoil laced his tone. "It means that hell could freeze over before I let Snopes have him."

She laid her face on his warm chest. Still shirtless, the muscles bunched and flexed beneath his skin. She felt the anger, the tension, in him. "Zack, he trusted you enough to talk to you. As far as I know, he hasn't spoken in at least three years. Don't you know how important that is?"

"Of course I know." Tremors raced through him. She recognized them as latent anger at the story he'd heard from Teddy. "It means that that son of a bitch Snopes scared him so damned much that he spilled his guts to me."

"No, Zack. It means that you reached him." Her hands smoothed away the knots in his shoulders. "It means he finally found someone he thinks can keep him safe. For twelve dollars and thirty-seven cents," she said, "he hired himself a champion."

Zack tugged her closer. "God, August. Did you know? Did you know what that bastard did to him?"

"No one knew. The only details in his file where how the social worker found him. Nobody knows what happened to his mother, or why he stopped talking."

He uttered a dark curse. "He watched his stepfather beat the living daylights out of his mother one night. Snopes threw her across the room, then cracked her on the head with an iron skillet. Teddy doesn't know where she is, just that the rescue squad came and she never came back." August pulled in a ragged breath. "He couldn't have been more than four or five at the time. Hell, she probably died and Snopes never even told him about it."

"Probably. Oh, Zack."

Restlessly, his hands roamed her body, as if seeking solace in her warmth. "Snopes threatened him within an inch of his life if he ever told anyone what had happened. Teddy was scared out of his mind. They moved to some hole-in-the-wall apartment where Snopes would leave him alone for hours. Teddy was so afraid of accidentally telling someone about his mother that he just stopped talking." Cradling her head in his hands, he tipped it back so that he could meet her gaze. She saw the ravaged hurt that flowed from his heart to his eyes. "Damn it, August," he said, "he told me that the slimeball hit him less when he didn't talk. How could he do that to a kid? How could anybody do that to a kid?"

The need in his eyes spoke to her as nothing else could. August pressed a warm, life-affirming kiss to his strong mouth. "Zack, the world's an ugly place. You know that. It's filled with Joey Palfitanos who care about nothing but their own greed and survival."

"Was it like that for you?" he asked her, his voice raw.

August hesitated. "I survived. That's all that mattered."

"No." His hands clamped on her waist like iron manacles. "No." With a gentle violence, he seized her mouth, rubbing, coaxing, plundering her lips until she shivered in his arms. "No one had the right to do that to you," he growled. "So help me God, I'll get even."

She clung to his shoulders. "It's over. Nothing's going to change the past."

Her protest seemed to fall on deaf ears. "I swear, August," he said against her mouth, "I'll never let them hurt you again."

By the time they broke apart, Zack had begun to feel his equilibrium return. As long as he kept touching her, as long as he could see and hear her, he could reassure himself that everything was going to be all right.

Together, they spent a subdued afternoon working with the boys and his brothers on the tree house. Every now and then, Zack would catch her watching him. Twice he leaned down from his perch on the ladder to drop a tender, reassuring kiss on her mouth. By mutual consent, August and Zack had not discussed the morning's events, or the uncertain future. They'd concentrated, instead, on helping the boys regain their equilibrium. But he saw the fear in her, and ached to comfort it the only way he knew how.

By that evening, he wanted her so badly, he hurt with it. He barely made it through dinner without tossing her over his shoulder and carrying her back to his house, but he contented himself with watching the way the growing fire in her made her eyes sparkle and her color heighten.

When they finally said good-night and retreated, by silent consent, to Jansen's house, he practically tossed her onto the bed. An unaccustomed wildness drove him. That afternoon, he'd taken the opportunity to phone Jansen with the news from Margie's fax. Once again, Zack had made the decision to delay telling August, as if he knew the fragile bubble of contentment he'd built around them would burst if he did.

When they came together in a frenzied, shattering passion, she clawed at his shoulders in reckless surrender. When it was over, she lay against him like a limp doll. He absently stroked her damp flesh, paused to drop an occasional kiss on her overly sensitized skin.

Most of the night passed in silence, with only murmured endearments carrying on the sultry night air. Both knew that the next morning would bring tough decisions. They learned each other's bodies. And Zack felt himself tumbling, like Alice down the rabbit hole, into an abyss of panic and yearning. He needed, the way he needed to breathe, to bind her to him so tightly that nothing would ever tear them apart again.

Dread like nothing he'd ever known engulfed him when he awoke the next morning, alone.

Quickly Zack pulled on his clothes and hurried next door. He found August sitting at the kitchen table, sharing the paper with Rafael.

Zack frowned. "What time did you get up?" he asked her.

She met his gaze over the top of the sports section. "Early. You looked tired, so I let you sleep."

His gaze slid to his brother's. "Everything all right?"

"Fine. Miguel and Sebastiano are outside, helping your boys build the Taj Mahal in the oak tree. You want some coffee?" He lifted a rakish eyebrow. "You look drained."

A blush stained August's skin. Embarrassed, she hurried across the room to the coffeepot. "I'm kind of in a hurry this morning," she muttered. Her knees still felt weak and wobbly from being wrapped around him most of the night. Inside, she felt hot, melted. "Bubba Lorden is bringing one of his calves out here this morning. He's supposed to be here by eleven."

"August." Zack placed two firm hands on her shoulders. They'd put off the pending discussion as long as possible. Jansen was due to arrive any minute, and if he didn't tell her now, he never would. "Sit down."

She ignored him. "I have to get my things ready before—"

"It'll wait," he ordered. "Sit down."

"But I can't—"

"August." This time his voice held an unmistakable command. "There are a few things we need to discuss."

Rafael's dark eyebrows lifted. "What were you doing all last night, *hermano?*"

"Callate," Zack growled.

August laid a hand on his chest. "That's not necessary," she said. "He's just kidding."

Zack gave his brother a warning look. Rafael had always known how and when to get under his skin. His nerves were stripped bare right now, and the last thing he needed was to renew the age-old argument. He dragged a hand over his face. "Listen to me," he urged. "We didn't talk about this yesterday because you were upset, but now is the time. There are some things we need to clear up. I know how Snopes found Teddy, and I know Odelia Keegan was behind it."

August gave him a shrewd look. "Can you prove it?"

"I don't think I'll have to."

She placed several more items in the black bag. "Do you think you can get Teddy to tell Judge Laden what happened?"

"I don't think I'll have to do that, either."

"Why not?"

"Because I know why Odelia wants you out of town, August."

He watched as the color drained from her face. She thrust a cup of coffee into his hands, then dropped, too quickly, into one of the chairs. "You do?" she asked.

"Yes."

Rafael reached to refill her own mug. "Drink this," he urged. "You look pale."

Zack took the seat across from her, then enfolded both her hands in his. "Do you want to know, August? I don't have to tell you."

Her eyes were wide and turbulent over the rim of the mug. She set it on the table with measured calm. "Of course I want to know. Why wouldn't I want to know?"

Zack didn't think he imagined the hysterical note that lurked behind her calm facade. "You're sure?"

"Perhaps I should go outside," Rafael suggested.

August shook her head. "Don't be silly. Zack's about to tell me who I am." She glanced at him. "Aren't you?"

"Yes."

"Why shouldn't you hear this? Why shouldn't everyone hear this? I mean, it's not like it's something to be ashamed of. I didn't do anything wrong." Her fingers fluttered in Zack's grasp. Her breasts rose and fell with the shallow force of her breathing. "It's not my fault."

"Honey, listen—"

"It's not," she insisted. "I had nothing to do with it. I was just a baby when they put me in that home."

"Stop." Zack would have pulled her into his lap, but she jumped from her chair and began to pace.

"I knew it, of course, when Enid left me the house, but I didn't want to think about it. I mean, admitting it would be terrible. I'd have to say that I stayed here, even knowing the truth. I couldn't have stood that. But now, Teddy depends on it." She met Zack's gaze. "Doesn't he?"

"August, it's not what you think," he insisted.

"No?" She looked at him. "Then why don't you just spit it out, Zack? I'm Odelia's daughter, aren't I?"

Chapter Fourteen

Rafael muttered a soft foreign curse. Zack eased out of his chair, placed a hand on each of August's shoulders, then guided her back to her seat. "No, honey," he said. "You're not."

A strange mixture of relief and terror poured through her. How could that be? She'd reasoned out the truth months ago, the first time she saw the portrait in Enid's attic. Red hair ran in the Keegan family. Odelia's had long since turned gray, Hiram's had fallen out, and Betsy May dyed hers blond, but that oil portrait had told August all she needed to know. For some reason, Odelia had given birth to her out of wedlock, then surrendered her to the state. Enid had known, and left August the house. It was all a simple equation, except that Zack didn't seem to believe it. "I'm not?" she asked him.

"She's not?" Rafael asked.

Zack shook his head. "Rafe, would you please leave us alone for a minute?"

He stood from the table, pausing to place a comforting hand on August's shoulder. "Trust him," he told her. "He can fix anything."

She glanced at him in surprise. Rafael laughed softly. "We haven't always gotten along, but I've never questioned his competence." The kitchen door creaked shut as he strode to the backyard.

August met Zack's dark gaze. "I thought—"

He shook his head. "So did I. I was sure you were Odelia's daughter until I talked with Betsy May one day."

"Betsy May knows about this?"

"No. She mentioned in passing that Odelia had an accident as a young girl. She could never have children. That confused me. I was certain I knew the explanation."

"Oh." The dark pit of longing in her belly had begun to unfold again. She'd had this feeling more times than she cared to count. Each time she believed she'd finally made a home for herself, this awful yearning had swallowed her whole. She swallowed hard, trying to still the turmoil.

"But I knew there had to be a connection," Zack continued. "I just didn't know what it was."

"How did you figure it out?"

His hand rubbed hers, offering silent comfort. "The telephone line that connects your house with Jansen's."

"The coffee cans?"

"Yes. Remember when I first asked you about it, you said the boys used it, but it had been there when you moved in?"

She nodded. "Yes."

"I asked Jansen about it. He told me he'd strung it as a kid, to communicate with Katherine Keegan."

At the unfamiliar name, August frowned. "Who?"

"Enid's younger sister, Katherine."

"I didn't know there was a younger sister."

"She died," Zack told her. "Jansen was in love with her. When she was sixteen, she got pregnant with his baby. Old man Keegan knew. So did Odelia. Keegan refused to let her marry Jansen. Jansen had been drafted, and was on his way to Vietnam when he got a letter from his mother saying that Katherine Keegan had been diagnosed with tuberculosis. The Keegan's sent her to Tennessee, supposedly to a sanitarium. Jansen believed that she died there."

August felt her body begin to tremble. "But she didn't?"

"She didn't." He pulled a folded piece of fax paper from his pocket.

August took the paper, unfolded it, and spread it on the table. It was a copy of a birth certificate. Her name and birth date were listed at the top, with Katherine Keegan and Jansen Riley listed as parents. The next page was a death certificate for Katherine, dated two days later. Cause of death: complications of childbirth. "Oh, God."

"Odelia knew," Zack told her. "Jansen never did. He had no idea you're his daughter."

"Oh, God," she said again, transfixed by the documents.

"When you came here, Odelia knew exactly what Enid had done. She was desperate to get rid of you. Her father left her with the family's money and reputation riding on her shoulders. At all costs, she was going to keep Katherine's skeleton in the closet, with the door as firmly bolted as possible. The longer you stayed here, the more dangerous it was. It was only a matter of time before someone noted the family resemblance, or put the story together. Odelia's money could only buy silence for so long."

August wiped a hand over her eyes. A ringing had begun to pound in her ears. "How long have you known this?" she asked.

Zack brushed a tendril of her hair back from her forehead. "Since the day we were married," he confessed. "I wanted to wait until the time was right to tell you."

"Does Jansen know?"

"I called him yesterday. He's on his way here."

She continued to stare at the table. "What about George Snopes?"

"I believe Odelia brought him to town in a last-ditch effort to get rid of you."

She sat in silence, listening to the sounds of hammering and sawing trailing in from the backyard. Her whole life, she'd wanted to know who she was, but a part of her now realized that wasn't exactly true. She hadn't wanted to know that she wasn't wanted, hadn't wanted to know that she'd been given away like a piece of old luggage. A deep, hurtful anger began to build inside as she considered Jansen Riley's role in this. Surely he had known that Katherine might be pregnant. Why had he allowed the Keegans to lie to him? Why had he believed them?

Why had Enid, knowing she was Katherine's daughter, allowed her to remain in foster care for so many years?

And why—her fingers shook as she touched the faxes—hadn't Zack told her, not just when he had proof, but before? Why hadn't he cared enough to prepare her, instead of springing this on her? Why had he waited until now, when Teddy's future hung in the balance? In a flash of insight, she saw Zack doing what he'd always done. His whole life, he'd made the decisions for his family. He'd decided where they'd live. He'd decided where they went to school. He'd decided their careers, their lives. He'd taken all the responsibility on himself and shared none of the burden. No wonder he and Rafael didn't get along. Rafe had been the one who stood his ground, demanded that Zack let him make his own mistakes and live his own life. And just as he'd done all along, he'd tried to run her life, too.

She saw it all so clearly now. Zack had orchestrated her meeting with Fulton Cleese. He'd chosen to infuriate Odelia with the restraining order. He'd demanded that August marry him, using emotional pressure to ensure that he got his way. From the beginning, he'd manipulated her into doing what he wanted, when he wanted.

And, fool that she was, she'd fallen for him like a ton of bricks. From the moment she saw him smiling at her across that damned fence, she'd tumbled head over heels in love with him. Her entire life, she'd struggled to prove to herself that she could make it on her own. She'd never had anyone she could depend on, so learning to depend on no one had been a question of survival. In a few short weeks, Zack had almost stolen from her the one thing that kept her sane. He'd taken her heart, but she'd never give him her soul. That was hers alone.

"Well, that's just great, Zack. I'm glad you felt you had the right to choose when to tell me this. Everyone got to know but August, is that it? Did you want to make sure I'd sleep with you first?"

"Don't get upset."

"Upset?" She stood up. "What makes you think I'm upset?"

"You're yelling."

"I haven't even started to yell."

"Your face is red."

"It's hot in here."

"*Querida,* sit down. I know this is a shock to you."

"A shock?" She bit off a half laugh. "Oh, that's rich. What makes you think I'm shocked? How dare you manipulate me like this!"

"I did not manipulate you."

"No?" She pointed to the backyard. "You played me like a fool, didn't you, Zack? Oh, you wrapped it up in a nice little package, but you were stringing me along the whole time. You've suspected this since the day we met with Fulton Cleese.''

"I didn't have any proof, and I didn't see—''

"You forced the issue with Odelia. You forced the issue with George Snopes, and when I wouldn't tumble into bed with you, you forced the issue with me, too. That's what this was all about, wasn't it? You wanted sex, and I wouldn't give it to you.''

Frustrated, he surged to his feet. "No, damn it. Will you shut up and listen to me?''

The insistent blare of a horn sounded from the driveway. "No.'' She grabbed the handle of her medical bag where it sat by the table. "I'm through listening to you. You've never told me the truth about anything, why should I start listening now?''

Before he could stop her, she stalked out the back door. With a muttered curse, Zack followed her into the yard. The hammering and sawing had stopped. Belatedly he noticed that Sam, Jeff and Josh had joined the building project. He gave his brothers a menacing glare as they regarded him with amused looks. "What are you looking at?'' he barked.

Sebastiano shook his head as Bubba Lorden rounded the house leading a two-month-old calf on a tether. "You, *amigo,* have really blown it this time.'' The boys, sensing the brewing argument, scrambled down from the tree fort.

August didn't seem to notice the growing crowd of spectators. "Just admit it, Zack,'' she demanded. "Admit that's why you married me.''

"That is not why I married you.''

"If you knew things were going to turn out like this, then you knew I didn't need your help to get Judge Laden to award me custody.'' She glanced at Teddy. "You already knew Snopes wasn't a real threat,'' she hissed.

"I didn't know that." He grabbed her arm. "And stop shrieking. You're upsetting the boys."

"What do you care?" She dropped her medical bag in the dirt with a thud. "You already got what you came for."

At the bitter statement, Zack threw up his hands in disgust. "You are the most hardheaded woman I have ever—"

"Is this a bad time, August?" Bubba Lorden stood watching them with a concerned expression on his face. "I know you wanted to do this out at the farm, but I figured—"

"Don't worry about it, Bubba," August assured him. "I said now. Now is fine." She reached into the bag. "Bring him over here."

Bubba looked warily at Zack, but led the calf forward. "You're sure he's not too young? He's just eight weeks."

"Positive," August said. "He'll be fine."

Zack took a step forward. "August, will you just listen to me?"

She held a syringe up to the light as she drained a medicine vial. "Bubba, he hasn't been ill, has he?"

"No, ma'am." The young man's Adam's apple bobbed when he saw Zack's harsh frown.

"You cannot ignore this forever," Zack said.

August stuck the hypodermic needle in the calf's rump. The young animal squirmed, but endured the expertly applied shot.

Sam's sneeze caught Zack's attention. He looked over his shoulder to see that his brothers and the seven boys had closed ranks around him to watch the procedure with the calf.

"Boy," Bo said, "is she mad."

"Yeah." Chip nodded. "I never seen August like this."

Jeff pushed his glasses up the bridge of his nose. "Not even that time we almost burned down the shed."

Sam wiped his nose with the back of his hand. "Or the time we let Mr. Farley's geese loose during that garden party at Ms. Keegan's club."

Lucas gave Zack a pitying look. "You blew it, man."

Even Teddy shook his head at him.

"Well, great," Zack said, "this is just what I need. I'm in the middle of a major crisis, and I'm getting advice from the Marx brothers." When Miguel started to laugh, he gave him a withering look.

The sound of a car in the drive momentarily distracted August from her examination of the young calf. Zack glanced up to see Jansen Riley making his way across the yard in measured strides. "Jansen," he muttered.

August stiffened. "The gang's all here."

Zack laid a hand on her shoulder, "August, please listen to me."

"I'm busy," she insisted. "Bubba, rope his back legs, we've got to lay him down."

Bubba deftly tied off the binding rope. August repeated the procedure on the now protesting animal's front legs. "The tranquilizer should help," she said, "but you're going to have to hold him still. He'll kick if you don't."

Jansen reached the backyard. "Zack, what's going on?"

"Morning, Jansen," Zack said. "I'm just having a little fight with your daughter."

Jansen looked at August. "Dear God, she's the spitting image of Katherine." He set his suitcase down on the ground as he took two steps toward her. "August, I can't begin to tell you what—"

"Bubba," August said, ignoring them all, "get the red-handled calipers out of my bag."

Zack saw the way her shoulders stiffened, knew she was struggling not to look at Jansen. He placed a restraining hand on the older man's arm. "Wait a minute, Jansen," he said. "You've waited thirty years, you can wait another couple of minutes."

"Zack, I—"

"I know," Zack said, "but just hold on." When he saw August struggling with the calf's front legs, he bent to help her. He grabbed the animal's head and forelegs, holding them still while August pulled on a pair of latex gloves. "Maybe you're right," he told her. "Maybe I should have talked to you about it, but if you'll just listen to me, you'll see that I—"

"Here ya go, August." Bubba had returned with the instruments she'd requested.

"Thank you. Bubba, hold his hind legs. Zack, if you're going to insist on helping, hold tight. He's not going to like this."

Zack felt the boys crowd close to his back as August took out an ominous-looking scalpel. Chip tapped him on the shoulder. "What's she doing?"

"Get back, boys," Jansen said. "That calf could kick you."

They moved inches away. August gave the scrotal sac between the calf's hind legs a tug. The animal yelped and struggled against Zack's confining grip. "Hold him, Zack," she insisted. "If he kicks me, I could cut my hand off."

"The reason I didn't tell you all this before," Zack insisted, "is because I wanted to be sure. How would you have felt if it had all turned out to be untrue? How would the boys have felt?"

Ignoring him, she made her first incision. As the knife sliced open the tender flesh, the calf bellowed. Behind him, Zack heard Sebastiano groan. With a deft swipe of the scalpel, she sliced off the testicle.

"I think I'm going to throw up," Miguel said.

The calf was whining now. "What the hell are you do-ing?" Zack asked.

"What does it look like I'm doing?" she snapped. "I'm doing a routine castration. I do about a hundred of these a year." She glanced at Bubba. "Hold him steady. One more to go." She made a second incision, then fingered the other testicle. When she cut it off, Zack saw Rafael's hand move protectively to his groin.

"All done," she said. She patted the calf's belly. "You did good, buddy." With a quick economy of motion, she swabbed the wound with a local anesthetic. Wiping off the instruments, she dropped each into her bag, then untied the calf's legs. He stumbled to his feet, giving her a somewhat wounded look, but seeming more or less recovered from the indelicate procedure. August dropped both testicles into a sanitized plastic bag. "You want them, Bubba?" she asked the young man.

His face paled as she watched her strip the bloodstained latex gloves from her hands. "Uh, no, ma'am. I'm just gonna take him home."

"He should be fine." She handed him a tube of medi-cine and a bottle of drops from the bag. "If he starts rub-bing at it funny, spread some of this on it. It'll stave off infection. And here are the antibiotics for his feed. The directions are on the bottle."

"All right."

She discarded the gloves in a garbage bag, then snapped the satchel shut. As Bubba led his calf away, she finally turned to Zack. "Just tell me one thing, Zack," she said, with a dead calm that made him feel panicky. "Tell me why you wanted to marry me."

He'd gotten so used to having her ignore him, he was unprepared for the abrupt question. "What do you mean?"

"I mean, why did you want to marry me? It wasn't

because of Odelia. It wasn't even because of the boys. Why did you do it?''

Relief surged in him. This she would understand. Somehow, he'd cleared the last hurdle, and once he explained to August that his only concern had been for her protection, she'd understand. He was sure of it. He reached out a comforting hand. "Because, *querida,* you needed me."

Her expression turned stone hard. He watched the anger flow through her with a renewed feeling of panic. "I don't need anyone, Zack. Not parents. Not a family. And especially not you."

"August—"

"You bastard. You arrogant bastard. Who gave you the right to play God with other people's lives?"

"I wasn't—"

"Who gave you the right to decide what was best for me?"

"Will you—"

"What makes you think you can stand there and tell me I *need* you? How dare you!"

"Damn it, will you—"

"Shut up, Zack. Don't you think you've said enough for one day? First you tell me you'll marry me to save my kids. Never mind how I might feel about it. You practically bullied me into it by scaring the wits out of me. But I'm supposed to *need* you? Well, thanks, but no thanks." In one hand, she still held the small bag with the bull's testicles. With a muttered curse, she slapped them against his chest. "Here, why don't you keep this as a souvenir? Every time you look at them, you'll know I wish it had been you." She turned and stalked into the house.

Zack faced the small crowd of men with trepidation. "Now what?" he muttered.

"Don't get too close," Miguel said.

Sebastiano shook his head. "And hide all the knives."

Lucas jammed his hands in the pockets of his shorts. "She's really mad, Zack. You better let her cool off."

Jansen glanced from the boys to Zack. "Nice going, Adriano," he said. "You went from attorney, to friend, to son-in-law, to fool, all in one day."

Zack exhaled a long breath. "Jansen, I'm sorry. I didn't mean for you to meet her this way."

"It's all right." He hefted the suitcase to his other hand. "I was prepared for it to take some time."

Sebastiano seemed inclined to agree. "You've just turned her world upside down, Zack. Give her a little time to adjust."

"*Mierda.*" Rafael stepped forward to grab Zack's shoulder. "Between the four of you, you don't know enough about women to fill a thimble. *Hermano*—" he gave Zack a shake "—you're about to throw away the only decent woman who'd ever have you."

"Hell, don't you think I know that?"

"For someone who makes his living arguing, you sure blew it this time."

He glared at Rafael. "Thank you for your support."

"You, *amigo,* are coming with me." He looked at Miguel and Sebastiano. "You two, watch the boys so Jansen can talk to August alone."

"Where are you going?" Miguel asked him.

"How'd you get here, Jansen?" Rafael asked.

"I flew. My private plane is at the airstrip."

"Good. We're borrowing it."

"Are you nuts?" Zack pointed at August's house. "I'm not leaving her now. Not like this"

Rafael pried the plastic bag out of his hand and tossed it in the trash. "You are if you want to keep that woman. My God, *amigo,* you're head over heels. Don't blow it." He propelled Zack out of the yard with a firm hand at his shoulder.

By the time they were settled in Jansen's plane, Zack was wallowing in self-pity. He'd ruined everything. He'd finally met a woman he could love, and he'd destroyed it with his own pride and arrogance. "You think I'm a fool, don't you?"

Rafael checked the panels as he prepared to take off. "Yes."

"You've always thought I was a fool."

"No." He flipped several switches, and the engine roared to life. "I've always thought you were too stubborn for your own good. You were so busy being everything we needed you to be, you never took a long look at yourself, Zack. You can't go through life scared to death that people are going to leave you. That's no way to live."

He looked out the window as Rafael began to taxi the plane. "Is that why you despise me?" he asked.

"Hell, Zack." He eased the throttle back. "Where'd you get a stupid idea like that?"

Zack met his gaze as the plane's nose lifted off the ground. "It's not a secret, Rafael. We've never gotten along."

"Listen. I am only going to say this one time. I may not have always agreed with you, but I admire you more than anyone I know. Now sit back and shut up, so I can tell you how to get your woman back."

On the afternoon of the third day after Zack's departure from Keegan's Bend, August brought two glasses of lemonade out onto the porch. Jansen sat, feet up, swinging gently. "Where are the boys?"

"Playing in the tree house," she said. "They're going to miss Miguel and Sebastiano." Zack's brothers had finally left that morning. Miguel's shore leave had run out, and Sebastiano needed to return to his business. Their presence had been an unexpected blessing in the wake of

Zack's departure. She'd needed the time to adjust to Jansen, to the truth. True to Zack's word, Odelia had backed off the instant Jansen confronted her with the truth. Snopes had disappeared from Keegan's Bend within hours, and Odelia had been forced into silence by Jansen's formidable presence. As far as he was concerned, she'd taken Katherine and August from him once, and he wouldn't tolerate it again.

Everything, August supposed, would have worked out fine, had it not been for the persistent ache in her heart when she thought of Zack, and his more-regular-than-clockwork phone calls. She didn't talk to him, couldn't bear to, but Jansen insisted on relaying the messages. The boys spoke with him each night. They plied him with questions about his return, and he always promised that, soon, he'd be back.

Her children had recovered with typical childish resilience. Teddy was talking more and more each day, and they'd readily adjusted to Jansen's presence in their life. August was the one who'd become a terminal basket case. She lived day to day, simultaneously dreading and wishing for the sight of Zack limping up her driveway. Her heart wanted him, ached for him, but the deep sense of betrayal she felt hadn't healed.

"Zack called again," Jansen told her when she sat on the swing next to him. "Said to tell you, hello."

"Please, Jansen, not now."

"August, you've got to deal with this sooner or later. I've known that boy a long time, and he's not going to go away."

"He already did," she said.

"Only to give you time to cool off. He wasn't trying to betray you, you know. He was trying to help."

She shook her head. "You just don't understand, Jansen.

He manipulated me to get what he wanted. How am I supposed to forgive him for that?''

"He married you, didn't he?"

"You heard why. He didn't want a wife, he wanted a dependent."

"Oh, hell. You don't believe that and you know it. How many times since you've known him has Zack told you he wasn't the kind of man who made commitments?"

"I don't know. A few."

"Don't you think he could have fixed your problem without marrying you?"

"He said—"

"I know what he said, but what did he mean? August, that boy had love written all over him. He was just scared to death to tell you that."

"That's ridiculous."

"Is it? His whole life, people needed him. Everyone around him wanted something from him. Zack spent over twenty years figuring out how to solve people's problems. In the back of his mind, he's scared to death that if you don't need him, it means you don't love him. He's going to need some time to understand that."

August felt a familiar tightness in her chest. "He wants me to need him. I've spent too long learning to survive on my own to let myself *need* anybody!"

"You know—" he stretched out his long legs "—you're as stubborn as your mother."

August glanced at him in surprise. They'd spent three days getting to know each other, but Jansen had rarely spoken of Katherine. The memories seemed to be too painful for him. "I loved her," he said, "so much, I'd have done anything for that woman." His eyes remained focused on the setting sun. "If she'd told me about you, I could have found a way to make it work, but she was bound and determined that she wasn't going to let me fight with her father."

"I'm sorry, Jansen."

"So am I." He glanced at her. "You'll never know how sorry I am. I've missed thirty years of your life, and now, you can't forgive me for it."

"That's not true."

"Yes, it is. August, don't you think I know how angry you are? Your whole life, everyone has disappointed you. First Katherine, then me, then the slew of people who were supposed to take care of you, and finally Zack."

"Don't be ridiculous. You didn't know."

"It didn't matter to you," he insisted. "I just have to hope that in the years to come, I can prove to you that I won't disappoint you again, that one day, you'll trust me."

Trust. She turned the word over in her head. How many times had Zack pleaded with her for her trust? She'd unfairly judged Jansen for the past, she realized. Hadn't she done the same thing to Zack? All he asked from her was her trust. She had given it, and with it, her heart. From the very beginning, she'd known that he was a remarkable man. She's seen it in the way he treated her kids. She'd seen it in the determined set of jaw and the strong tenderness of his hands.

He'd stolen her heart, and it had scared her to death. Years of practice had taught her to avoid caring at all costs. The people she cared about inevitably hurt her. She'd given love only to her boys. Until Zack Adriano stole it from her like the pirate he was. She hadn't wanted to love him, but he'd given her no choice, and in her blindness, in her driving need to protect herself, she'd pushed him away.

Finally, she realized, despite the anger his words had caused, that Zack had been right: She had needed him. She'd needed him to free her from the hurts of the past and give her a reason to cherish the future. She met Jansen's gaze with a tortured look. As clear as a morning sky she remembered Zack telling her he couldn't make a long-term commitment. Why hadn't she realized how much that had scared her? At the time, she'd focused on his pain, and completely missed seeing her own. In a corner of her heart, she'd always believed he'd leave her, and to protect herself from the pain his abandonment would cause, she'd left him first. Only now did she realize that she'd never given Zack the one thing he needed. Just as every person in her life had disappointed her, every person in his life had needed him. Zack equated need with love. He'd never had the opportunity to love and be loved for who he was, rather than what he could do. If she hadn't been such a fool, she'd have seen the desperation in him, recognized it in herself.

She raised tortured eyes to Jansen. "Do you think he'll really come back?" she asked.

In the glare of the afternoon sun, Jansen's face looked achingly loving. "He already has," he said, pointing toward the white panel truck coming slowly down the street.

When the horn blared, two dogs began an insistent barking. As the truck drew near, her seven boys filed onto the porch. "What's going on?" Teddy asked.

"It's Zack," Jansen said.

Lucas frowned at the approaching truck. "How do you know?"

Jansen let out a low laugh as Chip crawled onto his lap. "I just do." He gave August a gentle prod. "Go and say hello."

When the truck turned to back into the drive, August saw Zack and Rafael standing in the open cargo door. Rafael looked as disreputable as ever. Zack had an intense look on his face that made her heart rate trip into double time.

The driver backed the truck nearly up to the porch, and several passersby stopped to watch as Zack, Rafael and two other men began unloading dozens of suitcases from the back.

"What are you doing?" August asked him.

"I brought you something," Zack said absently. He indicated the growing stack of bags to his brother and the two men. "Don't get them mixed up." He tossed three more burgundy leather suitcases onto the pile.

The boys, eager to see Zack and Rafael, bustled off the porch. They picked their way through the piles to greet Zack with enthusiastic hugs and high fives. He scooped them up in turn, talking to them in low, conspiratorial tones as August watched the unfolding spectacle. They now had a respectable crowd on the sidewalk. She frowned at Jansen. "Do you know anything about this?"

He shook his head in an unconvincing denial. Slowly, August made her way down the steps as piles of suitcases in every imaginable color and shape landed in a heap on her lawn. "Zack, what's going on?" she asked.

The last of the suitcases joined the nine piles on the grass, and Zack pulled the cargo door of the truck shut with a hard tug. "Why haven't you taken my phone calls?" he demanded.

"I didn't think there was anything left to say."

He muttered something in Spanish, picked up a suitcase, then stalked over to where she still stood by the steps. "You're my wife, damn it, and you didn't think there was anything to say?"

"Not after the way you left."

"I left because you told me to."

"You had lied to me."

"I never lied to you, August. Maybe I didn't say a lot of things I should have, but I never lied to you."

She closed her eyes, suddenly weary. "Zack, why are you doing this?"

He thrust the suitcase at her. "Look at this," he said. She opened her eyes to find his gaze, angry and compelling, holding her captive. "Look at it. What do you see?"

"It's a suitcase."

"That's right." His finger jabbed at the monogram. "What are the letters."

She glanced at them, confused. What was he doing? "'A.T.A.'"

"That's right. You know what it stands for?"

"What are you—"

"It stands for August Trent Adriano, that's what. And everyone of these bags has one of the boy's initials on it." He picked up a blue one. "See. Lucas Gerren Adriano." He grabbed a red one. "Bo Mills Adriano." He seized a pink one. "Beth Mills Adriano." He dropped the bag at her feet. "You know who that is?"

August shook her head no. "Beth is Bo's sister. She's coming to live with us. We're adopting all of them." He planted his feet solidly apart. With his arms crossed over his chest, he towered over her. "And you're not going to say no."

"Why," she muttered, scanning the piles of luggage, "why are you doing this?"

"Because you pushed me away once, August. You did it because you were convinced I'd hurt you. You told me once that you spent your whole life feeling like you never belonged anywhere—that everything you owned fit into a suitcase." He frowned at her. "Well, now that suitcase has my name on it." With a sweep of his hand, he indicated the boys, who were gleefully pointing out their monograms on the luggage. "And their names. This is my family, damn you, and you're not going to take it away from me."

She felt tears sting at her eyes when she saw the rugged set of his face. She watched her boys laughing in the yard, felt Jansen's watchful gaze from the porch, saw Rafael's pleased smile as he observed from the shadow of the truck. "Oh, Zack," she whispered. "You're such a fool."

He took a menacing step forward. "You are not getting rid of me."

"I don't want to get rid of you, you big jerk. I love you."

A mixture of hope and distrust registered on his face. "You'd better mean it, August, because I swear to heaven, I'm not letting you go."

Two tears spilled down her face. "Of course I mean it. You were right all along. I did need you."

Something flared in his eyes. "No. I was a fool for saying that. You didn't need me, August. You're the strongest woman I've ever met. And because you didn't need me, I was afraid you couldn't love me. The only reason I married you is because I love you, and if you haven't figured it out by now, you're not nearly as smart as I think you are."

She pressed her hands to her face. "All this time, I thought you didn't really want us."

He gave her an incredulous look that sent fire to her toes. "Want you? *Want* you. I can't damned well live without you."

With a muffled cry of joy, she tossed her arms around his neck. "Welcome home, Zack."

Rafael's laughter carried on the hot afternoon. "Round up the boys, Jansen," he said. "I think we need to leave them alone."

Epilogue

August moved slowly through the large house, switching out lights. A quiet sense of contented exhaustion flooded her as she looked at the enormous Christmas tree in the living room. Zack had insisted that for their first Christmas together, they had to have the largest tree he could find. Fortunately, the extension Sebastiano had built to connect Jansen's house with hers had cathedral ceilings large enough to contain the monstrous spruce.

She tossed another log on the fire, then settled on the couch to wait for Zack. She shifted when the baby, now in its fifth month, kicked her hard on the right side. "Little hellion," she whispered. "You're going to be a soccer star, I know."

The clock in the hall chimed 4:00 a.m., and August tipped her head back against the sofa. She'd had trouble sleeping since Zack left on his business trip a few days ago. Jansen, three of Zack's sisters and their families, along with the four boys, slept upstairs. In a few hours, she expected the children to invade the quiet sanctity of the living room.

Zack had promised he'd be back by Christmas Eve, but had called her that afternoon to let her know he was running late. When he returned to Keegan's Bend that summer afternoon, he'd turned his life upside down for her. He had resigned his position in New York. He now practiced family law from their home. Sometimes, she worried that he missed the excitement of the city, but he was quick to assure her that he'd lost his desire for that part of his life. All he wanted, he claimed, was here, in the quiet, if occasionally chaotic, security of their home. Secretly, August hoped to persuade him to run for mayor in the next election. With the baby coming, she didn't want the dual responsibility of her practice and the mayor's office. Continental Motors was scheduled to open their plant in the spring, and the town was quickly growing. The mayor's job was becoming more and more important, and she could think of no one more suited to guiding the small town through the pending transition.

They saw little of Odelia. Since the day Jansen confronted her, she'd taken to staying out of the public eye. It saddened August that they couldn't resolve their differences, but she still maintained hope that one day, Odelia would be able to put the past behind them. In a strange twist of fate, Betsy May had approached August and asked to work with her in her veterinarian practice. She'd proved to have a deft touch with the animals, and August cherished the unexpected friendship that had blossomed between her and her cousin.

Her eyes drifted shut in sleepy contentment as she pondered the course of her life. How could she have known just a few short months ago that she'd soon be surrounded by the loving warmth of the large family she'd always craved?

In the corner of her mind, she heard the back door creak open, but was too sleepily content to open her eyes. "I hope that's you," she muttered to Zack.

"It is." His rumbly voice never failed to please her.

"Did you get everything done?"

"Yes."

She snuggled deeper into the couch. "I'm glad. Welcome home."

"It's good to be home. I'm sorry I'm so late." She heard him turn the lock.

"It's all right. The boys will be glad to see you in the morning." She couldn't stifle a yawn. "Just as long as I'm the first to wish you merry Christmas."

"Merry Christmas, sweetheart" he whispered as he pressed a soft kiss to her forehead. "Don't you want to see what I brought you?"

"Can it wait until morning?"

He chuckled softly. "I don't think so."

With a supreme effort of will, August forced her eyes open. Zack held a large, blanket-wrapped bundle against his chest. She rubbed her eyes. "What is it?" she asked on a yawn.

He set his burden on her lap, then peeled back the blanket. The sleeping face of the beautiful little girl looked so much like Bo that August felt tears begin to sting at her eyes. She glanced at the amazing man she had married and her heart almost exploded with her love for him. "Oh, Zack, it's Beth!"

"Yes."

"You found her." August's arms tightened on the slender body. "How did you find her?"

"With a lot of help from Kaitlin." He stroked a dark

curl off the girl's face. "And she's ours," he said. "I made Fulton sign the papers tonight."

With a muffled cry, August pressed her face against his neck. "I love you," she said. "I love you so much."

Zack shifted to the couch. So that he could cradle both August and Beth in his arms. "I love you, too, *querida*. Now go back to sleep. I'll be here in the morning."

*   *   *   *   *

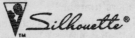
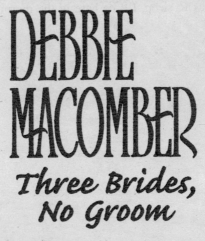

Take 4 bestselling love stories FREE

Plus get a FREE surprise gift!

SILHOUETTE® *Desire*®

15 YEARS OF GUARANTEED GOOD READING!

Desire has always brought you satisfying novels that let you escape into a world of endless possibilities— with heroines who are in control of their lives and heroes who bring them passionate romance beyond their wildest dreams.

When you pick up a Silhouette Desire, you can be confident that you won't be disappointed. Desire always has six fresh and exciting titles every month by your favorite authors— **Diana Palmer, Ann Major, Dixie Browning, Lass Small and BJ James,** just to name a few. Watch for extraspecial stories by these and other authors in **October, November and December 1997** as we celebrate **Desire's 15th anniversary.**

Indulge yourself with three months of top authors and fabulous reading…we even have a fantastic promotion waiting for you!

Pick up a Silhouette Desire… it's what women want today.

Available at your favorite retail outlet.

Bestselling author

JOAN JOHNSTON

continues her wildly popular miniseries with an
all-new, longer-length novel

The Virgin Groom

HAWK'S WAY

One minute, Mac Macready was a living legend in
Texas—every kid's idol, every man's envy, every
woman's fantasy. The next, his fiancée dumped him,
his career was hanging in the balance and his future
was looking mighty uncertain. Then there was the
matter of his scandalous secret, which didn't stand a
chance of staying a secret. So would he succumb to
Jewel Whitelaw's shocking proposal—or take cold
showers for the rest of the long, hot summer...?

Available August 1997
wherever Silhouette books are sold.

Silhouette®